GHOST
OF A
THREAT

Ghost of a Threat
Betty Boo, Ghost Hunter Book One
© 2011 Beth Dolgner

ISBN-13: 978-0984915613

Published by Redglare Press
Cover by Book Covers by Melody
Print Formatting by The Madd Formatter

BethDolgner.com

For Chris and Ashley Uno

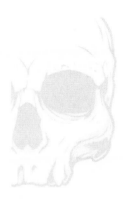

PROLOGUE

Sam MacIntosh's eyes snapped open, the dark interior of his bedroom coming into sharp focus. He wasn't sure what had awakened him as he lay there on his side, gazing at the closet door. He could hear the distant rumble of a freight train churning by on the tracks a mile from his house, and over that noise the soft, regular breathing of his wife sleeping beside him.

Sam's heart caught in his throat. Melanie had left him two years ago, and Sam hadn't shared his bed with anyone else since the divorce. He held his own breath, straining to hear. Still, the sound came from the other half of the bed behind his back. For a minute, he wondered wildly if he'd gotten drunk and brought someone home from the bar, but he knew he was alone in the house.

Clutching the covers in a terrified grip, Sam sat up abruptly and turned to face the other side of the bed. The newspaper was still lying on top of the quilt where he'd tossed it aside after giving up on the crossword puzzle and going to sleep, but there was no one in the bed. The sound of breathing had stopped, too.

Sam exhaled the breath he'd been holding, feeling both silly and glad that no one had witnessed his moment of panic. He'd have to lay off the beer if it was going to make him hear things. As he settled back down in bed, another noise began, but this time it was a low, ominous creaking sound. The closet door was slowly opening.

Sam couldn't see the door, his eyes staring up at the ceiling fan, his entire body suddenly frozen in fear. He recognized the sound, though. Melanie used to complain all the time about that squeaky closet door.

Then the footsteps began. They started at the closet and approached the bed, heavy and deliberate, but agonizingly slow.

Sam MacIntosh sat up and screamed.

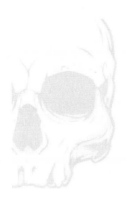

ONE

My phone was ringing. At first I thought it was the alarm clock, but I had just smacked the snooze button a moment ago. I rolled over and squinted at the clock. Who could possibly be calling me at 7:03?

Nobody would call me this early unless it was an emergency, I thought.

"Fine, I'm up!" I said, trying to talk my body and brain into wakefulness. I threw back the covers and swung my legs out of bed, leaping to grab the phone from the top of my dresser. I picked it up on the last ring before voicemail engaged.

"Hello?" I mumbled, willing myself to gain some sense of coherence. I put my hand to my mouth to stifle a yawn.

"Is this Betty Boorman?" said a man's breathless voice.

"Yes, this is."

There was a short pause. "I'm sorry if I woke you up," the man apologized. "I know it's early."

Before I could respond, he started speaking again, the words tumbling out of his mouth in jittery bursts. "I found your website online. You know, the one for your, um, group. And I live in Thunderbolt, so I'm not far away at all, and I have something weird going on at my house, and I just thought that maybe your group would be able to come out here and take a look around. I don't know what's going on, but I've been up since three a.m. and I'm a little shaken up. Nothing like this has ever happened to me. I don't even really believe in this stuff but I don't know what else could explain what happened last night."

The words spilled out so quickly that I had to concentrate to follow along. He sounded scared, embarrassed and wound up all at the same time. At least the fear in his voice had woken me up completely.

"Okay, no problem," I said, trying to sound reassuring. "Was last night the first time you've had any paranormal activity in your home?"

"Yes."

"Has anyone in your family died recently, or maybe a close friend?"

"No, no one. Well, my great-aunt died about three months ago, but I don't think she'd have any reason to," he paused, "you know."

"Haunt you?" I supplied.

"Yes. Sorry, it feels a little silly to say it out loud."

I smiled, and even though he couldn't see that through the phone, I knew he could hear it in my voice. "You don't have to worry about that with me. Just think, my idea of a fun Saturday night out is going looking for ghosts. Normal people my age are going to dance clubs on Saturday nights. Now, can you tell me what kind of activity you experienced last night?"

Again, he hesitated. I could tell it was really hurting his ego to admit all of this to me. I've seen it time and again. No one wants to admit they've been wrong all their lives; the older our clients were, the harder it became for them to change their beliefs and accept the existence of ghosts.

Not that all of our clients have to face that problem. We—The Savannah Spirit Seekers—have been investigating reported hauntings in Savannah, Georgia, for the past two years. Half of the cases we investigate turn out to be nothing but a combination of a noisy old house, rogue electromagnetic fields and very vivid imaginations. Sometimes I think it's even harder for those clients than the ones who actually have a haunting. When we confirm that a client really is experiencing a haunting, their first words are always, "Oh, good, then I'm not crazy!" But when we debunk a haunting, well, sanity suddenly doesn't feel so secure. One of our clients described it as being assured there's not really a monster under the bed, but when you're forty instead of four, it's a bitter pill to swallow.

The man on the phone sounded so freaked out that I hoped for his sake that he was just letting his imagination get out of control. I dashed to my dining room table to grab my pen and notebook.

"I woke up in the middle of the night last night," he began, "and I could hear breathing coming from the other half of the bed, but no one was there. As soon as I looked, the noise stopped. Then my closet door opened, and I could hear someone walking out of the closet, right over to my bed!"

"What happened next?" I prompted.

"The sound just stopped. I turned on the light, and of course I couldn't find anything. But then the footsteps started outside my hallway. And this morning when I finally got up, all of the pictures hanging in my hall were lying on the floor."

"Okay, this sounds like a lot of activity considering that nothing unusual has ever occurred before, but it's certainly not out of the norm," I assured him. "Are there any other details?"

"Let's see," he hesitated. "I think I fell asleep again at some point. I woke up because I felt something touch me." He paused again. "But that's it."

"What's your name?" I asked.

"Sam. Sam MacIntosh."

"Well, Sam, your case sounds like something we'd be interested in handling, but I'll have to confirm with the rest of my team members. Can I call you back this evening once I've had a chance to speak with them? We can schedule an investigation then, too."

"How soon can you be here?"

No one is ever patient when it comes to ghosts. "I'll have to check everyone's schedule, but it should be something we can do within a few weeks."

"A few weeks?" Sam MacIntosh was definitely one freaked-out man.

"I'm sorry, sir, but we all work during the week and have to schedule investigations on our free weekends. We'll do the best we can, and I'll have a firm answer for you this evening."

Sam couldn't really argue, so I took down his phone number and hung up. I looked down at my cat, who had sauntered up to be petted, and she gazed back with her wide golden eyes. "It's kind of strange, huh, Mina? This guy has lived in a house with no problems and all of a sudden he has a full-blown haunting?"

Mina let out a little meow in answer. I swear she understands me when I talk.

Just for the record, I don't claim to understand her in return. That's just a little too "crazy cat lady" for me.

I stood up and glanced at the microwave clock in the kitchen. "I've got to get moving!" I shouted. I showered in record time, towel-drying my long hair as vigorously as I could before I gave up and just swept it up in a clip. I threw on my gray pinstriped slacks and a pale blue button-down, giving myself a once-over in the mirror before heading for the kitchen. I can't live without my morning coffee, and luckily my coffee maker is set to turn on automatically each morning. I grabbed a travel mug and poured the steaming black liquid in, slopping it all over my hand in the process.

I howled, chiding myself for getting so clumsy in my rush. I cleaned myself up, my skin pink from the heat of the coffee, and headed out of my apartment.

My apartment has got to be the coolest place to live in Savannah. Okay, maybe just the coolest for those of us who aren't loaded. I'd love to live in one of the restored mansions that line the streets of the historic district, but until I win the lottery or marry a rich doctor, I'll be content in my little apartment. I live on the bottom floor of an old carriage house. The building is from 1861 and it, along with the mansion it sits behind, has been turned into apartments. I have the downstairs, and my neighbor Tim has the top floor. It's not a big place, but I'm right in the middle of downtown Savannah, surrounded by old buildings and tons of ghosts. Where better for a ghost hunter to live than in the most haunted city in the United States?

I made the drive from my place to the hospital administration building in twelve minutes, sliding through a few questionable traffic signals on the way. I'm the marketing assistant for Coastal Health Hospital: an entry-level corporate job with a paycheck that hardly covers my bills, but I'm grateful that I at least found a job right out of college. Of course, it probably didn't hurt that Coastal Health's HR manager goes to church with my mother. Anyone who doesn't believe the adage, "It's all about who you know," has obviously never lived in Savannah.

The morning passed quickly, and during my lunch break I called the rest of my team. Everyone was available Friday night, which was rare. There are four of us on the team, and we only schedule an investigation if at least three of us can be there. It's sometimes hard to work around everyone's schedules, with jobs, dates and social lives. But of course, those last two things don't really apply to me. What is it about guys that make them shy away from a girl who likes to wander around haunted buildings?

I called Sam MacIntosh back that evening, and he quickly accepted my offer for Friday night. It was already Wednesday, so he didn't have long to wait.

The rest of the week went by quickly. I stopped by the receptionist's desk on my way out the door Friday afternoon. "Got anything good planned this weekend, Betty?" she asked. Jeanie is only a year older than me, but she's already engaged. She says she can still be single by living vicariously through me. Considering how much of my "social life" revolves around ghosts, Jeanie doesn't hear the kind of wild tales she hopes for.

"We had a guy call about a haunting at his house in Thunderbolt. We're heading out there tonight to investigate."

Jeanie's face fell. Her idea of "good" is a hot date, or at least an activity involving a horde of good-looking single men. I wondered vaguely if her fiancé had his hands full trying to rein her in.

Jeanie perked up again. "Did you say a guy?"

"Yes. Why?"

"Do you think he's single?"

I laughed. "Oh, no, you don't! I don't mix ghosts and guys! He did mention that he was sleeping alone during all the activity going on in his house, though…"

I gave Jeanie a wink and turned toward the door. "I'll give you a full report on Monday!" I was still laughing to myself as I walked to my car. Finding a date through my work with The Seekers was the last thing on my agenda. We were a paranormal investigation team, after all, not a dating service. Considering my history with men, though, maybe it was something to look into.

During the short drive home, I tried to think of clever business names for a combination ghost-hunting team and dating service for single women. "Handsome and Haunted?" I mused out loud. "Dates and Demons. Hmm, no, that makes it sound like the dates are demons. Ghosts and Guys...Ectoplasmic Escorts."

When I got through the door at home, I dropped my purse on the dining room table and headed straight for my closet. I slipped on some old sweatpants and a tee and plopped down on the couch to finish watching a movie I'd started two days before. By the time the final scene ended, I was yawning. Getting used to the lifestyle of a ghost hunter had taken me a while, living "normal" hours during the week, then becoming nocturnal for the weekends.

I curled up in bed to sleep for an hour, then it was time to scarf down some dinner and head to Thunderbolt. I swapped my sweats for jeans and grabbed my case, which contains my tape recorder, flashlight, EMF meter, camera, and lots of extra batteries. No one really knows why, but ghosts seem to suck the life out of batteries. Some people think it's the spirits trying to draw energy from their surroundings in order to materialize. Whatever the reason, it's pretty annoying. I'm always joking that we need to get Duracell sponsorship for The Seekers.

I don't know what I was expecting of Sam MacIntosh's house, but I hadn't anticipated the grand mansion I pulled up to after a short fifteen-minute drive. The two-story house was at the end of a dirt lane, with pine trees surrounding it. The manicured lawn was absolutely flawless, and Sam obviously had professional gardeners maintaining the flowerbeds.

Several other cars were parked in a small paved area to the side of the house. I recognized the SUV that belongs to Shaun and Daisy Tanner, two of the other investigators with The Seekers. Lou Miles is our tech guy, but I didn't see his car there yet. He's better with finding evidence on our audio and video footage than he is at being prompt.

I pulled up next to a sleek black Mercedes and

wondered if all three of the cars I didn't recognize belonged to Sam. How much money did this guy have?

My case was sitting on the passenger seat, but I only grabbed my pen and notebook out of it. Before we got to the investigating part, we would interview Sam about the house and everything he'd been experiencing.

I walked up onto the wide front porch and rang the doorbell. A few seconds later, a short man who looked like he was speeding toward forty opened the door. From the dark circles under his brown eyes, I assumed it was Sam.

"Mr. MacIntosh? Hi, I'm Betty Boorman," I said, putting on my "new client" smile. I'm pretty shy, and meeting new clients is the hardest part about this job. You'd think encountering ghosts would be the worst part, but a living, breathing stranger is more awkward for me any day.

Sam's face broke into a smile, making him look years younger. "Ms. Boorman, please come in. And just call me Sam," he said, extending his hand to me. I shook his hand and stepped inside. "I'm so glad you all could come this quickly," he continued as he led me down a short hallway. The interior of the house was even more impressive than the outside. Beautiful antiques were everywhere, and the gleaming hardwood floor creaked softly beneath my feet.

"You have a beautiful home," I murmured, trying to take everything in at once.

"It's been in my family since 1902. We're very proud of it. The MacIntoshes came here from Scotland just after the Civil War, and they put in years of hard work before they were able to build this place."

We had reached the parlor by then; I could hear several voices inside the room, but I wasn't prepared for just whom I would find.

My eyes went instantly to Shaun and Daisy, who looked out of place seated on a gilt sofa. The flowered upholstery clashed horribly with the red hair that Shaun had inherited from his Irish family.

"Well, if it isn't Betty Boo," a man's voice said in a Southern drawl.

I felt my jaw clench just from the sound of his voice. Across from Shaun and Daisy, sitting in a wingback chair and looking like he ought to have a mint julep in his manicured hand, was my nemesis.

"Carter Lansford." I said it as nicely as I could, but I'm sure some of the iciness I felt slipped through. "I didn't expect to see you here."

"I didn't know how soon you and your team could make it, so I called Carter, also. I see you two already know each other," Sam spoke up, seeming to sense the tension. Of course he could sense it: Carter and I were practically glaring at each other.

Carter recovered his friendly demeanor before I could do the same. "Sure, Betty and I have met many times over the past few years. We've never gotten to work together, though, so this should be fun."

Fun. Right. I met Carter when I first began attending paranormal investigations. He's sort of a rock star in our strange little world. Carter's family has tons of money, and he's spent as much as humanly possible on all the latest ghost-hunting equipment. A lot of the small investigation teams can't even afford an infrared video camera for filming in darkened rooms. Carter owns twenty of them.

But the publicity department is where Carter has really gone overboard. He lectures at all of the paranormal conventions, which would be fine with me if he had more of a clue what he was talking about, and he's a bona fide media hound. Carter holds press conferences when he investigates high-profile buildings and homes, and the local media eats up every bit of it. Each Halloween, a local news crew will go on an all-night stakeout with him at a

11

haunted house, and I've even seen his "fans" asking for autographs.

Carter will never be as good of an investigator as me, and that fact drives him insane. He cares more about the spotlight than the actual investigating, and his ego keeps him from learning and developing that certain something that a good investigator needs. Call it intuition, or insight, or sixth sense…whatever it is, it definitely doesn't co-exist well with *arrogance*.

I had seen Carter for what he is the first moment I met him at a local meeting of investigators. I'm still working to develop my intuition when it comes to ghosts, but I've always been able to sense when another person isn't being straight with me, and Carter just makes the hair on the back of my neck stand up.

I also sort of told Carter what I really think about him once, and that probably didn't help our mutual dislike. The second time we met he asked me out to dinner. I politely declined, and Carter took it as a personal offense that a girl would turn him down. He's handsome—if you like your guys kind of slimy—and that coupled with his money and charisma means women are always falling all over him. It's really kind of disgusting. After he hounded me about a date for a month, I finally got fed up and told him I thought he was an arrogant hack. If that didn't make him hate me, I sealed the deal when I started The Savannah Spirit Seekers, and Carter realized that I could collect more evidence with just a tape recorder and a camera than he could with his twenty infrared video cameras. It all comes down to intuition, and unfortunately for Carter, you can't buy that.

There is definitely no love lost between me and Carter Lansford.

I realized I was still staring at Carter. I blinked and turned my attention back to Sam. "The more brains we have working on this, the better," I said, trying my best to smile naturally. Too bad Carter doesn't have one, I added silently.

Luckily the doorbell rang then, and Sam eagerly excused himself to answer it. He returned soon enough with Lou, plus two men and a woman I recognized as belonging to Carter's team, East Coast Paranormal Authorities.

Authorities, humph. I moved to squeeze onto the couch with Shaun and Daisy, rolling my eyes while my back was turned to Carter. Daisy grinned and gave me a wink. She has curly blonde hair and a personality so big that I don't know how it fits inside her petite body. Daisy has a wicked sense of humor, so I could only imagine what kind of mental torture she had in store for Carter. That thought made it a lot easier to smile naturally.

"My team's all here. Carter?" I began.

"We're ready. This is Jamie, Ron and Kerri," he answered, directing the introduction of his team to Sam.

I turned to Sam. "Why don't you start by telling us, in detail, about the paranormal activity going on here."

Sam related the same things he had told me Wednesday morning on the phone. When he finished, Carter asked the same question that was on my lips. "Have you experienced anything over the past two nights?"

"The same things again." Sam hesitated, then dropped his head. "I've gotten hurt, too," he said quietly, staring at the floor.

"When did that happen?" I was trying to maintain my calm exterior, but reports of paranormal activity that causes injuries are never a good thing.

Sam glanced up, his cheeks flushed. "It started that first night. I said that I could hear something walking toward my bed from the closet, but I didn't mention that before I turned on the light, something scratched me." Sam pulled up the sleeve of his oxford shirt, revealing an angry red cut that stretched at least four inches along his forearm.

"That's more than a scratch," I whispered.

"I know." Sam was still blushing, and he dropped his head. "I was afraid that if I told you I'd gotten hurt, you'd get scared and wouldn't come investigate. I've got more scratches, too. And this morning I fell down the last few stairs when I came down for breakfast. I'm pretty sure I didn't just lose my balance."

A malicious haunting. Well, this changed things. Still, we were already there, and I could see the terror in Sam's eyes. We were obligated to help him however we could, and I knew the others felt the same.

"We'll be sure to stay alert," Carter said, his voice confident. "Why don't you show us your bedroom and the hallway where you've experienced activity so we can start setting up?"

I frowned at Carter. Didn't he want to ask about the history of the house, or Sam's family? There have even been cases of ghosts attaching themselves to furniture, so maybe he'd acquired one of his antique pieces recently, and it was the cause of all this activity. Everyone was already standing up, though, prepared to troop upstairs after Sam. I shrugged to myself. We'd have plenty of time to talk details later. I was the last to follow, and I couldn't help imagining Carter getting some scratches of his own as I walked up the stairs.

TWO

After Sam showed us around his house, Lou began setting up our two infrared video cameras. In case a ghost really had pushed Sam down the stairs, we put one camera at the top of the staircase and the other at the bottom. If anything went that way during the night, we should see it.

Carter put his team to work setting up their own cameras in the hallway and master bedroom. I wasn't really surprised that Carter didn't do any of the work himself. When I went outside to my car to grab my case (my "paranormal pack," as Daisy calls it), I saw Carter standing out there talking excitedly into his cell phone. I gave Carter the meanest glare I could muster as I locked my car.

Thunderbolt is a tiny community right next to Savannah, but I'd never had reason to visit it before. I knew there were some mansions and even a few former plantation homes in Thunderbolt, but they're all tucked away in the woods and nowhere near the highway that connects the two cities. I'd only been through the town on my way to Bonaventure Cemetery, so my impression of Thunderbolt mostly revolved around fast food restaurants and gas stations. Looking at Sam's ancestral home, I knew I'd have to rethink my opinion. There probably wasn't even any reason to lock my car. If some thief really was going to come this far back in the woods, he'd probably go straight for the house or that expensive Mercedes.

Just as I thought that, Carter flipped his cell phone shut and walked over to the sports car, hitting a button on his key ring to open the trunk as he did so. It figured that the nicest car there would belong to Carter.

"What do you think, Boo?" he asked, pulling a gleaming black briefcase from the trunk.

Leave it to Carter to ruin a good nickname. When I was a teenager, smart-aleck classmates had called me Betty Bore. I must have asked my parents a thousand times if we could please change our last name from Boorman to something more generic, something the kids couldn't use as another excuse to tease me. Smith would have been nice. I guess I didn't help things very much since I wasn't the average teenager. I've never quite fit in with the "normal" crowd. I was smart and made good grades, and I even got involved with the drama department at school (though I always stuck to set-building and backstage work), but I just didn't really fit in with any of the cliques. Things got better in college, when I started doing the paranormal investigations and found a group of people that I finally related to. They had a new nickname for me: Betty Boo. It makes me smile when anyone uses it, except for Carter. The assumed familiarity coming from his forked tongue just made me twitch.

"I think we need to find out some more about the history of this house," I answered his question. "I've never seen a haunting that gets so strong and defined all of a sudden like this."

"Obviously you're not just experienced enough. It is strange, though. Usually activity starts gradually and shows enhanced manifestation over time. There needs to be a trigger for the haunting, too, a reason for a spirit to come back."

I nodded in agreement, as much as I hate it when Carter gets something right. I decided to ignore his snide comment about my experience; I didn't really want to get into an argument. "And Sam said there haven't been any recent deaths. He did mention a relative who died a few months ago, but that's not a likely haunting." I got a mental picture of an old woman perched on a cloud in Heaven suddenly sitting upright and shouting, "Wait, I forgot to tell my great-nephew something! I have to go back down there!"

Carter and I reached the front steps of the house, and I stopped to look up at the windows, glowing pale white with the reflection of the nearly full moon that hung in the sky. "The malicious nature of this haunting bothers me," I continued. "I wonder if Sam should go stay with friends or something until we know what's going on."

"No reason for that. We'll get some answers tonight and this will be over with in no time. I bet it's just an angry spirit. I'll talk some sense into it, get it to cross over."

Oh, boy, Carter Lansford, Superhero to the Spirits.

"Sounds like you don't really need my team's help if you've got this all under control."

"And miss my chance to work with the second most-famous ghost hunter in Savannah? Absolutely not. I can't wait to see the way you do things, Boo."

"Gee, thanks, Carter. I hope I'm not a disappointment to you," I answered, my voice dripping with sarcasm.

When we got back into the house, Sam was just coming down the stairs with a duffel bag in his hands. The residents of a house usually make themselves scarce when an investigation is going on, or if they do stick around, they usually wait in whatever area of the house we've got set up as a base of operations. In this case, that was the kitchen. We offered to let Sam stay there with Lou and Ron, but he

17

seemed anxious for any excuse to get out of the house. I couldn't say I blamed him.

"Don't you want to stick around for the fun?" I asked him, trying to sound nonchalant for his sake.

Sam gave me a tight smile. "No, thank you, Betty. I'm going to be in that charity run tomorrow, so I need to get a good night's sleep. I'll be at my brother's over in Savannah."

"Before you go, we'd like to ask you a few questions to get some more background."

Sam looked distressed. "But I've told you everything already."

"You were very thorough in telling us about the paranormal activity, but we wanted to get a better idea of your family's history and any events that might be causing this."

"Oh, ah, okay. Shall we go back into the living room, then?"

Carter came along, too, and he and I took the couch this time while Sam perched on the edge of the wingback chair. "There's no need to feel nervous, Sam. We're here so you don't have to live in fear," Carter began.

Sam tried to smile, but it looked more like a grimace on his strained face. "I know, and I really can't tell you how much I appreciate your being here. It's just, once it gets dark…" His voice trailed off and he shuddered as his eyes darted from one corner of the room to the other.

"Then we'll make this quick," I spoke up. "Have you ever heard reports from former residents about any unusual activity?"

"No."

"Have there ever been any traumatic events here at the house, maybe a death?"

"My grandmother died here, in her sleep. That was years ago when I was only ten or eleven. My parents and I were here then, but the adults kept pretty quiet about it so

18

I wasn't really aware of what was going on at the time. Before then, I can't think of anything right off hand. No murders or anything violent like that, certainly."

Now it was Carter who asked a question. "Sam, I don't mean to be intrusive, but has there been any history of mental illness in your family?"

"You think I'm crazy? You think I'm just making this up?" said Sam, sounding affronted as he pulled back his sleeve to reveal the nasty cut again.

"Certainly not," Carter said smoothly. "However, in the past the paranormal wasn't discussed as openly as it is today. There have been cases where people experiencing a genuine haunting were diagnosed as having mental disorders. It was a way for their families to keep fooling themselves about the existence of ghosts."

Sam relaxed. "Oh, I see. No, nothing in my family that I've ever been told about."

We asked Sam a few more questions, but nothing he said even hinted that there might be some odd history with the old house or its residents. We saw him to the door, and as he drove away in his red BMW, Carter and I turned to each other. I shrugged; I had no idea what could have brought about this haunting. "Only one way to find out," Carter said, reading my thoughts.

We gathered everyone together in the kitchen for a brief meeting before we started. There were eight of us, a pretty big group for one house. Since we didn't want to be getting in each other's way, we decided to split into three groups. Shaun, Daisy and I would take the stairs and hallway, leaving the master bedroom for Carter, Jamie and Kerri. Lou and Ron were only too happy to man the monitors in the kitchen, which were wirelessly connected to the video cameras.

"Everyone tune their radios to channel two," instructed Lou. "Now, let's do a test, starting with you, Kerri."

Each of us took a turn testing our radios, and then Lou spoke again.

"Try to maintain radio silence as much as possible. We'll radio to let you guys know if we see anything show up on the video screen other than the six of you. And remember, no whispering. Speak in a normal, clear voice. We don't want to mistake one of you whispering as an EVP on our recordings."

Lou Miles lives for the technical side of investigating. He's a tall, awkward-looking guy with straggly black hair pulled back into a ponytail. His parents were huge horror movie fans, and they named their son Lugosi, so I sometimes think that Lou was destined to live some kind of offbeat lifestyle like this. How can you be normal when you're named after the guy who was famous for playing Dracula?

As Carter's trio went up the stairs to settle into Sam's bedroom, I double-checked the video cameras we had set up on the stairs. They were both on and recording. Lou's voice crackled over our radios. "Everyone snug?"

"We're ready," I answered, and Carter gave his affirmative answer a moment later.

"Okay, everyone, lights out." At Lou's command, we shut off the lights in every room but the kitchen, pausing to let our eyes adjust to the darkness. Luckily the moonlight shone through the windows, providing a dim light for us.

Daisy produced her little digital tape recorder and turned it on. The tiny red light that indicated it was recording glared brightly in the moonlit room. "Is there anyone here tonight?" she asked in her high, clear voice. "Would anyone like to come and talk to us?"

Of course we wouldn't be able to hear a ghost if there was any response, but that's what we had the tape recorder for. For some reason, ghostly voices that we can't hear with our own ears sometimes register on tape. Electronic Voice

Phenomena—or EVP for short—is a hotly debated method of getting evidence of a haunting, but we usually got some great whispers and sounds on our investigations.

Daisy continued asking questions as I unslung my digital camera from around my neck and popped the dust cover off. I turned it on and took a few pictures of the stairway, the flash leaving bright spots in my vision for several seconds afterward.

After an hour of more questions and pictures, we didn't have anything. Of course, we wouldn't really know what we had until Lou analyzed everything, but Shaun and I had looked at the pictures from both of our cameras using the little preview screens on them, and nothing stood out.

It was more than that, though. That sense of something else being present just wasn't there. "Pretty quiet so far," Shaun commented.

Apparently Carter was thinking the same thing, because his voice came over the radio just then. "Anything on the stairs yet?"

Shaun pressed the button on his radio and replied, "Nothing. You?"

"No. It's so quiet up here I could take a nap."

"Let's switch, and see if we have better luck."

With that, the three of us walked up the stairs and into the cavernous bedroom. "Have fun," Kerri said to us with a bored tone as she trailed along after her two companions.

The bedroom was more of the same monotony. More tape-recorded questions and more pictures, but no sense of anything being present there with us. Sometimes ghosts get shy and it's hard to draw them out, so investigators often have to spend hours waiting for any activity, or even make several visits to a place. Being a ghost hunter is far from glamorous.

Shaun had brought my EMF meter up with us. It

detects electromagnetic fields, and the higher the EMF reading, the better the possibility that there is something paranormal present. Ghosts are believed to use nearby energy to materialize, so it makes sense that it would be detectable with an EMF meter, like other electric objects. Unfortunately, that was the downfall of using EMF meters: sometimes a "ghost" turned out to be nothing more than some stripped wires pulsing with electricity. It didn't seem to matter, anyway, since we weren't getting any unusual readings in the bedroom.

The investigation seemed to drag on for hours as boredom set in. We had started at ten o'clock, and by two in the morning we were all tired and very disappointed.

"Hey, kids, it's past your bedtime." Lou was obviously ready to head home.

"We may as well pack up," I agreed, yawning into my radio.

"No arguments here," came Carter's sleepy drawl.

We turned the lights on throughout the house, then dismantled the video cameras and the line of monitors in the kitchen. As Lou and Shaun carried out our video equipment, Jamie and Ron did the same for Carter's team.

I turned to Shaun. "Why don't you two head home? Your wife looks like she's going to fall asleep on her feet."

"Sorry, Betty," mumbled Daisy. "It's easy to stay up this late when we're on an active investigation. Tonight, on the other hand, has been like sitting through an after-school special marathon." She put her hand to her mouth to hide a wide yawn. "I'll see you tomorrow."

"No fair, those things are contagious!" I yawned, too.

Shaun and Daisy left with Kerri, Jamie and Ron on their heels. Carter and I did one more round of the hallway and bedroom to make sure we hadn't overlooked any of our equipment. We met up with Lou at the front door, and the three of us gladly stepped out, locking up behind us with the key that Sam had left with Carter.

"Good night, and drive safe," I called to Lou, who was folding his long legs into his beat-up truck.

He waved back. "I'll start going over this stuff tomorrow. I'll call and let you know what I find."

"Just don't call me before noon, Lou!"

As the headlights swept down the driveway, Carter turned to me. "Not exactly the most exciting night."

"I'm surprised. I wonder if the house isn't really what's haunted, more like Sam himself is…the target." It was the best word I could think of, and luckily Carter seemed to understand.

"Almost like a poltergeist, where the activity is generated around a certain person."

"Almost," I agreed. "But poltergeist activity is usually associated with teenagers and all of their roller-coaster emotions."

"Maybe Sam's going through puberty a little late in life."

I laughed, but immediately grew serious again as a new thought struck me. "Let's have Sam here the next time. Do you have anything scheduled for next Friday?"

"I'll clear the date on my schedule. And as much as I hate to admit it, Boo, having him along for the ride is a good idea." Carter paused for a moment, and it was obvious that he was debating whether or not to say something. Finally, he sighed. "You're not bad at this, you know."

"You didn't do too bad yourself, though I can't wait for the day I get to see an apparition pop up in front of your eyes. Ten bucks says you scream."

"I'm being serious. I mean, you have a lot to learn still, but you handle yourself pretty well. Have you heard of the Everett-Tattnall House?"

My eyes widened. "That gorgeous brick mansion on Bull Street? Sure, I've been by there dozens of times. You got asked to investigate there?"

"Coming up in two weeks. What do you think? There's going to be a lot of research involved, and that's sort of your thing, I believe."

I chuckled. "Yeah, that's me, the dorky girl who likes to hide in libraries and government records rooms. What's going on there that they called you?"

Carter shrugged. "They were really vague on the phone, but you know that place is a law office. Apparently one of the senior partners died a while back, and they think he's the one doing the haunting."

"All right, Carter, I'm in, so long as I can bring my team with me. I can't pass up the chance to investigate that place. It's one of the prettiest buildings downtown, and what little history I've heard of the building makes me curious about what other ghosts we might find there."

I wondered if I was going to regret agreeing to work on another case with Carter. Sure, he'd been tolerable tonight, but we'd been in separate areas of the house the entire time. A closer working relationship might not turn out so well, and I knew he was only asking me because he hated doing research himself. Still, the Everett-Tattnall House was a beautiful mansion in Savannah's historic district, and unlike Carter, I really do enjoy the research part of investigating, so it was impossible to pass up.

No sooner were the words out of my mouth than Carter made me regret my decision already. "The press conference will be Thursday evening at 5:30. Can you make it?"

He had to be joking. "Press conference?"

"Of course. We're going to announce the pending investigation on the front steps of the building. It will get the media excited, get people to go to my website, maybe sell some more copies of my book."

Carter and his stupid book. And all those adoring fans who actually wanted to read his stupid stories about being a ghost hunter. I hadn't thought his ego could get any bigger until he published his book last year.

"What if I say no?" I asked.

Carter gave me a disapproving look. "Well, I'll be announcing your involvement anyway, but it would be nice of you to show your commitment to the investigation."

"Don't ever doubt my level of commitment to an investigation," I said, my tone frosty. "I'm just not as much of a media whore as you. But if you're going to be talking about me, I at least want to be there to make sure you're not slandering my name or anything else. See you Thursday."

I turned and headed for my car without another word. I heard Carter chuckling softly behind me. He was going to make me regret signing on for this one, I just knew it.

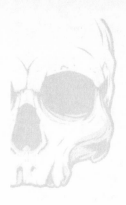

THREE

I love Saturday mornings. Despite a few bad dreams about being stuck on a never-ending road trip in Carter's Mercedes, I slept soundly. The bells from the cathedral just a few blocks away woke me up when they rang the hour with eleven chimes.

I stretched and rolled onto my side, pulling my sheet over my face to block the sun that was sneaking in through the slats in my window blinds. Mina walked up onto my pillow and meowed down at my head, her tone loud and demanding.

"I know, Mina, I need to get up." I reached up to pat her on the head, then snuggled further under the covers.

I needed coffee.

I slung my covers back and trudged out to the kitchen, but I had been so tired after the investigation that I hadn't gotten around to setting the coffee maker. By the time I had it percolating, I was beginning to feel somewhat like a human being. Daisy and I were having lunch at one, so at least I had a little bit of time before I had to really get moving.

Daisy and I have been best friends since we met in college. She married Shaun four months after we graduated, and since then she and I have gone out together for a little girl time at least once a week. I miss seeing her every day; we were roommates for the first three years of school —until she moved in with Shaun during our senior year— and we have always gotten along great. Now that she was married and settled down, Daisy always worried about my social life. I think she pictured me turning into an old maid, with nothing but a cat to keep me company.

Fresh coffee in hand, I wandered to the dining room table. Since my kitchen and dining room are pretty much the same thing, I didn't have far to go.

My copy of Savannah: A History in Architecture was already on the table. I had taken it off the bookshelf a couple days ago on the off chance that Sam's house was listed in its pages. It wasn't, but I knew the Everett-Tattnall House was. I found the page number and flipped the book open. The description of the house was only a few paragraphs long. It was built in 1821 for Josiah Everett, a local cotton merchant. Josiah's wife Mattie was the one who insisted that they build the house on Chippewa Square because she wanted to be far enough from the Savannah River that "no pirates would ever be a threat."

Josiah's son lived in the house with his family after Josiah died, but he later sold it to Elias Tattnall, another cotton merchant, and it stayed in the Tattnall family for three generations. The house was bought and divided into apartments in the 1920s, and in the 1980s it was renovated for use as a business.

I looked at the picture of the pale brick mansion in the book, wondering who was haunting the place. Carter had said the people at the law office suspected it might be a former partner in the firm, so hopefully we'd get some better answers soon.

By half past noon I was showered and ready to go in a denim skirt and white baby tee. It was already September, but summer seemed to be lingering. Today was supposed to be warm, but nothing like a normal sticky, humid summer day, so I was determined to enjoy it while I could.

Daisy and I were meeting at Soho South, a café only seven blocks away, and it was a perfect day for walking. Savannah is one of those cities that most people fall in love with, and I guess I'm one of those people. The downtown historic district is so beautifully restored that it's easy to envision the wealthy merchants and aristocratic South- erners of antebellum Savannah walking underneath the huge oak and magnolia trees, not to mention a rogue pirate or two stumbling through one of the grassy squares that dot the downtown area every two blocks.

I walked into Soho South just behind Daisy, who was already telling the hostess that there were two of us in our party.

"Hey, Betty, perfect timing! How you feeling this morning?"

"I'm feeling like I might have been crazy for accepting Carter's offer last night."

"Offer?" Daisy gasped as her eyes opened wide. "Oh, my gosh, you're going on a date with Carter? But you hate him!"

"Have more faith in me, Daisy!" I said, laughing.

"If you'll just follow me," said the hostess, looking at us impatiently. We followed her outside to a little table with an umbrella while Daisy peppered me with questions.

"But you said you accepted! Or was it something other than a date? When did this all happen?"

I just grinned at her until we were seated, amused at her anxiety on behalf of my love life. Finally I gave in and told her about Carter's investigation at the Everett-Tattnall House. "I'll understand if you don't want to participate since it means working with Carter more," I concluded.

"No way, I'm not going to sit out on that one even if I have to hold hands with that rat the whole time! Just don't hate me if I accidentally shove him down some stairs or something."

"I thought about doing that last night. You should have heard him, Daisy, going on about how he was going to single-handedly wrap up that investigation in record time."

Our waiter showed up just then to take our orders, and as soon as he left, Daisy was back to her original subject. "I'm glad you're not actually going on a date with Carter. I mean, I really want to see you get out there and date a man more than once every six months, but he's a little too sleazeball for you."

"Daze, if I ever go on a date with Carter Lansford, then call a priest because it will be obvious that I'm possessed." I shook my head, then told her about Jeanie's teasing at work on Friday and all of my potential business names for a paranormal dating service.

"Hotties and Haunts," Daisy suggested.

We were still coming up with names when our food arrived, and we were laughing so hard that a few people walking by on the sidewalk turned to give us odd glances.

We ate in silence for a minute before Daisy continued. "It's just that I worry about you, Boo. I've been your best friend since the first day of college, and I've only seen you go on maybe ten dates that whole time."

"Don't forget about Mark. He and I were pretty serious there for a while."

"'Mark the Mortician.' Please, spare me," said Daisy, rolling her eyes. "Why you ever picked him for a relationship, I'll never know."

"He's the one who introduced me to ghost hunting," I said in defense.

"Yeah, because that's a great reason to spend eight months dating a guy who looks like a long-lost cousin of the Addams Family!"

I knew I wasn't going to win. "I'll tell you what, Daze,

I'll do my best to get a date in the next month. Just remember that I'm doing it all for you, so you can stop losing sleep every night on my behalf!"

Daisy narrowed her eyes. "Not just a date. A date with a real man, not some creep from a crypt who owns nothing but black clothes from the Middle Ages."

I laughed. "Deal," I agreed.

———

I got a phone call from Lou later that afternoon, and even though everything he said was what I expected to hear, I still didn't like it. "I didn't find one scrap of evidence," he told me with a hoarse voice.

"That's disappointing. Still, I can't say I'm surprised after the lack of activity last night. What a strange investigation."

"Yeah. Not one damn orb picture or anything."

"Lou, you sound terrible. Have you slept?"

"For a couple of hours. I was anxious to start going through the video and the pictures you and Shaun took. I feel like the walking dead."

I giggled. "Don't you mean vampire? Now go take a nap and don't get up until sundown, Lugosi!"

"I don't want to hear it. I think my sense of humor disappeared somewhere around the third hour of video footage."

"You know I appreciate your work, Lou. I just wish we could have made your job more interesting this time around."

"Me, too, Boo. All right, bed calls. Talk to you later."

"Bye, Lou." I hung up the phone and glanced at the clock. It was only six, time to start dinner. Of course, with my lack of a social life, I had no plans for going out. A pint of Ben and Jerry's ice cream and one DVD was as exciting as it was going to get.

The rest of the weekend passed just as quietly, and too quickly for me. It's not just that I love the weekends: I was desperately hoping to slow down time so I could put off going to Carter's press conference. Talking to one stranger is hard enough for me, but the thought of having to stand up in front of a crowd of reporters and Carter's adoring fans made my stomach twist into knots.

I was still worrying about the coming "Big Event," as I was beginning to think of it, when I walked into the hospital's admin building Monday morning. Jeanie caught me so off-guard that it took me a moment to understand what she was talking about.

"What's the verdict?" she asked.

I stared at her blankly. "What?"

"On the guy you were going to meet on Friday!" Jeanie is a great girl, but she was way too perky for a Monday morning.

"No dice, Jeanie. Not my type, and there was no attraction at all."

Jeanie frowned. "Why not? What was wrong with him?"

I shrugged noncommittally. "Too old." Jeanie opened her mouth to speak again, but I raised my hand toward her to cut off the inevitable question. "Around forty-ish."

She nodded. "Looks?"

"He looked like a client. Not a potential date." Leave it to Jeanie to turn a night of ghost hunting into a search for a boyfriend. "You're lucky you found that special someone already. They aren't easy to find."

"I know," smiled Jeanie, her disappointment at my failure to pick up a rich, haunted man replaced by pride for her fiancée.

I turned to walk to my office, but then I stopped and

turned back to her. If anyone could help motivate me to keep my promise to Daisy, it was Jeanie. "Oh, by the way, I have a little wager with my friend Daisy."

"Ooh, what's that?" she asked, instantly eager.

"That I can get a date within the next month."

Jeanie clapped her hands and giggled. "Awesome! We'll totally make that happen!"

One thing I'll give Jeanie: I may not like morning people, but she did put me in a better mood for the rest of the day.

Unfortunately, her enthusiasm for my dating challenge wasn't much help as Tuesday and Wednesday flew by. Thursday's press conference was coming all too fast.

Suddenly it actually was Thursday, and I stared into my closet that morning with a feeling of panic. I had to go straight to the press conference from work, and I wanted to make sure I looked good. I knew that Carter would be wearing some kind of fancy designer clothes, but my income definitely didn't let me do the same.

I pulled out one outfit after another. If I didn't pick something soon, I'd either have to leave my apartment naked or risk being late for work. Finally, I settled on a navy blue dress suit—it was my "interview outfit," and the sole suit in my fairly casual wardrobe. It hugged my curves nicely without looking too sexy for the office, and I could ditch the jacket if I decided I was overdressed. Plus, Daisy had called to tell me that she and Shaun were going to be at the press conference, and they were taking me out for a drink afterwards. Good, I was going to need one. Or two. Or five.

The day sped past and at five minutes before five, my cell phone rang.

"Hello?"

"You hanging in there?" It was Daisy.

"I feel like my heart is going to pound my ribcage to bits. Otherwise, I feel great."

"Is Carter going to do all of the talking?"

"I assume so. We both know how much Carter likes being the center of attention."

"See, you'll be fine. You just have to stand to the side and look like a competent ghost hunter, and smile once or twice. You've got nothing to worry about."

Daisy had a good point. "You're right. I hadn't thought of it like that. You two still coming?"

"We'll be there! I just wanted to give you a call in case you're too busy to talk to us when we arrive."

"Thanks, Daisy. I feel better knowing you and Shaun will be there to suffer with me. I'll see you soon, okay?"

"You got it. Bye, Boo."

"Bye." I felt reassured. I could stand there and look good without too much mortification, and there was little chance that Carter would want to put me in front of the microphone. For once, I was thankful for Carter's giant ego.

I turned off my computer, grabbed my purse and headed for the bathroom at the end of the hall. When I got in there, I touched up my make-up, made sure I didn't have any remnants of my lunch stuck in my teeth and ran a brush through my hair, which I'd left down today so that it fell in auburn waves over my shoulders. I stared at my reflection in the mirror, and I had to admit that I looked good. I just hoped that no one would be able to see the anxiety in my eyes. Was it considered rude to wear sunglasses at a press conference?

I arrived at the Everett-Tattnall House ten minutes before the start of the press conference. As I walked up the grand front steps leading to the door of the house, I saw Carter standing next to a podium that had been set up with a microphone and was relieved to see that he was wearing a suit, too. At least I'd chosen the right outfit.

While I stared at Carter, wondering if he'd actually had his blonde hair professionally styled for this, he noticed me. "Betty, hi. You look nice," he said with a note of surprise. What did he expect, that I was going to show up in the usual tee-shirt and jeans that I wear when I'm ghost hunting?

I decided I'd just try to accept the compliment without over-analyzing his words. "Thanks, Carter. You, too. So, what's the plan?"

"Nothing fancy. I'll welcome everyone, then announce the investigation. You'll be introduced as a part of the project, so I just need you to stand next to me for the duration."

Whew. Exactly what I wanted to hear. I nodded. "Easy enough."

With the podium at the top of the stairs, the big front door of the house and the stained-glass windows on either side of it would be our backdrop. I looked down at the sidewalk below us and was surprised to see that there was actually a sizeable group of people gathering for Carter's announcement. His fans were easy to spot: most of them were young women in their early twenties, clutching cameras and waving frantically at Carter every time he turned in their direction. Directly in front were a few people with notebooks and tape recorders, obviously reporters, and there were even two cameramen. One stood next to a woman I recognized from the local evening news on Channel 2, and the other cameraman was with one of the hosts of a morning news show called "Good Morning, Georgia." Wow, Carter even got a statewide news crew to show up. He had more pull than I thought. Not that I would ever admit that to him, of course.

A gentle tug on my sleeve brought my attention back to

the scene at the top of the stairs. "Come on, Betty, just stand over here to my left," Carter was saying, pulling me into place. I followed along, my pulse pounding with fear. "No, no, not right next to me. I need you to step back so you're behind me a little."

I glanced to Carter's right, where a man in an immaculate tailored suit stood. When he saw me looking at him, he leaned forward and extended his hand past Carter. "Hi, I'm Alec Thornburn, one of the partners at the firm here."

I shook his hand and introduced myself in return. So this is what a rich, high-profile lawyer looks like, I thought. He had flawless olive skin, his dark hair was short and absolutely perfect, and his teeth flashed bright white when he smiled. Alec wasn't a handsome man, but he definitely had an aura of power and charm.

Carter cleared his throat and reached toward the microphone, and Alec and I took the cue to straighten up and look out at our audience, which had grown larger. I saw Daisy and Shaun in the little crowd of people, and Shaun waved while Daisy gave me a thumbs-up. I smiled, and actually felt myself relax a little bit. I had nothing to say, and since I was already in place, I didn't have to risk tripping down the stairs or something embarrassing like that, so what was there to worry about?

"Good evening, everyone," began Carter, speaking into the microphone. The audience instantly went silent, and the newspaper reporters held their tape recorders out to catch Carter's speech.

"My name is Carter Lansford, and I'm the founder and director of East Coast Paranormal Authorities. As many of you know, my team and I have been investigating the paranormal for five years now, and we have been able to bring peace to dozens of Savannah's business owners and citizens dealing with hauntings."

My mind wandered for a few minutes while Carter

went on and on about his paranormal credentials, even mentioning his book and his "popularity as an expert authority at paranormal conferences across the United States." When I heard that part, my eyes turned to Daisy again, and she made a face of mock awe. I had to bite my lip to keep a laugh from escaping.

"Whitney, Thornburn and Stiles is one of the most respected law firms in Savannah," continued Carter, "but even they aren't immune to the paranormal. When it became clear to them that a ghost was haunting this historic building, the beautiful Everett-Tattnall House, they contacted East Coast Paranormal Authorities to discover who is haunting here, and why. Alec Thornburn is joining us today as we formally announce our investigation." Carter turned and gestured to Alec, who flashed his ultra-bright smile at the audience.

"Also joining us in this investigation is Betty Boorman, who is joining East Coast Paranormal Authorities for this special project. Our investigation team advocates training and guiding people who are new to the world of paranormal investigating. It's a way for us to share our vast knowledge and to ensure proper ghost hunting techniques. Although Betty hasn't been in the paranormal field for very long, her research skills will be put to good use to find out what the history of this house and its residents can tell us that might help us identify the ghost here."

Carter turned and nodded toward me, and it was everything I could do to keep my smile pasted on my face. I looked out at the audience because I knew that if I met his eyes I wouldn't be able to keep my cool. I could get over the fact that Carter hadn't mentioned my involvement with The Seekers, but to imply that I was a fresh-faced investigator "under his guidance" was too much. Sure, I hadn't been investigating as long as him, but he made me sound like some kind of rookie who could only be trusted to handle the research.

The audience below began to applaud, and I realized that Carter must have wrapped things up. The host from "Good Morning, Georgia" raised his hand. "Mr. Thornburn, could you tell us what this ghost is doing?" he asked.

Alec moved to stand in front of the podium while Carter took a step closer to me. I glared up at him, and he returned my furious look with one of absolute confidence. "We've been hearing a lot of footsteps and knocking sounds," Alec said, "and a few of us are having problems with items being moved on our desks. It's gotten to the point that it's affecting our ability to do our jobs efficiently, which is why we decided to call Carter and his team in to investigate."

One of the reporters was the next to ask a question, and to my surprise he directed it to me. "Ms. Boorman, how did you get involved with this investigation?"

My stomach jumped; so much for just standing in one spot and looking good. I stepped forward and gripped both sides of the podium, but my fear virtually disappeared when I realized that this was my chance to set the record straight.

"I'm the founder of The Savannah Spirit Seekers, a paranormal investigation team based here in Savannah," I said. Gosh, did my voice always sound so thin and timid? "I began investigating three years ago, while I was still in college. Conducting thorough research is very important to The Seekers, and we've become the local experts at rounding up the history of a haunted site. Carter and I, plus our other team members, are currently working on another case together, and he asked me to lend a hand with this one."

I stepped back and flashed Carter a smug smile. He never misses a beat, though, and he was quick to pick up where I'd left off. "Yes, we're working on a most unusual case at a home in Thunderbolt," he said, taking his place in front of the microphone again. "The haunting started quite suddenly and violently, but our teams haven't uncovered any evidence so far. It looks like it's going to take our combined talents to discover the true nature of the haunting. We'll be updating the case report on my website, so be sure to go there for details about the investigation we'll be doing tomorrow night."

I looked out at the audience again, and my eyes drifted across the street to Chippewa Square. Dusk was setting in, and I could barely see a man standing in the shadow of an oak tree. He was obviously watching our press conference, but he was nearly hidden in the gloom. All I could see was a dark silhouette. As I watched, he took a single step forward, and I could see red eyes staring straight at me.

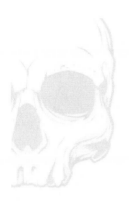

FOUR

"Thank you," I heard Carter say. I pulled my attention back to the press conference and saw that the crowd was breaking up. The event I'd been dreading all week was over, and I let out a breath I didn't realize I'd been holding. Carter said "Thank you" again, and it took me a moment to realize he was talking to me.

"Oh, um, you're welcome," I said, making it more of a question than a statement. "You're just lucky I didn't slap you for making me sound like a beginner who's only good for research. That would have made a nice picture in the paper." My eyes kept darting back to the oak tree where I'd seen the man, but the dispersing crowd blocked my view.

Carter actually laughed. "Come on, Betty, I've been doing this far longer than you. Besides, I can't let you show me up, now can I? I think I'm actually going to enjoy teaming up with you. I need a cute little sidekick."

"You need a cute little black eye." I whispered my threat so that Alec wouldn't overhear us. "I'm so looking forward to seeing you tomorrow night in Thunderbolt," I continued dryly. "Nine o'clock, or do you have a cute little secretary to remind you of things like that?"

"Why do I need one, when I have you to do it for me?" Carter smiled. "Good night, Betty."

I ignored Carter and tried to force a smile onto my face

for Alec, who was walking toward me. "So you'll be doing the research?" he asked. "We've got a lot of things for you to review."

"Really? I'm surprised. Most places we investigate don't have a lot of records on hand."

"We're a law office, we keep everything," he replied, smiling broadly.

I was beginning to like this guy, and I couldn't help smiling back. "I guess the big question is when can we all sit down and start going over details? Carter and I will want to hear all about the activity you're experiencing, of course, and I'd like to look through some of your records as soon as possible."

Alec looked over my shoulder. "Carter, what time is good for you next week? I've got Tuesday open."

"That works for me," said Carter.

"Me, too," I added.

"How about we meet at Big Bean Theory at seven? We can discuss it over coffee," Alec suggested.

Carter and I both agreed. Alec sure was a take-charge kind of guy, and I was looking forward to hearing the sophisticated lawyer talk about ghosts. He probably had a flow chart showing all of the paranormal activity over a thirty-day period, plus typed-up testimony from the rest of the staff.

I said goodnight to Alec, getting a firm handshake from him again, then headed down the stairs to meet Daisy and Shaun on the sidewalk. Daisy opened her arms and gave me a hug. "You look gorgeous! Carter was doing all the talking, but everyone was looking at you."

"You mean me, the inferior little research lackey?" After Daisy's compliment, it came out as more of a joke and I smiled despite myself.

"Carter's an ass," Shaun said matter-of-factly, loud enough that some of Carter's female fans looked over with expressions of horror. "But you defended yourself incredibly, and you didn't stoop to his level. Good for you, Boo."

I grinned at Shaun. "I was tempted to. I told Carter I nearly smacked him up there."

Daisy giggled. "I would have paid to see that! Maybe you can try it at the next press conference."

"No more press conferences! Right now all I can think of is food. Have you two eaten dinner yet?"

"We thought we'd grab something at The Burglar Bar since we're taking you there for a drink anyway," spoke up Shaun. "Does that work for you?"

"A drink and chicken fingers always works for me. I'm going to drive my car back to my house, then I'll walk over to the bar."

Daisy and Shaun headed for the bar to get us a table. I only lived about five blocks from the Everett-Tattnall House, but I'd driven straight to the press conference to save time and to avoid walking that far in high heels. Before getting in my car, though, I headed for the oak tree in the square across the street.

Of course, by the time I got there, no one was around except for a few tourists who were sauntering through the square. They were definitely not the shape of the man I'd seen. And they definitely didn't have red eyes.

I walked all the way around the trunk of the oak, as if the stranger might have been hiding behind it in some weird game of hide and seek. I even searched the spot where I thought he'd been standing, looking for what, I didn't know. As I stood in the spot he'd occupied, though, and looked up at the house, the setting sun's reflection in the windows glinted in my eyes.

"Betty, you're being so stupid," I said out loud. That red glow in his eyes had probably been a trick of the late-afternoon sun. I guess the anxiety of the press conference had gotten to me more than I'd realized.

By the time I arrived at The Burglar Bar, I'd slung my suit jacket over my shoulder. The bar had been our hangout since college, but during our early days there it was pretty much a dive. It took up the first floor of an historic building on York Street, and the bar had looked every bit its age back then. A year ago, though, the whole building had undergone a huge renovation after some new owners bought it. The Burglar Bar was a lot nicer now, with rock music playing quietly in the background and dark lighting that gave the place a mysterious air. Black and white mug shots of famous criminals hung on the exposed brick walls. The more sophisticated ambiance never would have suited us back when we discovered the bar during our sophomore year, but now it somehow fit. It was like the bar had grown up with us.

Shaun and Daisy were sitting at a high-top table near the back of the bar. He gave me a wave, and when I joined them, there was already a bottle of cabernet and three glasses on the table.

"Hope you don't mind I went ahead and ordered a bottle," said Shaun. "I thought it would be best if we drank up. Rumor has it that the Carter Lansford Fan Club is meeting here in a little while."

Daisy gave her husband a playful jab in the shoulder. "Obviously that rumor can't be true. Half of his fan club isn't old enough to drink, and the other half wouldn't dream of coming to a dump like this."

I poured the wine while Shaun and Daisy tried to decide where the "hoity-toity paranormal set" in Savannah would probably go for a drink. "Nowhere we want to be," I said, handing over their glasses.

Shaun raised his glass in a toast. "To our favorite researcher and media darling!" he shouted, and I saw several people turn their heads to stare as the three of us clinked our glasses together.

We had an enjoyable dinner, and I'm sure true wine aficionados would have shuddered at the combination of bar food and cabernet, but it seemed perfect to me. After our food had been taken away and Shaun had paid our bill, Daisy was quiet for a moment. "Do you think Sam MacIntosh is just making it all up?" she asked suddenly.

"What?"

"Think about it. He calls with this outrageous claim about being attacked, and says this all popped up out of nowhere. None of us has ever seen that sort of haunting begin without any forewarning, not even Carter's team. And then we show up there, and nothing happens. I think maybe Sam's making it all up."

It wasn't an option that I'd considered. "Maybe," I said slowly. "But why would somebody make up a claim like that? And if he is making it up, then how did he get those awful cuts?"

"That's what I can't figure out. Maybe he's just delusional and is subconsciously doing it to himself. Then again, maybe he just wants attention."

"It's possible, I guess, but it just doesn't seem right."

"Maybe he's lonely and figured this was a good way to get some company. You know, like a paranormal dating service," added Shaun, giving me a big wink. Obviously Daisy had told him of our conversation on Saturday.

"No dating clients!" I said, making a face at Shaun. "We'll see what happens tomorrow night when he's there with us. If nothing happens even with Sam around, then I'll be willing to consider other explanations."

"Shaun and I should probably get on home," Daisy said, glancing at her watch.

"Yeah, me, too. You two go ahead, I'm just going to finish my wine."

Shaun looked at me narrowly. "You sure you're okay here by yourself? You might be hounded by autograph seekers."

I smiled. "Bring 'em on! Have a good night, you two. And thanks again for the wine and moral support."

"We wouldn't have missed it. Bye!" Daisy gave me a quick peck on the cheek, and she and Shaun left.

I turned back to my nearly-empty glass of wine, staring into it absently as I thought. What were we missing in this case with Sam? Was it some sort of unusual poltergeist activity, or was he really making it up?

I was still gazing pensively into my wine glass when a smooth voice spoke quietly into my ear. "I don't think you'll find the answer in there."

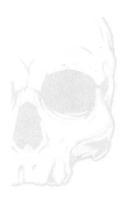

FIVE

Startled, I gasped and turned around to find the most beautiful man I'd ever seen standing just inches away from me. He was tall with a thin but muscular body that looked perfect in his white shirt and black pinstriped vest and slacks. The angular features of his pale face stood out sharply against his midnight black hair, which stood up in a messy, tousled style. It was the stranger's eyes that really took my breath away, though. They were the palest blue, like ice crystals, and they looked both inviting and a little sinister.

I couldn't respond for a moment, as I tried to absorb how incredibly handsome he was. I nearly asked him if he realized that he'd fallen off the cover of GQ and landed in a bar, but luckily my good sense stopped me. Talk about a cheesy pick-up line.

"The answer to what?" I asked a little breathlessly.

The man smiled, which made him look even more handsome, and I took a deep breath in an effort to clear my head.

"The answer to what's haunting Sam MacIntosh," he answered, "and how to help him."

"How do you know about that?"

"It was on the evening news," he said smoothly. "You and that pretty-boy Carter Lansford are investigating a house in Thunderbolt, and since it's such a small town, I knew it had to be the MacIntosh estate."

I nodded my head. "That's the one. And you say you know what's going on there?"

"Yes."

"How do you know what needs to be done to help Sam?"

"Let's just say it's my job," he said, handing me a crisp white business card. I took the card and read the only two words printed on it: Maxwell, Demon.

There was a phone number below that, and I'm not sure what struck me as more funny: that this guy called himself a demon, or that a demon would have a phone number.

I couldn't suppress a wry smile. "Your area code is '666'?"

"Just because I'm evil doesn't mean I don't have a sense of humor," he answered. Maxwell gave me an appreciative nod. "I'm a big fan of your work, Betty. You're the best paranormal investigator in this city. When you decide you want to know what's haunting Sam MacIntosh, give me a call."

With that, he turned and left. I stared after him, fighting the compulsion to follow. Great, I mused, I meet the most beautiful man in the world, and he's completely crazy. Or he really is a demon, like he claims.

I wasn't sure which would be worse.

He had to be crazy. Demonic hauntings were one thing, but a flesh and blood demon showing up in my neighborhood bar? Give me a break. That was the kind of thing you'd see on a TV show, not something from real life.

Then again, I realized, there was a third option: maybe he was joking, and he liked to flirt using humor. It would have to be an elaborate joke, though, since his business cards were obviously professionally printed.

Definitely crazy. A well-informed crazy, at that. Any news story based on the press conference would have focused on Carter, not me, so how had this Maxwell recognized me? He'd mentioned he was a big fan of my work, so obviously he knew some of my background. Creepy.

I took the last sip of my wine and left, wondering about the mysterious Maxwell during my three-block walk home.

I was still thinking about him when I fell asleep that night.

Friday flew by, like the rest of the week had, and all day long co-workers popped into my office to tell me they had seen the piece about the investigation on the news. With all of the congratulations, I was beginning to understand why Carter hoarded the spotlight. It felt pretty nice.

I went home from work and fell into my usual Friday routine: relax on the couch, nap and eat dinner. Sam was going to be at the investigation with us tonight, and I hoped that we would witness some sort of paranormal activity so that we might have some idea about how to help him.

I was so anxious to get some answers that I arrived at Sam's house fifteen minutes early. As I walked up onto the front porch, the front door opened and Sam rushed out.

"Thank goodness you're here! It's been an awful week!"

"Sam, are you okay?" I asked, alarmed. "Have you gotten hurt again?"

Sam blushed. "No, I haven't. I actually haven't been out here since Saturday. I came back and packed my things, even though you said that you didn't find any kind of evidence. I've been staying at my brother's in Savannah."

"Then why has it been an awful week?"

"I can't stand my sister-in-law."

A laugh escaped me before I could help it. "Oh, so your problems aren't of a paranormal nature, then. I am sorry you don't feel safe in your own home right now, Sam. I hope we can get some answers tonight."

As Sam led me inside, a sudden thought struck me. "You didn't have any paranormal experiences at your brother's, did you?"

He shook his head. "No. I had some pretty crazy dreams, but no weird stuff like what happened here."

I frowned at Sam's back as he walked to the living room. Carter and I both thought that the ghost might be haunting Sam himself, but if that were the case, it should have followed him.

Sam and I shared a few minutes of small talk before the doorbell rang, and soon Shaun and Daisy joined us in the conversation. "So, Betty, you have any rabid fans come after you last night once we left?" Shaun asked.

"Funny you should mention that," I said, not sure how to begin telling them about my encounter with a so-called demon. "I did get a phone number from a…" I hesitated, "a fan, but he was only interested in business."

Daisy instantly perked up. "Oh, does he have a case he wants us to look into?"

"Not exactly. I'll tell you all about it later. It was an odd encounter." For some reason, I was reluctant to mention Maxwell in front of Sam. I found it strange that Maxwell knew it was Sam's house that we'd referred to in the press conference, and I was worried how he might react to Maxwell's offer of help on this case.

The doorbell rang again just then, and Sam went off to let in the next arrivals. As soon as he was out of sight, Daisy leaned toward me and whispered, "So spill it, Boo!"

I laughed at Daisy's curiosity. "Seriously, Daze, I can't

even begin to describe this guy before Sam comes back. He was either crazy or a minion of hell."

Daisy's eyes widened, and Shaun gave me a disbelieving look.

"But he was absolutely gorgeous," I added.

"Well, then, that solves it," said Daisy, as Carter and his team trooped through the door. "He's a minion of hell, for sure."

"You're not talking about me, are you?" Carter broke in.

"No, we're not. Believe it or not, it's not always about you," I said.

"Yes, I've missed you, too, Betty. By the way, have you seen all the great press coverage we've been getting? Lots of pictures of you and me standing together. I told you I needed a cute sidekick."

I rolled my eyes.

Lou arrived soon after, and everyone began setting up the cameras in the same locations as the previous week. We broke up into the same teams, and decided that Sam would tag along with Carter, Kerri and Jamie first. After a radio check, they headed upstairs while Shaun, Daisy and I took up our vigil near the staircase.

Shaun turned on his camera while I got my own set up, but Daisy had other things on her mind. "Okay, tell us about the hunka hunka burnin' love from hell!"

I described my strange meeting with Maxwell, and they were both as intrigued as me. "He's got to be off his rocker," Shaun asserted when I was done.

"Well, that seems more likely than him being a living, breathing demon," I said. "But there was something about him. He knew it was Sam's house, which was a little odd, but I figure it's Savannah after all, and there aren't many secrets the way people around here gossip. But the way he called me by name and seemed so sure that he knows how to solve this case…it was a little eerie."

"So he's off his rocker and he's a stalker," Shaun amended. "You're going to have as many adoring fans as Carter before long."

"You going to call him?" Daisy was looking at me expectantly.

"I doubt it. I hope we can figure this case out tonight and help Sam before any more time goes by. Besides, it's probably not even a real phone number. I bet it's some weird joke or something."

"Maybe it's how he picks up women. At least it's more memorable than all those cliché pick-up lines guys try to use." Shaun grinned at me.

"I actually thought of that."

"You like guys with a good sense of humor. He might be fun to go out with."

"Shaun, are you on the 'get Betty a date' bandwagon now, too?" I tried to look exasperated, but I failed miserably. I held up my hands to close the subject. "No, I'm not calling him."

Daisy settled down then and turned on her tape recorder. "Is there anyone here with us tonight?" she asked.

The entire house was silent for a moment, and then we heard a crash from upstairs. "Was that in the hallway?" I asked. The three of us rushed up the stairs, and saw Carter and his team facing us from the other end of the hallway.

"Was that you guys clunking around out here?" asked Kerri, a note of superiority in her voice.

"Not us. We were down at the foot of the stairs," answered Shaun.

Carter pumped his fist. "All right, looks like we might get somewhere tonight."

They returned to the bedroom with a wide-eyed Sam,

and we stayed at the top of the staircase so we could keep an eye on the upstairs hallway. Whatever had made the loud noise remained silent, though. Shaun and I didn't find anything on our cameras, and Daisy was growing weary of asking questions when she, as she put it, felt like she was talking to an imaginary friend. "I'm just not feeling anything," she said.

We sat silent for a few minutes, straining to hear or see anything in the darkness that might break up our monotony. I was just lifting my radio to my lips to ask Carter if we should all trade places when a scream came from the bedroom.

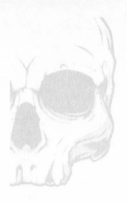

SIX

The three of us looked at each other, then we scrambled to our feet and hurried down the hall. When we entered the bedroom, Kerri was sitting on her knees on the floor with everyone huddled around her.

"Here, use this!" shouted Sam, tossing a tee-shirt at Jamie. He hastily folded the shirt and reached down to wrap it around Kerri's arm, and I saw by the shine of Carter's flashlight that she was bleeding profusely. Already blood was dripping from her arm, leaving dark splotches on the cream-colored carpet.

"What happened?" I asked, flipping on the bedroom light.

"It attacked her!" said Sam, looking like he was on the edge of hysteria.

"Nothing at all was happening," said Carter, who looked plenty shaken himself. "Then Kerri sat down next to Sam, and as soon as she put her hand on his shoulder, something sliced her arm open."

The two guys stationed downstairs came thundering into the room then. "We heard screaming. What happened?" asked Lou.

Carter gave them the same account. "We need to get her to the emergency room for stitches," spoke up Jamie. "I'll drive." Carter's tech guy Ron volunteered to go along, too, and in a few minutes they were on their way out the door, with Sam following and apologizing the whole time, as if the paranormal attack was all his fault.

After they were off, we went to the kitchen to look over the videotape of the bedroom. There was nothing but Sam and the investigators in the footage, when suddenly Kerri screamed. The camera wasn't angled correctly for us to see the actual cut opening on her arm.

"Well, my entire team is gone for the night," said Carter. "Do we call this off or give it another go?"

"I say one more go," said Shaun. "Daisy, why don't you stay here with Lou?"

Daisy would have normally argued against sitting on the sidelines, but for once she just nodded her head. "Be safe," was all she said, squeezing Shaun's hand and looking grimly at each of us.

Carter, Shaun, Sam and I started upstairs, but halfway up I felt Sam's hand clamp down on my arm.

"No!" he shouted, and he began to jerk frantically at my arm. For a split second I thought he was just trying to make me stop ascending the stairs. "Sam, what's—" I began to ask, but then Sam tugged so hard at my arm that I had to grip the railing to keep from falling down the stairs.

He gave an incoherent shout, then his fingers slid from my arm and he went sailing backwards, landing on his back a few stairs down and tumbling violently to the floor below.

"Sam!" I shouted, following after him. I heard him groaning, so at least he was still conscious. "Are you hurt?" I started to look over him, and thankfully all of his limbs seemed to be in proper order.

"Hit my head," grumbled Sam.

I leaned over to see if his scalp was bleeding at all, and my loose hair slid over my shoulder and skimmed his face.

"That tickles," he chuckled, then groaned again. "Ow, it hurts to laugh."

"Sorry," I said. As I pulled away, I saw a bright flash out of the corner of my eye. I jerked backward quickly as a ball of flame hurtled past, right through the narrow space between my face and Sam's. As I watched the orange flame crash into the wall, I realized that there was still something glowing directly in front of me. My hair was on fire.

I screamed as Shaun tackled me to the ground, beating my hair into the carpet. It was just the ends of my hair that had gotten caught in the path of the fire, I realized, as I sat up and looked with dismay at my charred locks. Little tendrils of smoke were rising from the blackened strands.

Luckily the wall hadn't caught fire, but there was a big black circle where the flames had singed the paint.

"I think it's time we called it a night," said Shaun, his voice shaky.

I nodded my head, too shocked to speak.

Sam sat up, looking a little dazed. "Think someone could drop me off at my brother's house in town? I'm feeling a little woozy."

Shaun nodded. "Yeah, we can take you. Come on, let's turn on all the lights and pack this stuff up. Betty, you okay?"

I nodded again. "What was that?"

"It's new to me. I've never seen anything like it," said Carter. "There's no way we're giving up now; we're finally getting results!"

"Results as in Sam falling and me getting lit on fire? And you want to keep going?" Maybe the ghost would light Carter on fire.

"Absolutely! This is whole new territory for us. When have you ever seen a ghost make fire materialize like that?"

Carter was practically giddy, and I had to put my hands in my pockets to keep from shoving him.

Before either Shaun or I could stop him, Carter was talking again, this time addressing the ghost. "Are you still here with us? In the past you've only haunted Sam, but tonight you've gone after two people who were right next to him. You only got Betty's hair, though. Come out and show us what else you can do."

"Carter! Are you asking it to try to hurt me again?" My hands, I realized, were no longer in my pockets. Instead, they were curled up in fists.

Carter shrugged. "I'm just trying to provoke it a little. Sometimes that gets results."

"No, no more 'results' tonight," Sam finally spoke up. "We're leaving."

Carter gave me a stern look, his lips set in a tight line. "Fine." When he turned to Sam, his face transformed into one of condescending pity. "Of course, Sam, we'll start packing up. I'd love to see what we got on video, but we'll wait to review the tapes elsewhere."

Daisy met me at the kitchen door, a horrified expression on her face. "Oh, your beautiful hair!" she kept lamenting as we packed up our equipment in record time.

Within twenty minutes all of our cars were packed and ready to go. Sam was standing with a bag full of clothes next to Shaun and Daisy.

"Sam, I'm so sorry," I told him. "I had hoped we would learn the nature of this haunting tonight, so we could get you some peace and quiet. But this is beyond our experience, and I think we're going to have to do some research to find the answer to this. I'm really, really sorry."

"At least I know now that it wasn't all in my head," he answered. "I'm just sorry your friend got hurt and that your hair caught on fire."

"We'll be fine. Take care of yourself, Sam, and call

me if anything happens. We'll be in touch with you soon." I shook Sam's hand before getting a hug from Daisy.

Carter stepped forward and lifted a strand of my hair with his perfect fingers. His angry expression changed to one of pity, which only made me mad. Sympathy from Daisy made me feel better, but sympathy from Carter just made me want to throw my own fireball at him. "Tough luck, Boo," he said.

"Yeah," I answered, and it was all I could get out. I climbed in my car and drove home in a daze. Once I was inside my apartment I headed straight for the bathroom, where I looked at myself in the mirror. The ends of my hair were black and crisp (not to mention reeking like burned steak), and if I touched them little strands would break away. If I went to sleep like that, I'd wake up to a bed full of barbequed hair in the morning. I pulled my long hair into a braid, grit my teeth, and cut the blackened ends off with a pair of scissors. I fell asleep that night with tears running down my face.

I woke up earlier than usual Saturday morning, and even though I was groggy, I forced myself to get up. I had two phone calls to make, and although I wanted to put one of them off as long as I possibly could, the other even took precedence over my morning coffee.

I flipped open the address book on my dining room table and dialed the number, reading it through unfocused eyes. On the second ring, someone picked up. "A Shorn Thing," a distracted voice said.

"Hi, I have a little bit of a hair emergency. Does Sheila have anything open today?"

"Maybe. Can you hold for a minute?"

"Sure." I crossed my fingers, hoping I could get in to see Sheila, my hairstylist, today. I wasn't sure how bad my hair looked now, but I figured it must be horrifying.

Looking in the mirror was not high on my list at the moment.

After what seemed like an age, the woman at the salon picked up the phone again. "Can you get here in about twenty minutes? Sheila can squeeze you in this morning."

"Yes! Thank you!" I nearly shouted into the phone. I gave the woman my name and hung up the phone, then dashed into the bathroom for a quick shower. I skipped putting on any make-up, and of course there was no point in styling my hair, so I managed to make it to the salon right on time.

When I walked in the door, Sheila wandered up to the reception area as I was giving the woman there my name. She eyed my damp, uneven hair and frowned. "Honey, what did you do to yourself?"

I smiled grimly at her. "It wasn't me. I just hope you can work some sort of magic on this mess."

"Well, of course I can," she answered with a note of pride. Sheila is of Gullah descent, an African-American culture from the low country areas of the Southern coast, and she has a light accent in her voice. Sheila has been my stylist for a few years, and she's well versed in my adventures as a ghost hunter. I can't say she necessarily approves of it, but she's definitely a believer. Gullah culture is steeped in superstition, so she never gives me a skeptical look like a lot of people do.

Sheila sat me down in a chair, draped a cape over me, then began running her fingers through my hair. "Did you cut this yourself?" she asked.

"I had to," I explained. "The ends were breaking off."

"Hair doesn't just fall off on its own. What did you do?" Sheila sounded every bit like a scolding mother.

I shrugged. "My hair kind of caught on fire last night."

"Kind of? Did this have anything to do with one of your ghosts?"

I told Sheila about Sam's mystifying situation, culminating in my brush with a phantom pyromaniac last night. Her frown deepened as I told her more details, and by the time I was done she was shaking her head disapprovingly.

"Honey, you got something more than a ghost on your hands," she told me.

"I think maybe I do," I agreed.

"Regular old ghosts don't try to tag people with fire. If it's getting that dangerous, you're probably dealing with something from the devil. And you listen to me when I say you shouldn't be messing with that at all."

"I try not to." Even as I spoke, an image of Maxwell flashed through my mind.

"And I think you should tell that nice man you're sorry, but you can't help him anymore."

I nodded my head once, because I knew it was good advice even if I had no intention of following it. We had an obligation to Sam, and I didn't see myself telling him that the only solution to his problem was to move out of his house. Besides, if he did leave, there was no way of knowing that whatever was haunting him wouldn't follow.

Sheila had been snipping off bits of my hair while we talked, and finally she fluffed up my hair with a brush and asked me what I thought. I hardly recognized myself in the mirror: the long hair I'd had for so many years was gone, and instead I had a layered cut that followed my jaw line.

"It's different," I said hesitantly.

"You'll get used to it," Sheila assured me. "It's flattering on you, and it's a great style for your facial structure. Sometimes change is good. Just don't go lighting this hairdo on fire, or you're going to wind up with a high and tight like those Army Rangers around here."

I thanked Sheila for saving the day, then paid and left. I drove home slowly, checking my reflection in the rearview mirror at every stop sign. I felt like I was looking at a stranger.

When I got home, Mina met me at the door with a loud meow. "I know, it's different," I told her. "Do you like it?"

Mina just rubbed her head against my ankles, so I figured that must mean "yes."

Now that my hair had been taken care of, there was that second phone call I had to make. It was barely noon, though, and I figured I could put it off a while longer. Instead, I called Lou.

"Good timing, Betty," Lou said when he picked up the phone. "I haven't finished going over everything yet, but I've found a couple of video clips you're going to love. Why don't you come over here? I think Daisy and Shaun are going to come by, too, so I can show you all at once."

"Okay, I'll be there in a bit," I promised, and hung up the phone.

Lou lives over in the Victorian district, so he's near the even older historic area I live in, but walking to his place would have been a hike. I drove over instead, pulling up in front of a slightly-shabby Victorian mansion on Whitaker Street. Lou rents an apartment on the second floor, and his living room is techno-geek heaven, with all of his computers and video equipment taking up every inch of space. Daisy always refers to his apartment as the Mad Scientist's Lair, and she isn't far off the mark.

Lou met me at the door with a grin. "You're going to love this!" he said, grabbing my arm and hurrying me up the stairs and into the living room. Daisy and Shaun were already huddled around a video screen, so I crowded in and poked my head between them. "Hey, Boo," Shaun mumbled absently, his eyes never leaving the screen.

"What have you got, Lou?" I asked, noticing that everyone had the same intent look.

"Ta-da!" said Lou, rewinding the video and replaying it for me. The screen showed the staircase and was obviously from the camera we had stationed at its bottom end. Suddenly, the five of us who had continued to investigate after the others left for the hospital came into view, and we began climbing the stairs.

No, there hadn't been five of us last night. Only four. I realized that the fifth body in the picture was just a dark shape, and it was following Sam's ascent. After several paces, the shadow crept closer to Sam, just as he began to tug on my arm.

The shadowy figure disappeared as Sam tumbled down the stairs.

"What was that?" I asked.

"Just keep watching," said Lou.

I watched myself run down the stairs, and I expected the figure to reappear as I knelt down to check on Sam, but the fireball that streaked across the screen was all I saw.

Just as I was about to say something, I heard the faint noise of laughter. It sounded more like a cackle, something befitting an evil witch in a children's fairy tale.

Lou turned to me with a smirk. "How about that for evidence?"

"It's convincing," I said, "but we still have no idea what's going on. The figure looked almost like a shadow person, but this just isn't typical ghostly behavior. And whatever it is obviously took delight in scaring the wits out of us with that fire. I think we've been too narrow-minded, simply thinking of this entity as a ghost."

Daisy turned to me for the first time since I'd entered the apartment. "Then what should we think of it as?" she asked, and then she gasped. "Your hair! It looks great!"

Lou and Shaun looked up then, too, and added their praise. "Thanks," I said, feeling embarrassed. "I had to go get all the burnt bits cut off. But anyway, Daisy, I'm thinking this might be demonic."

Shaun nodded slowly. "Maybe we should have a priest come out to perform an exorcism then. That might help. I can call Father McInnis. He's an old friend of my family's, and I know he's done a few exorcisms around here."

"Okay," I said slowly. "Let's try it. But forewarn him how dangerous this entity is. I don't want him to get caught off guard."

"Maybe the fire department can come along, too," joked Daisy, giving me a grin.

I groaned and tugged at a lock of my short hair. "I think it might be too soon for jokes. Let my hair grow out an inch or so, and then I might be ready for you to tease me."

We sat around for a while longer, going over the experiences at Sam's house and trying to make some sense of it. During the conversation I wandered to the kitchen to get a glass of water, and Daisy followed me.

"You okay, Betty?"

I thought over her question for a minute. "I guess so. I'm frustrated and a little scared. My hair stylist warned me away from this case altogether when I told her what happened. I can't help but wonder if she wasn't right."

"But you feel like we owe it to Sam to do as much as we can," Daisy prompted.

"I do."

"Good. So do I, and so does everyone else. We can't give up yet. We'll try the exorcism, and if that doesn't work, well, then we'll find some other specialist somewhere who might be able to help us. There's no danger in that."

"That's true," I agreed. "Between the four of us I know we've got some untapped resources. We'll figure this out."

We all left shortly after, and once I got home I popped a movie into the DVD player and was settling onto the couch when I noticed it was already after three in the afternoon. I sighed and paused the movie as the opening credits began. It was time to make that second phone call.

I picked up my cell phone and dialed the number off the business card that was sitting on my coffee table. I should have had the number memorized by now, since I'd been staring at it so much.

I'm not sure what I expected to happen, but I was surprised when someone actually answered.

"Maxwell," said a smooth, deep voice.

At the sound of his voice, my stomach instantly knotted up as I remembered his piercing blue eyes. I swallowed and did my best to speak in an even voice. "Hi, Maxwell, this is Betty Boorman. Um, we met Thursday night at The Burglar Bar."

"Betty, hi. I didn't expect to hear from you so soon after the skeptical looks you kept giving me on Thursday. What can I do for you?"

"I want to know what you can tell me about the paranormal activity at Sam MacIntosh's house, and what I can do to stop it."

"And here I thought you didn't believe me," Maxwell said, and I could tell he was smiling on his end.

"I don't believe you, but at this point, I'm willing to try anything," I told him honestly. "I'm not convinced you're a demon, but you obviously know something about our work."

Maxwell laughed softly. "Well, I guess I'll have to prove it to you. Why don't we talk about this over dinner? Are you busy tonight?"

"No," I began, and was going to suggest we do something a little less date-like when he began speaking again.

"Wonderful. I can pick you up. Eight o'clock?"

"Oh, ah, how about I meet you at the restaurant?" I asked. Call me paranoid, but I just wasn't ready to hand my home address over to a self-styled demon. Rule number one: never tell the crazy guy where you live.

Maxwell gave a quiet laugh again. "So tell me, Betty, what would make you feel more comfortable? To believe I'm just a compulsive liar, or to see proof that I am what I say?"

"If you can actually help Sam, I'll be comfortable either way."

"Why don't you meet me at Ristorante Roma on Broughton? That's not too far from you."

How did he know that wasn't too far? Did he already know where I lived? I shuddered. His knowledge of both the investigation and me was making me nervous. Still, if he could really help....

"Okay, I'll see you at Ristorante Roma at eight. Thanks, Maxwell."

"You're most welcome, Betty. Goodbye."

"Bye." I ended the call and sat there staring at my phone for a few moments. Maxwell's voice was nearly hypnotic and every bit as sexy as his looks. And we had what sounded an awful lot like a date tonight, at a trendy Italian restaurant that wasn't a typical place for a simple meeting.

I was suddenly nervous, but it was different than the nagging feeling that Maxwell knew too much about me and was obviously some kind of oddity. This was the nervous feeling of having to meet up with an incredibly handsome stranger at a nice restaurant on a Saturday night. What in the world does a girl wear to impress a demon?

SEVEN

Needless to say, a lot of my afternoon was spent alternating between staring into my closet with a feeling of panic and telling myself I was crazy. The only reprieve I got was when Carter called to let me know that Kerri had gotten stitches in her arm, but was otherwise fine after last night's violence.

Carter's normally haughty tone was subdued today, and I wondered if he was as shaken as me. I didn't ask because I knew that Carter would never admit to being scared, and this whole investigation had to be tough on someone who was used to being a know-it-all.

I told Carter about Shaun's suggested exorcism, and he reluctantly agreed, even though none of us was sure that this was a demonic haunting. At least we had some alternative to try, one that didn't involve Maxwell. I didn't know what he was going to say to me tonight, but I was hoping we could help Sam without bringing Maxwell into the investigation. I had an unsettling feeling that he wasn't the kind of guy you wanted to be indebted to.

I considered calling Daisy to tell her about my dinner plans, but I didn't know how she would react to the news. She would either be thrilled and think I'd made good on my promise to get a date within a month, or she would forewarn me about the dangers of dating a hellion. I wasn't in the mood to deal with either opinion, so instead I hopped into the shower early, figuring I'd need extra time to figure out how to style my hair.

Eventually, I decided to go with something simple, pulling one side of my short hair back with a silver barrette. I lingered on my make-up, trying to look nice without looking like I was trying to look nice.

"This isn't even a date!" I mumbled as I brushed on my mascara. "What am I so worried about?"

After staring blankly into my closet some more, I finally chose a black knit dress, one that showed off the curves of my torso and then flared into a flowing skirt that stopped just above my knees. I figured it was nice but casual, so I would look appropriate no matter what Maxwell showed up wearing. I chose a simple silver chain and matching bracelet, and stepped into a pair of strappy black heels.

I'd started getting ready so early that I still had half an hour before I was meeting Maxwell. I admired myself in the mirror for a few minutes, turning this way and that as I scrutinized every angle. But it's not a date, I reminded myself. It's a dinner, to talk about an investigation.

Since I was so early, and since parking downtown can be a nightmare on Saturday nights, I decided to walk to the restaurant. The distance was a little long for heels, but since I wasn't in a hurry I figured I could get away with it. The evening was mild: fall was finally starting to make its presence known, and a light breeze helped clear my head as I walked.

I smoothed my hands self-consciously over my hair, making sure it was still in place as I neared the restaurant. Maxwell was already there, standing just outside the door to Ristorante Roma, and he was impossible to miss because everyone on the sidewalk was staring at him. "Wow," I breathed as I took him in. He was dressed more casually tonight, with tailored black slacks and a sliver-gray button down shirt, but he still looked amazing.

Only two days had gone by since we'd met, and I'd already forgotten just how handsome he was.

No, handsome wasn't the word. He was breathtaking.

Maxwell's face lit up in a smile when he caught my eye, and all of the women staring at him turned to glare at me. Maxwell was undaunted as he greeted me with a hello and held the door open.

I returned the greeting and walked inside, feeling my cheeks flush.

The girl standing at the hostess's booth glanced up at Maxwell, and her face took on the look of awe that matched what I'd seen on the faces outside. "Oh, Mr. Damon," she said, "right this way."

I turned and looked at Maxwell with a raised eyebrow. He smiled in return, "I come here once in a while," he said smoothly.

"I'm more intrigued by the fact that you apparently have a last name," I shot back.

Maxwell laughed. "The word 'demon' comes from the ancient Greek word 'daimon.' It's amazing how you can fool people when you change the spelling a bit. Besides, I can't go around introducing myself to everyone the way I did to you. That sort of thing hurts a man's reputation, you know."

At least he had a sense of humor about it. Maybe Shaun was right, and the whole demon thing was an elaborate way to pick up women. As we were seated across from each other at a table overlooking the busy street outside, I tried to steal a glance at him, but I found myself staring straight into his pale eyes.

"Your hair looks beautiful. It suits you," he said.

"I…thanks," I said, not willing to delve into my reasons

for getting it cut, and feeling a little embarrassed by his flattery.

"White or red?" he asked.

I blinked, and it took me a moment to realize he wasn't talking about my hair anymore. "Red."

A waiter came over just then, as if he'd been beckoned. "Bring us a bottle of your best malbec, please," Maxwell instructed.

As the waiter turned away, I smiled at Maxwell. "We need a whole bottle of wine just so you can tell me what's going on with my investigation?"

He returned my look but kept his expression serious. "No, we need a whole bottle of wine so we can enjoy a nice quiet dinner together."

I wasn't sure how to respond to that, so I just said, "I have a lot of questions for you."

Maxwell smiled. "I imagine you do. But first, I think you have one very important question for me that I need to answer before we even begin to talk about Sam MacIntosh." He leaned over and blew out the candle that sat between us on the table, but just as I was about to ask what he was doing, the waiter came back with our wine.

Once we both had our full glasses in front of us and the waiter was out of earshot, Maxwell continued. "Here's your answer," he said quietly. He cupped his hands together, then opened them up slightly, extending his arms toward me. Inside his hands there was a tiny but brilliant flash of fire. I gasped, involuntarily reaching up to clutch strands of hair that were long gone, as Maxwell moved his hands to the candle. With a gentle flick, the miniscule fire-ball slid out of his hands and onto the wick, igniting the candle.

I stared at him, speechless. "How did you know?" I finally asked.

"Don't you mean 'How did you do that?'" Now Maxwell was the one who looked mystified.

"No, how did you know?" I insisted. "Last night, at Sam's house, there was a ball of fire that just came out of nowhere."

"Ah," said Maxwell, leaning across the table to brush his fingers lightly through my hair, sending a shiver up my spine. "Had a close encounter with it, did you?"

"A little too close." I didn't know how Maxwell had done his little flame trick, but the fact that he considered fire a way of proving his supposed demonic power was too much of a coincidence for me to be entirely comfortable. How long was he going to keep up this charade that he was really a demon? At this point, I decided, it didn't really matter, as long as I got help for Sam. "So the activity at Sam's house is demonic."

"Yes, he's being harassed by a demon. A lesser demon, one that's more like a troublesome imp than, well, me."

"Is there some kind of demon hierarchy?" I couldn't keep a hint of sarcasm out of my voice.

"Yes. Some demons are almost unconscious of what they do; they can't really think for themselves. Others, like Sam's new friend, exist solely to cause chaos, and although they can think and act on instinct, they don't really reason. They're almost childlike in their behavior. Demons like me are far fewer, especially those of us existing in human form."

"Why do you look human? The thing at Sam's showed up on one video clip as a sort of shadow, but otherwise we can't see it."

"Hell isn't really a fun place to be, as I'm sure you can imagine." Maxwell spoke casually, as if he were discussing a trip to the doctor's. "Only those of us who have been of great service and find favor with the boss man get permission to come to Earth in human form."

The boss man. Right. Complete with horns and a long red tail, probably. Even though I was skeptical, Maxwell spoke like he really believed what he was saying. I'm usually so good at reading people, but Maxwell was proving to be difficult.

"How long have you been here?" I asked.

"Since I got permission." Maxwell gave me another stunning smile, but his eyes were teasing.

My next question was on my lips when our waiter returned. I hadn't even looked at the menu. I snapped it open distractedly, then looked at Maxwell. "Since you come here so much, what do you like?"

"The pork tenderloin with linguine is one of my favorites."

I looked up at the waiter. "That works for me," I told him.

Maxwell put in his order, and as I watched him I realized that he just didn't strike me as crazy. He was apparently knowledgeable about demons, but I'd never heard of one running around in human form. Maybe he really was what he claimed.

And maybe that made me a little crazy, especially since I was still here, drinking wine and about to eat dinner with a possible demon.

"Tell me, Betty, how did you become interested in the paranormal?" Maxwell asked, turning back to me.

"I actually used to date a guy who did some paranormal investigations. I had just started college, so I didn't know a lot of people and wound up hanging out with all of the ghost hunters he knew. Then I found out my roommate, Daisy, had an interest in the paranormal because she'd seen her grandma's ghost when she was little."

"And what happened to your boyfriend?"

I grimaced. "He turned out to be pretty nuts. After he claimed that all of the women executed in the Salem

Witch Trials were trying to communicate with him, and that I'd best be on my guard because they were jealous of me, I figured it was time to end things. Eventually he moved, but I don't know where. Probably Salem so he could be closer to his paranormal girlfriends."

"Let's hope your taste in men has improved." The corners of Maxwell's mouth turned up, and his hypnotic eyes were gleaming.

"I think it's safe to say it has." My taste in demons, on the other hand, I wasn't so sure about.

We continued to chat, and mostly Maxwell asked questions about my work as a ghost hunter. I found out that he is actually a successful businessman, running a company that works with international exporters. It was mostly confusing legal jargon that he mentioned, but he told me enough that I realized he makes tons of money, but has the right people working for him so that he doesn't really have to do much work himself. I actually got the idea that he was a little bored with his lack of responsibilities.

The food was good, I assume, but I was so engrossed in my conversation with Maxwell that I hardly noticed how it tasted. Finally, when our plates had been taken away and we were slowly finishing the bottle of wine, I brought up the subject of Sam and his demon again.

"Is there really a way to help Sam? We were thinking of an exorcism," I began.

"An exorcism is a great short-term fix, but it would only send the demon back to hell temporarily. He could always come back later to torment Sam some more."

"So can't you just go talk to it and ask it to leave Sam alone? You know, demon to demon?" I had to bite my lip to keep from laughing; asking a question like that sounded so silly to my ears.

"I could," Maxwell smiled, "but where would be the fun for you in that?"

"I'm going to have to do it myself, you mean."

"Yes. Like I said before, I can't broadcast the fact that I'm a demon. For one thing, it wouldn't do a lot for my reputation, because at the very least people would think I've lost my mind, like you originally believed. Plus, there are certain people out there who would use that knowledge against me. I can't just walk into Sam's house and risk being exposed."

"If you're worried about being exposed, why did you introduce yourself to me as a demon?"

"I trust you. I've heard enough about you to know you're an honest person, and someone who understands that there are things out there beyond normal human perceptions. Plus, I had to give you reason to believe that I can help you."

You could have just said you were an expert in demonology, I thought. "Okay. Then tell me what I need to do."

Maxwell put his hands out, palms up. "It's easy," he said, and I saw a faint glow in each of his hands. "Fight fire with fire."

"I think that trick is a little beyond my abilities," I said, eyeing him with apprehension. If he was a demon, I wondered how many people Maxwell himself had "haunted" over the years. I wasn't sure I wanted to ask.

"Light a white candle, and put this in the flame," Maxwell said, pulling something out of his pocket. He dropped a little red square into my hand, and even though it was small, it felt heavy in my palm. "While it's burning, blow on the smoke to send it away from you. That's it. The demon will know it's from me, and he'll leave immediately."

I frowned. I guess I at least expected something a little more elaborate. "Okay," I said slowly. "How will we know if it's worked?"

"You'll know."

I put the little square, which felt like it was coated in wax, inside my purse, and when I looked up again, Maxwell was gazing at me with something like triumph.

"Why are you agreeing to help me?" I was suddenly a little suspicious of my handsome date. Was I selling my soul to the devil by accepting Maxwell's help?

"I wondered when you'd finally ask that." Maxwell seemed pleased at my question. "A demon's job is to spread fear and chaos, to make people question their God and eventually to secure them a long future retirement in hell. Back in the good old days, people were so superstitious that it was easy. They thought every little thing, from a lunar eclipse to what weekday a baby was born on, had some supernatural meaning. They believed in vampires, and ghosts, and, especially, in demons. Unfortunately for me, the Middle Ages are long gone."

"You refer to the Middle Ages as 'the good old days'?" I interrupted.

"Supernaturally, of course. Today, though, people scoff at those very things that once affected the daily life of people in Europe. Anything that seems supernatural has a rational explanation, they think, and they've replaced their God with science. As you can imagine, it makes doing my job pretty tough. But you, Betty, you're one of the people who keeps those old superstitions alive, whether you know it or not. Your research into ghosts proves there is life after death, and it makes people wonder what else is out there. There are those who never once thought about religion, until seeing a ghost made them believe in God. And people who believe in God believe in Satan. When people have faith, it makes me a lot more effective at my job."

"So you're helping me because..." I prompted, struggling to understand how I figured into his plans.

"Because you make people believe, or at least begin to

wonder about things outside the corporeal. And if they believe, then they don't just make up excuses for, shall we say, things that go bump in the night."

"You think that by helping me, more people will believe in the paranormal, and you can use their belief to spread some sort of fear of the unknown; shake people's faith."

"That's exactly what I think."

"That's ridiculous," I snapped. I felt like I was being backed into a corner by Maxwell's calm rationale. "I don't have to help you do anything like that."

"What choice do you have?" he asked, his voice smooth and alluring. "You've been helping me since you became a paranormal investigator, whether you knew it or not."

I frowned. If Maxwell's solution really was the only way to help Sam, then I had to try it. But that didn't mean I was going to help him terrorize people. Sam was scared enough as it was, and I wasn't going to risk upsetting him even more. Whatever Maxwell—human or demon—wanted to accomplish, I wasn't going to be a part of it. At least not consciously.

"All right," I agreed, feeling a little more sure of myself. I knew I could find some loophole, even though the opening lines of "The Devil Went Down to Georgia" were playing in my head. "I'll try this at Sam's house."

"You'll be very pleased with the results."

Our conversation returned to a more normal one after that, as Maxwell paid our bill and we left the restaurant.

"Where are you parked?"

"Oh, I just walked," I told him. "I'm not too far from here."

"Let me drive you home, then. There are worse things lurking out there than ghosts and demons." Maxwell said it lightly, but his joke sounded ominous to me.

I agreed, and he walked me around the corner to his

car, a stunning Audi R8, painted bright red. "Wow, that doesn't stand out or anything," I laughed as he held the door open for me. When Maxwell was settled into the driver's seat and the engine was rumbling happily, I turned to him and said, "I live off of Abercorn, not far from here."

"I know," was all he replied, and he drove us to my apartment without once asking for directions. He'd definitely done his homework on me.

Maxwell parked in the tiny alley behind my carriage house apartment and came around to open my door for me again. If he was a demon, at least he was a polite one. I hesitated for a moment after I stepped out, wondering if I should invite him in for coffee. Did a demon have to be invited in before he could enter? No, that was a vampire myth, I reminded myself.

Maxwell offered his arm, and I could feel heat radiating from the skin beneath his long-sleeved shirt. He walked me straight to my front door, never hesitating about where to go.

I unlocked my door and turned to Maxwell. My little apartment was probably the size of his master bathroom, if his house was as nice as his car, but I'd at least ignore my nervously-pounding heart and ask him in. "Did you want to come inside for some coffee or anything?" I sounded as timid as I had at the start of Carter's press conference.

"Sure." That smile was going to make me melt. I opened the door and motioned him in, but an ear-splitting yowl stopped me in my tracks. Mina was standing at the threshold, her tail fluffed to about five times its size and her tiny fangs bared. Her gaze was on Maxwell.

"I'm so sorry," I told him. "She's usually really friendly to people."

Maxwell gave me a grim smile. "I'm not 'people,' remember? I think I'd better take you up on your offer some other time. Some time soon, I hope." He reached up and put his hand lightly against my cheek, looking into my eyes.

"You're warm," I said. It sounded silly out loud, but his hand felt fevered. I realized with surprise that it was the first time his skin had made contact with mine.

"It's my nature," he replied easily, his hand still resting there. "Call me after you help Sam. I'll take you out to celebrate."

"I will. Thank you for dinner, Maxwell."

"You're welcome," he whispered. He moved his face closer to mine, his eyes locked on my own, but a hiss from Mina stopped him. "Good night, Betty," he said, and he was gone before I could answer. "Good night, Maxwell," I said to my empty front stoop.

I shut the door and flicked on the living room light. I locked up and turned around, and I instantly knew that something was wrong.

.

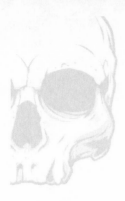

EIGHT

The first thing I noticed was that my address book and weekly calendar weren't sitting on the dining room table where I had left them, and the only time I ever put them somewhere else was on the rare occasion that I had someone over for a real sit-down meal at the table. It seemed like a silly thing to get upset about, but their absence sent a jolt of dread through me.

I almost opened the door to run after Maxwell, if he was even still outside. He had made his exit so quickly that it almost seemed supernatural, like he had taken a few inhumanly quick paces and then vanished entirely. But even if he was still out there, what would I tell him? "Please come inside because my address book is missing!" would sound even more pitiful than my coffee invitation.

At that thought, I glanced down at Mina. If it weren't for her temper tantrum, Maxwell would be in here with me right now. Or, at the very least, I would have gotten a goodnight kiss from him. Even amid my worry I could still curse my bad luck at having missed out on feeling those full lips against mine.

I turned back to the off-kilter scene before me, straining to hear any little noise in the apartment. My first thought was that something paranormal was going on, that maybe my once-quiet apartment had become home to a transient ghost. Had I brought something home with me from Sam's house?

My feet felt heavy as I forced myself to walk to the dining room table. "I'm being silly," I told myself firmly. "I bet the cat just knocked my books off the table and they're under here on the floor."

I bent down and peered under the table, but they were nowhere to be seen. A quick glance at the floor in the kitchen didn't show any wayward books, either.

As I straightened up, my gaze fell on the window in the living room, the one that faced the little alleyway behind the carriage house. The blinds were hanging at an odd angle, like someone had yanked on the cord to open them but only one side had risen.

I definitely hadn't left them like that.

The feeling of dread deepened, and I was shaking so badly by the time I reached the blinds that I could barely lift them up to look at the window. The pane was open by just a few inches. With the lingering summer weather, I hadn't opened my windows in months since I'd been running the air conditioner every day. Someone had broken into my apartment through the window during my dinner with Maxwell and taken off with my address book and calendar.

Wait, that didn't make sense at all. Who would want to steal those things? There had to be something else missing. The near-paralysis I had been feeling suddenly turned into a flurry of anxiety as I swept through my little living room, mentally checking off my belongings. The TV was still there, and even though it was old I'm sure a thief would have been happy to take it off my hands. My DVDs looked like they were all accounted for (though, really, what self-respecting criminal would see a pile of old chick flicks and think, "Jackpot"?), and even my laptop was still sitting on the couch, right where I'd left it after checking e-mail earlier in the day.

I ran into my bedroom, but everything looked like it was in order there, too. The cedar jewelry box on my dresser was in its place, and I turned it upside down, pawing through the things inside. Everything was still there, right down to the diamond earrings I had inherited from my grandmother.

"What happened?" I asked aloud. I went back to the living room, where I had dropped my purse by the front door. I pulled my cell phone out and dialed "911."

"911 Emergency Services," a dispatcher answered.

"I'd like to report a break-in at my apartment," I said.

"Are you there now?"

"Yes."

"Is the intruder still there?"

"No."

"And what is your address?"

I gave the woman my address and phone number, and she assured me that a police officer would be along shortly to take my statement. I guess they couldn't really justify rushing over with sirens blazing for a break-in that had already happened, especially since whoever had done it might have been miles away already. Still, I was anxious for the officer to arrive, and I paced back and forth between the living room and the dining room while I waited.

Even though I was expecting it, I still jumped at the sound of someone knocking on my front door. I peeked through the front window before opening the door and was relieved to see a tall, heavyset policeman there. I motioned him inside, happy to have someone else there with me, especially a someone with a gun.

"Have you been harmed at all, ma'am?" he asked me, after identifying himself as Officer Roberts.

"No, sir, I wasn't home when it happened. I just came in the door and found out someone had broken in earlier."

Officer Roberts surveyed the room slowly, then moved into the kitchen and dining areas. Finally, he turned to me. "They come in through the door?"

"No, the living room window, over here." I led him to the window and showed him how the blinds were skewed, and pointed out that the window was slightly open.

The officer nodded, "And was anything of yours taken?"

"My address book and calendar are gone. They had been sitting on my dining room table, but now they're missing."

For the first time since I'd walked in the door, I realized how weak my claim sounded. A calendar marked with friends' and relatives' birthdays plus some past investigations, and an address book of nothing but those same friends and relatives: it sure didn't seem worth the risk of breaking and entering.

Officer Roberts gave me a slightly doubtful look. "Have you inspected the rest of the house to see if anything else is gone?"

"Yes, everything else seems fine. My nice jewelry, my laptop, all of it is still here."

"Okay, ma'am, I'll see if I can lift some fingerprints for you." The cop looked even more skeptical.

I bit my lip, feeling tears threaten. The reality that someone had been inside my home while I was gone was beginning to sink in, and I felt personally affronted. I suddenly had the urge to clean the entire apartment, followed by the longest, hottest shower of my life. I just felt violated, even though most of my things were completely undisturbed. Officer Roberts's obvious doubt of my claim was just making me feel worse.

He believed enough of my story that he went to his

patrol car and retrieved his fingerprinting kit. He dusted the powder on the window first, and then he waved me over to look at the two fingerprints that were outlined in the bottom pane of glass. By their position, I could tell that the hand they belonged to had obviously reached under the window from outside, grasping the pane to push it open. The bottom of each print was blurry, but the tips of both fingers were clear.

"Is that enough to identify someone?" I asked.

"Possibly. It's a partial print for two fingers, so they might be able to match it up. We'll check your table, too." I watched as the officer lifted the prints off with a sort of tape, which he placed against a glass slide and stored in his case. He went through the same process with the top of my dining room table, but there were no definite prints there.

With his fingerprinting case packed up and stowed under one big arm, Officer Roberts pulled out a business card and handed it to me. "You'll be able to pick up the report within two days at the station on Oglethorpe," he said. "And if you have any more problems, or find something else missing, you call me."

"Thanks. How long until you'll know if the fingerprints are a match?"

He grimaced. "Unfortunately, it can take up to a few months."

"A few months?" If they really had a chance of catching this guy, why didn't they start looking for a matching fingerprint on file the very next day?

"I'm sorry, miss. There are so many open cases that we've got a backlog. I'll call you if we find anything."

"Okay, thanks," I said, trying not to sound too disappointed. After all, it wasn't his fault, and he'd been pretty patient with me.

"Make sure you close and lock that window, and

double-check the other windows in your home. Good night."

"Bye." I shut the door and locked it, then did just as Officer Roberts had advised. Every window in the apartment was already shut and locked, and I paused just long enough to wipe the fingerprinting dust from the open window before I secured it, too.

Too wound up to sleep, I made a mug of hot chocolate and wrapped myself up in an afghan. While I sipped my hot chocolate, words that Maxwell had said to me earlier came to mind, something about there being worse things in the world than ghosts or demons. How right he was. On the bright side, at least the intruder hadn't broken in and burned off my hair. I smiled at the mental image, and the tenseness I'd been feeling began to dissipate. I finally drifted off to sleep, and I awoke at dawn, when pale daylight began to seep through the blinds. I stretched, thought about getting up and crawling into bed, then finally gave up and fell back asleep on the couch.

The next time I awoke, my stomach was growling and I had a faint headache. I vaguely wondered if that was from the wine or the dramatic events of the night before as I stood up and stretched my stiff body. My right foot had fallen asleep, and I limped into my bathroom as pins and needles shot through it. I swallowed a couple of Advil to stave off my headache, then moved into the kitchen for my coffee. The microwave clock told me that it was nearly noon. No wonder I was starving.

As soon as a cup of coffee was in my hand, I grabbed my phone and called Daisy. Good thing I have her number programmed in since my address book is gone, I thought wryly. Daisy must have recognized my number on her caller ID, because her voice soon bubbled into my ear. "Well, hey, Boo!"

"Hi, Daisy."

"You sound half asleep. You have a late night or something?" Daisy said it with a teasing edge to her voice, but she had no idea how right she was.

"Daze, you won't believe the night I had. First of all, everything is okay, but my home got broken into while I was out with Maxwell."

Daisy was silent, which is a rare thing for her. She started to speak several times, and finally she got a question out. Her voice was much more subdued than it had been when she'd picked up the phone. "Is your apartment in bad shape?"

"Nope. They took two things that seem absolutely trivial. Everything else is fine. They opened up a window to get in, but it's not broken, so I guess I had forgotten to lock it. I'm pretty shaken up, but for the most part it doesn't even look like anything happened."

"What did they take?"

"My calendar and address book."

"Weird. Your jewelry is still there? They didn't make off with your TV?"

"Nope. They came in through the window, snatched those things off my table, and left."

Daisy's sigh was audible even over the phone. "That's good; I'm glad it wasn't more serious. Since you're okay, I don't feel bad asking another question. Did you say you were out with Maxwell? Isn't he your little demon friend?"

Only Daisy could switch gears so quickly. I wondered if she was trying to take my mind off the break-in or just anxious on behalf of my love life. "Supposed demon," I reminded her. "And yes. He and I met so we could talk about Sam MacIntosh. Can I come over? There's too much to tell over the phone."

Daisy and Shaun live in the stretch of suburbs between Savannah's downtown historic district and the Southside, where two malls plus pretty much every chain restaurant and store can be found. Their subdivision was only a few blocks off Victory Drive, and the neighborhood was old but still nice. Shaun's parents had given them the house as a wedding present. It had once belonged to his grandparents.

I parked on the street in front of Daisy and Shaun's brick ranch home, and I had only walked halfway up the driveway before Daisy came bursting out the front door. She nearly ran over to me, throwing her arms around my shoulders in a tight hug. "Are you okay?" she asked.

"No, I'm not. Some crazy woman is suffocating me." Daisy laughed and I joined in. It was a relief to feel a little more lighthearted.

Once we were sitting on the back porch, each armed with a giant glass of sweet tea, Daisy sobered as I described the break-in and the odd circumstances of it. She reached over to pat my hand several times, mumbling, "How awful." When I was done, I put down my empty tea glass and spread my hands. "So, what do you think?"

"It's just weird, Betty. Why would anyone want to break in just to take your books? It almost seems like a practical joke or something. Though you're assuming it was an ordinary thief who broke in. Maybe it was just some crazy, or even a homeless guy looking for somewhere to sleep."

I frowned. "I'm not sure that makes me feel any better. But at any rate, there's nothing I can do about it right now. Nothing valuable was taken, and I'm safe. That's what counts, right?"

I was nursing my second glass of sweet tea when I brought up the other subject weighing heavily on my mind. "We need to get back to Sam MacIntosh's house as soon as possible," I said. "I want to try this 'solution' that Maxwell gave me."

"It might not really do anything," Shaun said, walking out to join us. "Or it might be dangerous."

"I know, though I really think Maxwell was sincere about wanting to help. Still, to be on the safe side, I don't think we should have everyone present when I try this. Sam needs to be there, of course, since the demon doesn't seem to respond if Sam is elsewhere."

Daisy nodded and gave me a narrow look. "I hate to say it, but Carter should be there, too."

I agreed grudgingly. If we sent the demon on its way without letting Carter in on it, there's no telling how he would react. There was no way I was going to put my chance to work on the Everett-Tattnall House investigation in jeopardy, and I wouldn't put it past Carter to slander my name to his media contacts if I made him feel left out.

"Got a phonebook I can use?" I asked.

"Somewhere. We hardly use it anymore," said Daisy. Daisy rooted through a few drawers before she finally snapped her fingers. "I put it in the cabinet with the plates we got from Shaun's great-aunt!"

Once the phonebook was in front of me, I flipped anxiously to the "M" section of the white pages. It seemed like half of Savannah and its outlying little towns had a last name beginning with "Mac" or "Mc," which made sense considering the huge Irish and Scottish population in the city. The "MacIntosh" listings accounted for a full three inches on the page, but there was only one named Samuel with a Thunderbolt address.

I dialed my cell, but as I waited for someone to answer I realized in a panic that if Sam wasn't staying at his house, then calling his home number wouldn't do us any good. Just as I thought that, his answering machine picked up. I left a message, but had little hope that Sam would retrieve it any time soon.

"Do I have to call Carter?" I was whining, but I figured

that I could get away with it under the circumstances. My rival's number was actually programmed into my phone, and I waited for him to pick up while I drummed my fingers impatiently on the kitchen counter.

I turned to Daisy. "Maybe he's on some rich-boy trip out of the country and—Carter? It's Betty Boorman. I need a favor. Actually, I need two."

Fortunately, Carter had Sam's cell phone number. Unfortunately, Carter was eager to come out to Thunderbolt with us that night to see what I planned to do. Carter plied me with questions, but I just told him that I'd explain later. I didn't really know what to tell him, anyway.

Sam was less enthusiastic when I called him since it meant walking into his house after dark yet again, but he was happy to hear I had something to try, at least. I warned him that it might not work, but when I said, "I have a possible solution that might get this entity out of your house," Sam seemed to hear, "I am going to fix everything tonight."

I sure hoped I wouldn't let him down.

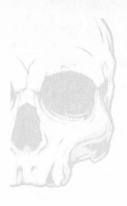

NINE

We had agreed to meet at Sam's house at nine, and by the time I needed to begin getting ready for the trip to Thunderbolt, my apartment was gleaming from a thorough cleaning. I was also dirty, sweaty and exhausted. Still, I felt like my home was mine again, as if wiping down every surface somehow erased all memory of the intruder.

A second shower was in order, and when I was done, I threw a frozen pizza in the oven for dinner. It wasn't just that I didn't feel up to cooking; I didn't want to mar my shiny kitchen countertops.

I was yawning on the drive to Thunderbolt, but I hoped that we wouldn't have to be at Sam's house for long, especially since I couldn't sleep in the next morning. I pulled into his driveway at the same time as Shaun and Daisy. Shaun hefted a black bag out of the backseat of their car. "Video camera," he said, patting the bag. "I thought we could at least film this, and see what turns up."

"Works for me. I really don't know what to expect."

Carter arrived next, and he strutted from his Mercedes over to our group. The first words out of his mouth annoyed me, making me wish even harder that things would be over with quickly. "Betty, you should get your hair fried more often. That's a great 'do for a sidekick."

"Lay off, Carter," I said. I was getting tired of playing nice with him.

Carter just grinned in response, his arrogance impenetrable. I was about to fire off another retort, pointing out that it was me who had come up with a solution and not him, when Sam pulled in. It was probably a good thing I never got the words out of my mouth since the last thing I needed was open warfare between Carter and me.

Sam nearly leaped out of his car and hustled over to us, his face flushed. "Can you really take care of all this tonight?" he asked.

"Sam, we're going to try our best. Unfortunately, ghost hunting isn't an exact science, so I can't guarantee you anything." Demon hunting wasn't exactly my forte, either, but I decided to leave that little tidbit out.

I turned to Carter, Shaun and Daisy. "Sam should go inside with me, but I don't think we should all go. I don't know exactly what's going to happen, and in case this solution backfires, I'd rather not put all of us in danger."

"I'm going in," spoke up Carter. Of course he was.

Shaun nodded grimly. "All right. If you're certain of this, Boo, we'll set up the video camera, then Daisy and I will wait out here."

Sam led the way inside, and I suggested that we set up in the living room. I was carrying a thick white candle with me that normally sat in a hurricane glass on the mantle above my fireplace. When we got to the living room, I sat on the couch and instructed Carter and Sam to sit on either side of me.

While I put the candle on the coffee table in front of us and lit it, Shaun put the video camera on a tripod and aimed it at us. "You're sure about this?" he asked me.

"Where did you find this solution?" added Sam, before I could respond to Shaun.

I sighed. "An acquaintance of mine suggested this."

"Who?" This time it was Carter asking a question, and he had a note of suspicion in his voice.

"Someone who's an expert when it comes to this kind of haunting." That was putting it mildly. "He wants to remain anonymous for personal reasons."

Carter looked at me through narrowed eyes, clearly mistrustful. "Do I know this expert?" Carter spit the word out like it was vulgar.

"If you aren't comfortable with this, you're welcome to leave," I told him.

"No, thanks," he said stiffly.

Daisy reached over and squeezed my shoulder before she and Shaun went out the door, turning out the lights in the house as they went. We were left in near darkness.

"Let's get this over with," I said under my breath. The tiny red square that Maxwell had given me was in my pocket and I fished it out. I held it up so that Carter and Sam could see it in the dim light from the candle. "See this? I have no idea what it is, but I think there's something very powerful inside it. I'm going to put this into the flame of the candle, and I want both of you to be on your guard when I do. This entity might go quietly, but on the other hand he might go kicking and screaming. Or, for all I know, he won't go at all, but he'll be more pissed off than ever. Got it?"

Carter nodded solemnly but Sam just sucked in his breath and scooted a few inches closer to me, so that we were shoulder-to-shoulder on the couch. I gripped the little square by one edge and held it forward, silently praying that Maxwell's solution was going to work.

As soon as I positioned the square over the flame, the red coating began to melt, dropping fat red blotches of wax onto the white candle. It looked like drops of blood, and I kept the edge I was holding at an upward angle so the wax wouldn't drip onto my fingers. I should have brought tweezers to hold this with, I thought, just as the little square began to glow.

It began as a soft golden glow, just like what I had seen in Maxwell's hands at dinner on Saturday. After several seconds, though, the glow brightened, turning white. Soon it looked as though a light bulb had been illuminated, and the entire room was dimly visible. I held my breath, waiting for my fingers to grow hot, but the edge I was touching remained cool against my fingertips.

Suddenly, the light flared outward, startling me so much that I dropped the square and jumped backwards on the couch. Sam cried out and clutched at my arm. The square landed right on top of the candle flame, giving off a brilliant sphere of light that was almost too painfully bright to look at directly. I squinted, looking for the smoke Maxwell had mentioned, but I didn't see any.

We watched, terrified and mesmerized, as the light began to rise up, coming to a halt about a foot above the candle and even with our line of vision. Then the light began to fade, and as it slowly returned to the orange glow we had seen earlier, a thick column of black smoke began to rise. I did as Maxwell had instructed: I leaned forward, drawing as much air as I could take into my lungs, and breathed gently on the smoke.

As the smoke drifted away from me, it began to change shape. Tendrils of it floated downward, while the top of the column continued to rise. Soon it stretched from the floor to a height of at least six feet, taking on the basic shape of a human standing on the opposite side of the coffee table.

"Wow," Carter whispered, while Sam mumbled something unintelligible in his fear. I remained silent, too fascinated to say anything. I knew that whatever seemed to be standing there was of Maxwell's doing, and that knowledge made my fear subside.

Whenever amateur ghost hunters come to me for advice, I always tell them that ghosts sense fear and tension, and that the best way to experience paranormal activity is just to relax and stop looking so hard for it. "Something always happens when you're least expecting it," I'll explain.

I should have been taking my own advice there in Sam's living room.

The soft glow had nearly faded away, and with a quiet "pop" it extinguished altogether. The candle snuffed out at the same time, leaving us in inky blackness. After the bright light, my eyes were momentarily blind as they fought to adjust to the sudden darkness.

I breathed a sigh, thinking that it was over with, when I heard three loud noises on the other side of the room. It sounded like some of Sam's huge antiques being hurled to the ground. There was a shriek, high-pitched like the evil laugh we'd captured on video after Sam fell down the stairs, then a voice that commanded, "Get down!"

It wasn't Carter or Sam who had spoken. I recognized the disembodied voice as Maxwell's, and I reached my hands out to my companions and grabbed their arms. "Do it! Get down!" I shouted.

I slid to the floor, crouching behind the coffee table as the shrieking began again. There was a rushing sound, and I felt cold air blowing over my head, and then all went silent for a brief second.

I risked peeking up then, but as I did the smoke was replaced with a bright flash as an explosion lit the room and flames erupted out in all directions. The noise was like that of a freight train, and the air grew hot and thick. I shut my eyes and crouched further down, wondering if we would be able to escape the house before the fire surrounded us or brought the roof down on top of us.

And then everything went silent again.

The air felt cooler, and when I opened my eyes, the room was in darkness. Sam was the first one to speak. "It's over," he said, and his voice was filled with relief.

"How do you know?" I whispered.

He shook his head. "I just know. I can feel it, like I've been released from something. I feel lighter."

I cautiously raised my head, and nothing around us was burning, so I stood up slowly and weaved my way past Sam toward the light switch. I hesitated before turning the lights back on, afraid of what I might find, but when the room was illuminated, there wasn't a single sign of the explosion. Everything was in its place and the smoke was gone. Whatever had made the crashing sounds, it wasn't Sam's antiques.

I walked back over to the coffee table, looking at the rug beneath it for any sign of the smoke or the explosion, but there was nothing. My white candle was the only thing that showed any sign of our experience, with the red wax now dried and blended with the white in pink swirls.

Carter straightened his polo shirt and ran a cautious hand through his still-perfect hair. "That was intense."

A laugh welled up inside me, and it broke out of my mouth with almost hysterical force. Maxwell's solution had given all three of us a scare, but it had apparently worked. He had said that we would know whether or not it had been successful, and I took Sam's confidence as our sign.

Sam and Carter started laughing, also, and the three of us hurried outside to assure Shaun and Daisy that we were okay. They both had strained expressions, and our laughter as we trooped out the front door made their eyes widen in confusion. The three of us told the story, haltingly, and as Sam concluded for us I felt my laughter suddenly turn to tears.

I turned away from the group and pushed my fist against my mouth in an effort to hold in the sob that I felt building inside. Tears ran down my cheeks and I took several deep breaths. I guess the stress of the past couple days had finally broken me down, and I suddenly felt utterly exhausted. I heard light steps behind me, and Daisy was at my side, her arm around my shoulders.

"What's wrong? I thought it worked?"

"It did." My voice shook and I sniffed loudly. "It's just been kind of a crazy weekend. I think my emotions are going haywire." I put my arm around Daisy's waist and we stood looking at Sam's house while the others continued to laugh and celebrate behind us.

"Come on, Betty, you can't let Carter of all people see you cry!" Daisy said, giving me a sly look.

I wiped my cheeks with a shaky hand and swallowed hard. "You're right. I'd never hear the end of it. It was weird in there, Daisy. I heard Maxwell's voice, warning us to get down before the explosion."

"It must be some sort of trick. Maybe there was some kind of audio recording in that little package." Daisy's voice was skeptical. The little wax-covered square had been too small to hold any kind of a tape recorder, even a digital one.

I shook my head. "Whatever happened in there, it wasn't some sleight of hand trick. Demon or not, Maxwell knows what he's doing."

"I'm just glad it worked. I didn't know demons ever did good deeds."

"They don't, unless they think they can get something in return. In this case, I think scaring the pants off Sam MacIntosh was enough. Don't ask me why."

"That's a question for you to ask Maxwell. I guess you're going to give him a full report?"

"Yes. I need to thank him. Besides, he told me we'd go out to celebrate our success."

Daisy laughed. "He's just making up excuses to go out

with you, isn't he? I wonder how long it will take him to just ask you on a real date."

I smiled wryly. "He's too good-looking to want to date a normal girl like me. I bet he usually goes out with supermodels."

Daisy grabbed my hand and began to pull me back to the others. "Silly Boo. When are you going to realize that you're not normal?"

Sam looked at me as I approached. "I feel normal again!" he shouted triumphantly, which sent Daisy and I into a fit of giggles. "What did I say?" Sam asked, looking at both of us in amused confusion.

"Nothing. Daisy here was just trying to convince me that I'm not normal, so I'm glad someone here can make that claim."

"Well, I've got all of you to thank for it. You have no idea how much this means to me. Isn't there something I can do for you? Do I owe you money?"

"We don't do this for money," said Carter. "We're just happy we could help. If you're willing, I'd appreciate your permission to post details of this case on my website. I can keep your name anonymous, of course, if you prefer."

Sam smiled. "That's fine. Just make up a good name for me." He shook hands with Carter, then turned and gave me an awkward hug. When he stepped back, I noticed that he looked years younger now that he wasn't afraid anymore.

"I'm going to go inside and sleep soundly in my own house tonight," Sam announced with pride. He had been terrified during the exorcism, or demon banishing, or whatever Maxwell's fiery trick had been, but now he seemed relaxed and happy. In Sam's mind, we'd simply rid his home of nothing more than a pesky ghost. In a place like Savannah, that was no big deal. As I watched Sam heartily shake hands with Shaun and Daisy, I smiled to myself. Instead of promoting Maxwell's hellish agenda, I'd accomplished just the opposite, helping restore peace to Sam's life. My soul was definitely still my own.

We all wished Sam a good night, then went our separate ways. I had just reached my car when Carter called my name. I turned to see him only a few feet away, his lips pursed disapprovingly. Oh, he's so good at being a snob, I thought.

"What is it, Carter?"

"Who told you how to do that? Whatever that little thing was, it packed a lot of punch."

"I told you, the person wants to remain anonymous."

Carter wasn't going to give up that easily. "I've worked with the best exorcists in the country, and none of them have ever done something that...flashy."

Okay, it had been pretty flashy. Surely Maxwell could have devised something more low-key but still effective, though that just didn't seem like Maxwell's style. "It worked, didn't it? What else matters?"

Carter's eyes narrowed. "Yes, it worked, but it also seemed like it was designed to be terrifying. I don't know who your anonymous expert is, Betty, but I don't like him."

"I guess that's why he's working with me, and not you," I answered, giving Carter a tight smile. Without waiting for a retort from him, I turned and climbed in my car.

When I got home, I did another check of all the windows, mentally kicking myself for still being worried. Sam might have slept well that night, but I lay awake for a long time.

TEN

I dragged myself into work on Monday morning, and Jeanie greeted me at the front desk with a perky smile. "You look tired. Busy weekend, Betty?"

I grimaced at her. "This ghost hunter feels like a zombie. I haven't slept well the past couple of nights. Someone broke into my apartment Saturday night, so I've been a little jumpy."

Jeanie's usual bright smile disappeared. "Oh, no! Are you okay? Did they take a lot of your stuff?"

"Yes, I'm okay, and no, they only took some trivial little things. All in all, it was very weird. I'm beginning to think it was just some crazy passerby or something."

"You need a security alarm."

"Probably." I agreed, but I doubted that was something I could talk my landlord into installing in the old carriage house. I could always ask for bars on the windows, maybe, or install them myself.

By lunchtime, pretty much the entire office knew about my break-in. Jeanie is the one person who connects the staff since she sees everyone at least twice a day: when they're coming and when they're going. People in other departments whom I'd only met once or twice began sending me concerned emails, and I knew Jeanie had been spreading my news.

Great, I was the hot office gossip.

I'd been physically tired when I walked in the door, but as I left to grab lunch at a diner a few blocks away, I was mentally weary, too. I picked at a salad with disinterest, staring at a book that I wasn't really reading.

When I finally gave up and got back in my car to return to the office, there was still plenty of time left in my lunch hour. I didn't want to go back until I absolutely had to because I needed as much of a break from everyone's well-meaning attention as I could get. I sat in my car for a moment, debating what to do, and I finally decided to give Maxwell a call.

When he picked up and I heard his voice saying, "Maxwell," my heart skipped a beat. For a few moments I felt just as light-headed as I had there on my doorstep Saturday night.

"Hi, Maxwell, it's Betty."

"I didn't expect to hear from you so soon." He sounded pleased. "I guess you didn't waste any time in returning to Sam MacIntosh's house."

"No, I didn't. We went last night. It worked, Maxwell. We were scared half to death in the process, but it was well worth it. Thank you."

"No problem. Betty, are you okay? You sound…different."

Great, now I was going to have to go through the whole scenario with Maxwell. So much for getting a little bit of a reprieve.

"I'm okay, just really tired. Things got a little exciting after you left Saturday night."

"Oh?"

I told him about the break-in, giving him the same story I'd been rehashing all day long. Today had to be the longest Monday of my entire life.

I expected Maxwell to respond with the same sympathy everyone else had, so I was surprised when he remained silent.

"Maxwell?"

"It's odd. I wonder if there's something more to this that you haven't considered yet."

"Like what? It's completely random, isn't it? It's not like I have top-secret phone numbers in that address book."

"Maybe you've got someone who wants to know what you're doing, and who you're doing it with." Maxwell sounded concerned, but I couldn't understand who or what I could be involved with that would be of interest to anyone. It's not like I had a popular social life or knew the movers and shakers of Savannah. As for my calendar, investigations were about all that were listed there, and Carter had pretty much broadcast my upcoming work at his press conference, anyway.

I said as much to Maxwell, and he paused before he spoke again. "Maybe someone wanted to know about any plans you and I might have had."

I was beginning to feel a little annoyed with this line of thinking. Or maybe "nervous" was a better word than "annoyed." I didn't even want to consider that there was something deeper behind this, let alone anything involving Maxwell.

In an effort to lighten things up, I said, "What, do you have a jealous ex-girlfriend who's stalking me?"

Maxwell chuckled. "That's not exactly what I was thinking. You could be right, Betty, maybe Saturday night was just a weird coincidence. It would make me feel better if you promise to be on your guard, though."

That lightheaded feeling began to return. "I promise."

"Of course," he continued, "there's really no better

safeguard than having a demon at your side. I believe I promised to take you out in celebration of your success at the MacIntosh estate."

My insides started to do a victory dance, but I tried to keep my voice calm. "Not my success, our success. And yes, I believe you did."

"We could do something on Friday, but I'm terrible at waiting. That's almost a week away."

"Friday's no good, anyway. I have to be at the Everett-Tattnall House that night for the start of our investigation there."

"And I'm in Atlanta tomorrow and Wednesday, so how about Thursday night?"

"That works for me. Where will we be going?"

"I was thinking we'd have dinner at a favorite restaurant of mine. I'll pick you up around 7:30."

That didn't tell me much, or give me any idea how to dress, but I agreed. Daisy was right; this was the second time he had asked me out using my ghost hunting as an excuse. If he wants to celebrate, I told myself, then who am I to stand in his way? We said our goodbyes and I drove back to the office, and I smiled the entire way. With a night out with Maxwell to look forward to, my Monday was definitely going better.

As the afternoon wore on, I kept an ever-growing mental list of why I was falling for Maxwell. On the downside, he was still keeping up the demon charade, but I figured I could worry about that later.

By the time I got off work, my weariness had dissolved, and I was feeling positively giddy. After I got home, I checked my answering machine and found a message from my mother, wanting to know if I was okay. How had she heard the news? I called her back, and it turned out that she had heard it from Shaun's mother. They both live down on the Southside, and the two acquaintances ran into each other at Wal-Mart Sunday night. I made a mental note to warn Shaun not to share such stories with his talkative mother in the future. There really are no secrets in a city like Savannah. No matter how much this city grows, it still has that feel of a little town where everyone knows everyone else's business. I half expected Mom to ask me how my dinner with Maxwell had gone. I'd emailed her since then, but I hadn't mentioned him to her. I just wasn't sure what to say about him yet, especially since I didn't even know if we were actually dating or not.

After I assured Mom that I was just fine—and that there was no need for me to temporarily move into her house with her—I filled her in on the investigation at Sam's house. She was impressed, and I was reminded how lucky I am that she is supportive of my ghost hunting, even though the idea struck her as strange and possibly dangerous the first time I told her about it. After my first paranormal investigation, she had finally admitted to me that we had a ghost in our house while I was growing up. We'd moved out of that house when I was five, so I had few memories of it, but Mom said that there were constantly thuds and footsteps emanating from the attic. I had a slew of "imaginary friends," too, and Mom often suspected that some of them weren't so imaginary. Sometimes I wondered if it wasn't some early experience buried deep in my memory that had put me on the path to being a ghost hunter. I'm sure a psychiatrist would have a field day with me.

The rest of my evening was quiet, and I finally crawled into bed early. Between sheer exhaustion and my excitement about seeing Maxwell again, I was able to sleep much better. I still woke up a few times during the night, imagining I'd heard noises at my window, but by Tuesday morning I was feeling like myself again.

I knew it was going to be a long day since Carter and I

had our first meeting with Alec Thornburn in the evening. Alec had given me the impression that there was more to his story than what he'd discussed at the press conference. The occurrences he'd described—knocking, things being moved, the usual ghostly activity—certainly warranted his law firm calling for an investigation, but I suspected that there was some other kind of activity going on, too. I attributed my feelings on the subject to my ability to see past the façades people put up, but it may have also had something to do with Sam. After all, he'd called me up saying a ghost had touched him, when what he really meant was "a demon has been slashing up my skin." There was no telling what claims of a ghost "moving things" might translate to in this case.

Putting on jeans and a tee-shirt had been my first order of business when I got home from work on Tuesday, but it somehow felt too casual for a meeting with Alec Thornburn. The lawyer probably didn't even own a pair of jeans, and I knew Carter would be his usual well-groomed self. I finally made a compromise, putting back on the navy blue silk blouse I'd worn to work. It looked nice with my jeans and my tan boots, so I wouldn't feel too underdressed at our meeting.

One of the things I love about living downtown is that I don't actually have to drive to get anywhere in the historic district. The Big Bean Theory isn't far from the Everett-Tattnall House, so I walked over there as the sun dropped below the tops of the buildings, turning the sky a pale peach color. Twilight has to be one of my favorite things about the fall.

My route took me past the Everett-Tattnall House, and Alec was walking briskly down the front steps as I approached. I waited for him at the wrought-iron fence that surrounded the house, noting that he was once again dressed extremely well, this time in a crisp black suit.

Alec noticed me and smiled as he let himself out through the gate. "Good evening, Betty. I didn't realize that I was going to get an escort to the coffee shop tonight." He extended his hand to me.

"Hello, Mr. Thornburn. It's nice to see you again," I said, shaking his hand.

"Please, just call me Alec. You know, when I was growing up, other kids would always ask me if my first name was 'Smart.'"

I laughed as we began our walk together. "I can relate. I was called Betty Bore all through grade school. It wasn't until I became a paranormal investigator that I got the nickname Betty Boo."

Now it was Alec's turn to laugh. "Very catchy. Tell me, Betty, do you spend as much time marketing yourself as Carter?"

"No. Carter and I are very different when it comes to that." I hoped I was keeping my voice even so that Alec wouldn't sense my distaste for Carter's antics. "There's a website for The Seekers, and I've been asked to speak at some paranormal conventions, but nothing like Carter. He keeps threatening to make me his sidekick, but I think he really just wants someone to keep track of all of his promotional appearances for him." I gave Alec a big smile, and he seemed to appreciate my joke.

"What do you do for a living?"

"Oddly enough, I work in marketing. I like to think I'm good at promoting other people and companies, but it turns out I'm not very good at marketing myself. I just graduated last year, and I'm working at Coastal Health now."

Alec nodded approvingly. "They're a good company. We've done some work with the hospital in the past. What do you want to do eventually?"

Alec sure had a lot of questions. Luckily, he was a good

conversationalist so I didn't feel like the lawyer had me on trial. "Eventually I'd like to own my own marketing firm. In a perfect world, my company would be so successful that I'd be able to open an office in one of the historic mansions around here."

"Which would be haunted, of course."

"I'm not sure there's a single building here in Savannah that isn't!" I paused, giving Alec a sidelong glance. "How long has your firm been in that house?"

Alec gazed ahead, as if he was looking at a big calendar. "It will be seven years this December," he finally answered.

"I'm supposed to save questions like this for our meeting with Carter, but is this the first activity you've experienced there?"

"Oh, no. We've had little occurrences since the day we moved in. Nothing significant, though. Our receptionist swears there's a presence in the ladies' restroom, and when any of us is there late at night we can hear footsteps from the upstairs master suite."

I bit my lip. If Alec considered phenomena like that to be trivial, then the activity he'd described at the press conference wouldn't have been a big deal to him, either. There was definitely something more going on than he was telling.

"Are you a lifelong resident of Savannah?" I asked. I guess it was my turn to grill the lawyer, but Alec chuckled warmly.

"Is that your polite way of asking me if I've believed in ghosts my whole life?"

"Guilty as charged, sir."

"The answer to both questions is 'yes.' My childhood home had an old cook who didn't realize that the family she served had been dead for generations." I should have guessed that Alec was a native; his pleasant manners and soft accent were indicative of Savannah gentility.

We arrived at the door of The Big Bean Theory, a cozy little coffee shop that had an interesting clientele. During the day, sharply-dressed business people rubbed shoulders with the off-kilter students from the Savannah College of Art and Design. By this time of night, the students outnumbered the other customers, but there was a small table surrounded by four plush chairs in one corner, and Carter was already sitting there.

Carter stood up and greeted us, then offered to get our drinks. Alec requested something with such a long title that I doubted Carter would be able to remember it. "Iced mocha for me," I said.

Alec and I settled into our chairs, and he pulled a pile of manila file folders out of his briefcase. They were all bound together with rubber bands, and he handed the stack over to me. "I told you we keep everything," he said.

"Wow. Is all of this relevant to the haunting?"

"Probably not. But these are the things Jasper Whitney was working on before he died. And, by the way, I'm going to need you to sign a confidentiality agreement that you won't share these details with anyone."

"Of course."

Alec gave me a quick wink. "We've removed any sensitive material and blacked out names. We still have to respect our clients' privacy, so you're getting censored copies. Still, we hope it might help point you and Carter in the right direction."

I was about to ask a question when Carter returned with our coffees. I took a long sip of my mocha while I considered the meaning of Alec's words. "You think it's the former partner haunting you," I prompted.

"Yes."

"And you think he's haunting you because of something going on with one of these cases he was working on."

Alec sighed and waved a hand at the file folders. "We think maybe he has some sort of unfinished business. That's one of the reasons people come back as ghosts, right? And we thought it was significant that he's haunting the office, not his own home."

Carter finally spoke up. "How do you know it's your former partner?"

Alec settled back in his chair and crossed one leg over the other. "Oh, there have been hints," he said. I knew then that we were finally getting to the real story. "Jasper died unexpectedly. He had a heart attack about three months ago, and within a week there were strange things happening around the office. The biggest thing was how much paperwork was getting moved around. I'd come in to work and there would be one of Jasper's files sitting on my desk. Or the receptionist would go to the kitchen for a cup of coffee, and his old notebook would be in the drawer with the spoons. We figured Jasper was the one moving all this stuff, trying to get our attention, but we didn't know what was so important. I've been through his open cases, but nothing stands out. Hopefully having an outside observer like you, Betty, will help us find something that we've overlooked.

"The things I've said prior to tonight about the nature of the haunting have been understatements." Alec gave me an appreciative glance. "I think you knew that from the start." I nodded, and noticed Carter's jealous glare out of the corner of my eye.

"Anyway, we could have dealt with the things moving around on their own. It was a little disconcerting, but certainly nothing to be alarmed about. A few weeks ago, though, Jasper decided to step up his efforts. A client of ours was sitting in the waiting area, and all of a sudden the old gentleman screamed like a girl. Annabelle, our receptionist, went running in there, and she says he was so pale that she thought he might faint. Once he calmed down, he claimed to have seen a man standing in the corner who just disappeared. The description sounded like Jasper."

"Was the client one of Jasper's?" asked Carter.

"No, one of Terrence's, our third partner." Carter nodded, making a "go ahead" gesture with his hand. "I was the next person to see Jasper's ghost. He showed up in the mirror that hangs at the landing of the staircase. I was walking out at the end of one day, and there he was, just standing behind me in the reflection. I turned around, but no one was there. Since then we see him almost daily. Whatever he wants us to know, he seems urgent about it. That's why I finally called you, Carter. I'm hoping that with your expertise you can help. If Jasper doesn't have some kind of unfinished business, then maybe he just needs help getting on his way."

"We've seen that a lot," said Carter. "Sometimes a ghost doesn't know it's dead, or is scared about moving on, and just needs some help and encouragement."

"What's the ghost doing when you see it?" I asked. "Can you tell if he's gesturing or trying to talk?"

Alec thought for a moment before he spoke. "Usually he's just standing there, but I've seen his lips move before, like he's speaking, but I can't hear anything."

Carter broke in again. "One of the things we do on an investigation is use tape recorders, which sometimes pick up the voices of the spirits even when you don't think they're talking. I bet we can hear what Jasper is saying that way."

I looked down at the pile of folders sitting on the table in front of me. I felt like a freshman who'd just been handed a huge stack of homework. "What about the other partner, Mr. Stiles?"

"Terrence?" Alec's mouth tightened into a thin line. "He's said from day one that he doesn't believe in ghosts. I remember being in the office with him several years ago, and you could hear the footsteps pacing back and forth in the master suite. He sat there and told me it was probably rats, or the air conditioner making noises. Terrence has been a little jumpy lately, because even he can't deny that things are getting misplaced, but he blames it on Annabelle or me. He says he hasn't seen Jasper since the day he died, and he thinks the rest of us need professional help. He wasn't happy when I called all of you in to investigate, but he knows people in Savannah eat this kind of thing up so he hasn't been too difficult about it. After all, it's a popular marketing gimmick these days. And who doesn't like a little bit of self-promotion?" Alec turned his head toward me and gave me another wink. I clamped my teeth down on my straw, trying not to giggle. The joke had been aimed at Carter, but he didn't seem to realize that anything had passed between Alec and me.

Actually, Carter was sitting across from us looking very thoughtful. "Was Jasper married?"

Alec seemed a little surprised at the question, but he answered in the affirmative.

"Have you tried talking to his widow about this? Maybe she knows of some unfinished business Jasper may have had, or what kind of a message he might be trying to relate."

"No, we haven't talked to her about it. The thought hadn't even occurred to me. I guess I just assumed he wanted to tell us something dealing with his work since he's haunting the office. I doubt his wife would be able to help us with any information involving a case."

"Carter makes a good point," I said. Carter gave me a smirk when I said that, as if he knew how much it pained me to admit it. "His presence at the office doesn't necessarily dictate why he's there. There are a lot of factors that can affect a haunting. Some locations are more conducive to haunting than others, so maybe for some reason Jasper's ghost is drawn to the office more than his home. Or maybe he's afraid that if he pops up in front of his wife he'll scare the daylights out of her."

Alec stared down into his steaming mug of the coffee with a long name. "You have a point. It would be worth exploring, but I feel like I need to forewarn you. Rebecca took Jasper's death really hard. None of us had any reason to believe he was anything but perfectly healthy, so the suddenness of it was really hard for her. It might be difficult to discuss this with her."

"She has no idea his ghost has been seen?" Carter asked.

"No, because we saw no reason to tell her. We didn't want to upset her if we didn't have to. If you want to talk to Rebecca, that's fine, but I would like to request that you make it a last resort. Please, go through the case files first, and don't contact her until you see what you find at the investigation on Friday night."

"We can do that," Carter assured him.

"Alec," I said, "even if we get satisfactory evidence on Friday, or from the files, to confirm that this haunting is work-related, I'd still recommend that you tell Mrs. Whitney about this. If she sees something on the news, or hears through the grapevine that the firm has a team investigating, she's likely to figure it out anyway. It would be better for her to hear it from you directly." I was thinking of my conversation with my mom the night before. If word was getting around about my Saturday night, then there were certainly people talking about the firm, especially since Carter had called the press conference. I couldn't imagine the horror of finding out through idle gossip that a loved one had come back as a ghost.

"Are there any other details you can think of that we haven't discussed?" Carter asked.

Alec gazed forward again, like he had earlier when calculating the firm's tenure in the Everett-Tattnall House. I wondered what he was seeing in his mind. The details he had shared were definitely more than he had mentioned at the press conference, but I was glad that Alec hadn't been holding back details about any malicious activity. A ghost with a message I could handle. After Sam's demon, a whole courtroom full of dead lawyers would seem like a cinch. "No, I think that's everything," Alec finally said. "We even tried to figure out if Jasper was showing up in certain places or at certain times, but it seems like he's been touring the whole house. We just hope we can help him."

"So do we, Alec," Carter said. "Don't worry; we'll get some answers soon for you. You're going to feel a lot better after our investigation on Friday." Carter and his ego.

"I'm glad to hear it. Oh, one last thing." Alec produced a few sheets of stapled paper from his briefcase. Tiny print covered the papers, and he laid them on the table in front of me. "Our standard waiver for anyone outside the firm who reviews case files," he said.

I glanced at the text, but after the first "whereas" and a "shall" or two, I gave up and looked at Alec. "What does all this say in non-lawyer words?"

"That you won't tell anyone what you read in those files and you won't let anyone else read them."

"That I can understand." I took the pen Alec offered me and filled in the appropriate lines with my name and address, then signed the bottom of the final sheet and handed the waiver back.

Alec neatly tucked the papers inside his briefcase before he stood up. "I believe we're done. Betty, call me if you have questions about any of those files. I'll see both of you Friday night at eight o'clock."

Carter and I both stood to shake hands with Alec. I began to gather up the pile of file folders so I could follow Alec out the door when Carter stopped me. "Betty, can you wait a minute?"

"Sure." I hesitated, then sat back down. "What's up?"

Instead of answering me, Carter's gaze suddenly focused on something behind me. He gave a wave and smiled broadly. I turned around and saw a rumpled-looking young man hurrying toward us.

"Who's this?" I asked under my breath as the man approached.

"Reporter." Carter's voice was as low as mine, as he gave me a quick glance. "Hope you don't mind." His grin looked inviting when it was aimed at the reporter, who had reached our table, but when he turned it on me it just looked evil. Maxwell might be a demon, but Carter looks like one, I thought.

"Carter, good to see you again," said the breathless reporter. "I appreciate this."

Carter shook hands with the man, then gestured to me. "Brian, this is Betty Boorman. Betty, Brian is a lifestyle reporter for the Savannah Morning News."

A lifestyle reporter? I wondered. What, is he doing a story on "a day in the life of a paranormal investigator"?

"Hi, Betty," Brian said, shaking my hand. "I'm doing a story about Carter and his investigation team for our 'Career Paths Less Taken' series." Ah-ha, so I had been sort of right. "I wanted to talk with you for a few moments, if you have time."

"With me?"

"Sure. Since you and Carter work together sometimes, I want to get some details about things the two of you have done together."

"Oh, I...um, sure."

Carter went to get another round of coffee, and the

reporter dropped into the chair that Alec had recently vacated. He had his tape recorder out as soon as Carter turned his back. "So, Betty, I understand that Carter is training you to be a paranormal investigator?"

"Here we go again," I mumbled.

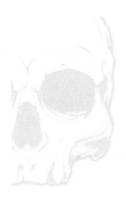

ELEVEN

I should have been tired by the time I got home from the coffee shop, but after two iced mochas I was pretty wired. I was also still riled up about Carter ambushing me like that with the reporter, but I couldn't be too mad. Once again, I'd had an opportunity to set the record straight when it came to my involvement with Carter and his team, so I looked forward to seeing the finished article. Brian the rumpled reporter had said it would run in Sunday's newspaper, and I made a mental note to read the story before telling anyone about it, just in case it was a little too biased toward Carter.

It was only 9:30, so I sat down at the dining room table with the stack of files that Alec had handed over to me. Mina jumped up onto the table and perched next to the stack, and I absent-mindedly petted her with one hand while I opened the top file.

I'm not sure what I expected, but the files were all photocopies of the originals, and many were nothing but notes written in a spiky scrawl. I figured that Jasper must have written notes during his meetings with his clients, or while on the phone with them, and then he just stuck the sheets into the folders without typing up the information first.

Unfortunately for me, legal jargon is almost like

another language. There were a lot of notes that made absolutely no sense to me. Still, I tried to find anything in the files that might have prompted the haunting. I went through the first few manila folders, but none of them seemed particularly urgent. The first two in the stack were corporate clients, and it seemed like standard business dealings. The third was for a case involving a dispute over an inheritance, but again it didn't strike me as being worthwhile for a ghost.

The caffeine might have revved me up, but the case files made me sleepy. Normally I really enjoy doing research, but this was a different kind of information than I was used to. Usually, I looked into the history of a place: when a house was built, who the various owners of a building had been, news reports involving the address where we were investigating, any deaths there. Occasionally I deal with legal records, but when I do they are always typed up in a neat and intelligible manner. Until now, anyway.

I gave up on the research, my "already read" pile painfully small compared to the rest of the stack, and went to bed.

Wednesday was another swift-moving day at work, and I was excited about the days ahead. Thursday night I was going out with Maxwell, and on Friday I would be investigating at the Everett-Tattnall House. A date and an investigation definitely counted as exciting in my book.

But before either of those things could happen, there was that huge pile of manila file folders waiting for me at home. As soon as I got off work, I hurried home, slipped into sweats, and settled in at the table for a marathon reading session.

The first dozen or so files were agonizing, but by then I was learning to differentiate one type of case from another. After I knew what to look for, the process went much faster.

I took a break halfway through to eat dinner and watch the news, and when I took my plate back to the kitchen I noticed that the message light on my answering machine was blinking. I hit the "play" button, and the first call was just a hang-up.

So was the second. And the third.

In all, there were seven messages on my machine, but they were all hang-ups. It was like someone was trying to get in touch with me, but they didn't want to leave a message. Probably sales calls, I figured. I often got messages like that, though seven in a row had to be a record.

I went back to the much-smaller stack of files to be read, and the pile was finished within an hour. I was glad to be done with the task, but I hadn't come across one single case that seemed likely for Jasper Whitney's "unfinished business." The possibility that Jasper just really loved his job and wanted to stick around occurred to me, and I made a mental note to ask Jasper if that was the case during an EVP session on Friday.

After I checked my email on my laptop, I swapped my sweats for pajamas, then went into the bathroom to get ready for bed. My mouth was full of foaming toothpaste when the phone rang. "Gee, perfect timing," I mumbled. I spit into the sink but didn't rinse, then made a mad dash for the phone.

"Hello?"

"Betty Boorman," a gruff voice said into my ear. "A word of advice. Sometimes you don't want to find out the truth about someone, so stop trying."

There was a click, and I heard the dial tone.

I slowly put the phone down, wondering who had called and, even more importantly, whom they were talking about. Find out the truth about whom?

Maxwell. The mysterious voice had to be referring to

Maxwell. I already knew he claimed to be a demon, so what more could there be to the truth about him? Maybe Maxwell had been right when he said someone might have broken into my apartment to find out what was going on between us, and now that person was calling to warn me away from Maxwell. He was definitely not the average guy, and surely a businessman as successful as him had made a few enemies on his way up. What kind of secrets did Maxwell have? I knew I should be wary of him, but instead I was looking forward to seeing him again.

I considered calling Maxwell to tell him about the anonymous caller, then decided against it. I'd be seeing him in less than twenty-four hours, anyway, and there wasn't much Maxwell could do about it tonight.

If Maxwell was a demon, I didn't want to think about what evil deeds that entailed. Even if he was just another mortal man, he was still fully capable of evil acts. You don't have to be a true demon to do demonic things. The caller had been right, in a way: I didn't want to know the truth about things Maxwell had done in his years (Hundreds? Or was it thousands?) on Earth. He had been such a gentleman so far that I found it hard to even envision Maxwell doing something evil. Of course, he had mentioned his ulterior motives for helping me rid Sam of his demon, but that was hardly something to warrant an anonymous phone call. I went to bed satisfied that I had nothing to worry about, and I didn't have a single dark thought about Maxwell as I fell asleep.

During my lunch break on Thursday, I called Alec to let him know that the case files he had passed along hadn't yielded any results. He was understandably disappointed, but I asked him if he could gather the things that Jasper's ghost had been moving around the office and let me look at those. Alec told me some of the things were trivial, like a picture of the partners when they had the ribbon-cutting ceremony on the house, but I told him to throw it all in a box and I'd pick it up that evening. It meant more tedious research for me, but I had to explore the possibility that Jasper was moving items around for a specific reason.

I was out of the office at five o'clock on the nose that day, and I drove straight to the Everett-Tattnall House. The receptionist, Annabelle, greeted me when I walked through the front door.

"Ms. Boorman? Mr. Thornburn is at a meeting that ran late, but I have a package for you." She reached behind her and lifted a big box, setting it on top of her desk.

"Wow," was all I could say. If the box was full of more files, then I was going to be reading legal documents all weekend.

Annabelle smiled politely. "Don't worry, it's not even close to full, and it doesn't weigh much. Do you need help carrying this to your car?"

I looked at the petite woman, who was probably thirty pounds lighter than me, not to mention half a foot shorter. "No, thanks," I told her. "I'm parked right outside on the curb, so I can manage."

I thanked Annabelle and hefted the big box, which was awkward but not heavy at all. As I tottered toward the door, a small elderly man in an olive-colored suit stepped in front of me, blocking my path. I stopped short, but the man gave me a thin smile. "You must be Betty Boorman, one of those ghost hunters," he said. I could detect the barest hint of sarcasm in his voice. "Please, allow me." He turned and opened the door, sweeping his arm grandly to usher me outside.

"Thank you, Mr...." I began.

"Stiles. Terrence Stiles. Pleased to meet you face to face, Ms. Boorman. You have quite the high reputation among your set."

I could feel my cheeks flush. Was he being serious, or making fun of me? Alec had already warned me that Terrence thought the claims about the building being haunted were just the result of overactive imaginations. I'm usually such a good reader of people, but the third partner in this law firm was skilled at masking his true feelings. Must be a good lawyer, I thought wryly. Whatever he really felt, I smiled and replied, "Thank you. It's nice to meet you, too."

Terrence's small dark eyes looked at me as if he were studying a legal document, and I brushed past him as quickly as I could without looking like I was trying to flee from his gaze. His manner was the opposite of Alec's warm, friendly demeanor.

Outside, I squeezed the box into the trunk of my car, and within minutes I was at home. I perched the box on my dining room table and took a peek inside. Alec had been right about the ghost moving an odd assortment of things. There were some more case files, though less than I had anticipated, but the rest of the items included some notebooks, what looked like financial records, and even a stuffed teddy bear holding a big red heart. I raised my eyebrows at the jumble of stuff, then closed the top of the box.

Maxwell was due at 7:30, so I hopped in the shower. I didn't really need one—it's not like I got sweaty sitting in my air-conditioned office all day—but it perked me up after a long day of working. I dried my hair and put on a wide green headband. It looked pretty against the auburn shine of my hair. Luckily, choosing an outfit didn't take nearly as long as it had Saturday night. I chose a soft green sweater that matched my headband and paired it with black slacks. I was putting on my lipstick when there was a knock at my door. "Maxwell's here!" I said to Mina. "Please be nice to him this time. I like him."

"You look great, Betty," Maxwell said, his pale eyes appraising me as I opened the door. "I'm glad you're wearing a sweater; it might be a little chilly where we're going for dinner."

"Where are we going?"

"Out to Tybee. A friend of mine owns a restaurant overlooking the ocean, and around this time of year it's a little breezy out there."

I locked up and took a good look at Maxwell as we walked to his car. He looked drop-dead gorgeous, of course, and tonight he had on a black button-down shirt and slacks, making him look like a sort of demonic Johnny Cash. The clothes coupled with his black hair made his blue eyes stand out even more, and I sighed. I wasn't sure I could make it through dinner without drooling.

Maxwell and I talked easily on the drive out to Tybee Island, and once we were clear of the city and out on the long highway that leads to the coast, he sped up to nearly twice the speed limit. The last bit of daylight still lingered, throwing an eerie glow over the marshes that were blurring past. The whole time, Maxwell's gaze barely seemed to leave my face, even though he was driving so fast.

"You might be missing your true calling as a race-car driver," I said.

"I've tried it, back in the 1960s. I won my fair share of races, and crashed a few times, too." Maxwell said it so casually, like the fact that he was alive and racing cars long before I was born was no big deal.

"That was a little before my time. You might have to consider making a comeback so I can come cheer you on."

Maxwell smiled at me. "That would be nice."

We reached Tybee Island in what had to be record time and pulled into a parking lot next to a small restaurant right on the beach. We were seated on the patio, where the only light came from the candles on each table and a string of tiny white lights looped along the patio railing. Maxwell had been right about it being chilly, and I was glad I'd chosen a sweater and slacks. The rhythmic sound of the waves breaking against the sand was soothing, and the breeze had that wonderful salty sea smell. I inhaled deeply.

"You like the ocean?" Maxwell asked.

"I love it. I used to come out here all the time before I became a ghost hunter."

"Why don't you come anymore?"

I shrugged. "Well, now I'm up during the night on weekends, and I sleep most of the day. It's kind of a strange schedule."

"You could come out here at night, then."

"Wandering a dark beach alone isn't really high on the list of safe things for single girls to do."

Maxwell chuckled. "Good point. Then how about you and I go for a walk on the beach after dinner?"

"That would be great."

Maxwell reached across the table and took my hand, the warmth of his skin a sharp contrast from the cool air blowing in off the water. "Of course, it may not be safe for you to be on a dark beach alone with me, either."

"I survived the adventure at Sam's house. If I could do that, then I can handle anything else you might try."

"Pride goes before a fall," Maxwell answered mockingly.

Our conversation shifted to Sam MacIntosh, and I told Maxwell the details of Sunday night. He laughed at the thought of Carter being frightened by the banishing he'd devised for me. "And what did you think of it, Betty?"

"It was beyond my expectations. I'm impressed, but I have to admit that it scared me pretty good, too. I really thought Sam's house was blowing up and that we were all going to get caught inside there. Then when we turned on the lights and there was no fire, no smoke, nothing, I realized I should have trusted you. At least, I'm hoping you're not trying to kill me." I gave Maxwell a wink.

"Definitely not. Having dinner with you is a lot more fun, I think." While Maxwell talked, he absently rubbed the thumb and forefinger of his free hand together. A few bright sparks of flame erupted from his fingers; tiny pinpoints that disappeared nearly as quickly as they were created.

I'd thought that his trick during our first dinner together had been just that: a clever trick that would have made a veteran magician jealous. Now, though, Maxwell seemed almost unaware of what he was doing, and he certainly wasn't doing it to impress me.

Maxwell followed my gaze and his fingers stopped moving. "Sorry, it's a bad habit."

"What are you?" The words just popped out of my mouth before I could stop them.

"We've covered this territory before, I believe."

"Yeah, that's the problem," I said carefully, hoping I wasn't throwing away all politeness for the sake of honesty. "You believe, but I'm not sure I do."

"I generated fire for you. I got rid of Sam's demon for you. How much more proof do you need?"

"I thought the fire was a trick of some sort, like maybe you had a lighter hidden in your shirt cuff or something." Saying it out loud, I realized how unlikely that was. Maxwell had held the flame in his hands; there had been no hidden lighter.

Maxwell didn't respond, so I continued awkwardly. "As for Sam, well, I just thought you were really experienced at dealing with paranormal entities."

Maxwell's eyes were intent on mine, and for the first time since I'd met him I felt real fear. I couldn't look away and I couldn't shut my eyes against the sight of his face, his jaw rigid and his pale skin almost glowing. My hand was growing hot, and I realized that it was still entwined with Maxwell's. His grip hardened, and the searing heat flowed up my arm and into my shoulder. I would have cried out if I hadn't been transfixed.

TWELVE

It felt like hot coals were coursing through my body. I'm going to be burned to death, I thought. My skin will be charred and my blood is going to boil.

The image of Maxwell's face blurred as the heat slithered up my neck and into my head. I realized I must be passing out and felt relief: at least I wouldn't be conscious when my body burned.

My relief soon turned to a new fear, though, as images crept into my mind. I saw flames leaping up from a dark pit, smoke curling around me so thickly that I could feel it brushing against my face. I tried to hold my breath, but still the stench of smoke and sulfur filled my nose. The heat was nearly unbearable, pressing at me from within and without now. I looked down but couldn't see my body. Instead, I saw the precipice on which I seemed to be standing, the dirty rock scored with long gouges. There were two sets of long scratches, and somehow I knew that fingernails had made those as someone fought against whatever had dragged them into that pit of fire.

I shut my eyes against the sight, and the heat dissipated immediately. There was only one part of me that still felt warm, and that was my hand, which was still clinging to Maxwell. I opened my eyes and he was looking at me grimly, but with sympathy in his eyes.

"Now you see why I wanted to get out of hell," he said quietly.

I looked down at my arm and realized with a little surprise that my sweater was still green, not blackened. I pulled back the hem of my sleeve slowly, but the skin underneath was unblemished. Still not convinced that I was unharmed, I put my hand against my cheek. I was okay, even though my hand was shaking.

I inhaled deeply, letting the cool ocean air fill my lungs and clear my head. The breeze felt chilly after the temperatures I'd just experienced. "That's what it's like there?" I asked.

"Never ending."

"I believe you."

Maxwell smiled as if nothing had happened. "Good, I'm glad we finally got that settled."

"That was awful."

"I know, and I'm sorry, but you're terribly stubborn."

I looked around at the few other diners still on the patio. None of them were staring at us or running for their lives, so I knew we hadn't created a scene. I guess it was a good thing that I hadn't been able to cry out or I would have been screaming like a doomed girl in a horror movie. That image rallied my spirits a little. "Skeptic," I said.

"Still?"

"No, I mean I'm not stubborn, I'm a skeptic. I try to look at all possible options before believing something is really paranormal."

"And it makes you very good at what you do." Maxwell's gaze was admiring.

"Even if it takes me a while to figure out what's really going on," I conceded. I took another deep breath and tried to smile. "This is my first date with a demon, you know."

"And this is a celebration, so we need a bottle of champagne." Maxwell caught the waiter's eye and ordered the champagne. When it arrived, he held his glass up to mine. "To the demon and the ghost hunter," he said, "and our first victory."

The rest of dinner was pleasant, though I certainly had a new appreciation for Maxwell's power. Maxwell's friend, the owner of the restaurant, came out after we ate to say hello. I could hear the note of pride in Maxwell's voice when he introduced me, and his friend kissed my hand gallantly. "Betty, I've heard so much about you. You're the prettiest ghost hunter I've ever seen."

After he left our table, I finally brought up the one topic that I'd been dreading. I wasn't sure how Maxwell was going to react to the warning phone call I'd gotten. "Maxwell, I think you may have been right last week when you said someone might want to know what you and I are up to."

Maxwell instantly looked serious, and he leaned toward me. "Why do you say that?"

I told him about the cryptic phone call, adding that I didn't know who else the caller could have been talking about. When I finished, Maxwell sat back and looked out over the ocean. He was silent for a few moments before he spoke. "Not many people know what I am. Betty, there's something you need to know." Maxwell turned his eyes back to me, and they had a sad look.

Oh, no, I thought. This is the part where he tells me some dark secret from his past that I don't want to hear.

"There are people out there who look for my kind. Demon hunters," he said. "It's possible one of them has tracked me down, and knows you've been out with me."

Wow, that wasn't the deep, dark secret I had expected. "I see," I said slowly.

"Most demon hunters will try to keep any mortals from harm, if they can help it. Although, sometimes, one or two

123

have to be sacrificed for 'the greater good.'" Maxwell's tone was condescending.

"They go around banishing demons, then," I prompted.

"Yes, and they all consider themselves holy men. Men of God. But some of them aren't much more than bounty hunters. They work for money, usually. The more trouble-some the demon, the bigger the payout."

"I take it you'd be worth a pretty hefty sum."

"Well, not to brag, but there's a church in Germany that offered five thousand marks for me a hundred years ago. That was a lot of money then." Maxwell's face lit up at the thought, but his expression quickly sobered again. "If the man who called you is a demon hunter, then we need to be careful when we're together."

I nodded. "Understood. I guess that means our walk down a dark lonely beach is out then?" I said it as a joke, but I was sad to think that our date might have to be cut short. Part of me regretted telling Maxwell about the caller, but if he was right and someone was hunting him, then he needed to know.

"I'm sorry, Betty. I'll have to make it up to you." At least Maxwell sounded genuinely disappointed. I was disappointed, too: I was convinced Maxwell had been on the verge of kissing me when our first date was cut short by Mina's frantic hissing. Now, our second date was going to end early, too.

Maxwell paid and we retreated indoors. I walked toward the front door of the restaurant, but Maxwell put his hand on my elbow and gently steered me through a doorway on our left.

The kitchen glowed brightly, but it was mostly deserted; a dish-washer was huddled over the sink, his body moving in time to the music blaring from his head-phones. He didn't even look up as we walked past.

"You giving me a tour of the place?" I asked.

"Something like that." Maxwell led me through yet another door, this one constructed of heavy wood. The storage room beyond had a faint musty smell, and the wooden floorboards beneath our feet were scarred and stained.

"Are you ready?" Maxwell asked. Before I could answer, he turned to the room and raised his voice. "Margaret, are you here? Come out and say hello."

Nothing happened for a heartbeat, but then I felt the air turn cold—the cold that indicates a paranormal presence. The frigid temperature wasn't surprising, but when a woman materialized directly in front of me, I let out a shriek.

"Betty, I'm disappointed in you. You should be used to this sort of thing." Maxwell's tone was teasing.

"I'm not used to a ghost who materializes on demand." I couldn't take my eyes off the apparition. She was much shorter than me, and her expression was a combination of shock and despair. Her dark brown gown reached to the floor, and she held her hands in front of her waist, her fingers laced together tightly. "She looks so solid. And so sad."

"This building was once part of a larger complex, and during the Civil War, scouts were stationed here to monitor ships sailing along the coast," Maxwell explained. "Margaret's husband was stationed here, but he became ill—cholera—and a rider was sent for Margaret. She came out here as quickly as she could, but she was traveling all the way from Savannah, and I was quicker."

"What do you mean?"

"Let's just say I speeded his exit from this world."

"Maxwell!" At my outburst, the ghost's eyes turned to me for the first time, and a shiver worked its way from my tailbone up to my shoulders.

"Margaret was devastated when she arrived. She had lost the chance to say goodbye to her husband by only five minutes. She asked the other soldiers to leave the room so that she could have some privacy. After they left, she cursed the war, the South and, finally, God. It was quite the impassioned speech; I wish you could have heard it. When she was done, she took a knife from her husband's belt and stabbed herself. She fell over on top of her husband and died."

I felt a tear spill down my cheek. "Oh, how terrible," I whispered.

"Yes, it really was," Maxwell answered with satisfaction. "I knew she wouldn't take his death well, but I had no idea she'd commit suicide right then and there. Evil is like art: sometimes you think you're just making random brush strokes, but when you stand back and look at the canvas, you've created a masterpiece.

"They had three children, who of course went to an orphanage. One died of smallpox in less than a year, the second turned into a petty thief. The middle child—a girl —turned out all right. Oh, well. You can't destroy them all."

I finally turned to Maxwell. "How could you?"

Maxwell spoke slowly, as if I were a stubborn child. "I'm a demon, remember? It's what I do."

More tears were welling up in my eyes, but they weren't for Margaret. They were for me. Of course he was a demon. However kind he'd been to me all night, no matter how attracted to him I was, he was still a creature of evil. Maxwell treated me well because he was attracted to me, but how long would it take before he grew tired of me? And when he did, what kind of evil would he bring to my life?

I looked at the ghost of Margaret again. Her hopeless eyes were green, the same color as mine. As I watched, she sighed and faded away, leaving nothing but the cold air.

I sighed, too, and whispered to Maxwell, "Take me home."

On the trip back to my apartment, Maxwell drove a lot slower, as if he wanted to stretch out his time with me. He rested his hand on my thigh, and once in a while I saw him rubbing his fingers together. Whenever he did, I stiffened, expecting a spark to ignite my slacks. Maxwell was quiet while we drove, and I couldn't stop thinking about Margaret's sad eyes, and the pain and death Maxwell had brought to that entire family. By the time we got back to Savannah and he walked me to my front door, it was already far past my usual weeknight bedtime.

I unlocked my front door and went inside, just to make sure I hadn't had any more uninvited visitors. Everything was in place, though, and I turned back to the door and stopped short. Maxwell had stepped inside, too, and I had nearly walked right into him. We were standing just inches apart.

"I forgot to mention that I ran into Sam MacIntosh today," he said.

I blinked. "What?"

"I ran into him downtown."

"I didn't know you knew Sam," I said. I had the feeling that this was going somewhere bad, and I wasn't sure I wanted to hear the rest.

"Sam and I do business together from time to time. I asked him how things were going, and he mentioned he was having problems with a ghost, and that you came in and saved the day."

"Okay," I said, still not sure what Maxwell was getting at.

"Well, I just thought it was interesting that Sam said it was a ghost haunting his house, and not a demon."

Uh-oh. "That's because I didn't tell Sam that it was a demon." I was either being straightforward or stubborn, and neither option seemed right, but I figured there was no way I could talk my way out of this one.

Maxwell's voice was soft. "Well, you see, holding back details like that doesn't really help me spread fear, and that's the whole reason I agreed to help you."

I had known that from the start, but it still made me angry. "You said you wanted to spread fear, and I guarantee you Sam was scared," I retorted. "And Carter, and me. If you wanted everyone to know it was a demon, maybe you should have teamed up with Carter, and he could have held a press conference for you."

"No, thanks, I'd rather have a little fun and Carter is anything but that. I just assumed you would tell Sam; that you would feel like you owed it to me since I agreed to help."

"Owed it to you? If that's what you wanted, then you should have said that up front. Just because a guy buys a girl dinner doesn't mean she owes him a kiss good night. If you expected me to do something specific in exchange for your help, then you should have said so." I was definitely angry now.

Suddenly Maxwell grinned. "You're mad."

"Yes."

"Don't be. I'll get over it."

I sighed. "I'm sure you will. You'll just find someone else to help you with your reign of terror." And someone else to go out with, I added silently. With that thought, my anger dissolved into disappointment.

Maxwell was quiet for a moment, then he gave me a wicked smile. "Now that you mention it, I bought you dinner but never got a kiss," he said. "In fact, I've taken you to dinner twice now. Like you said, it doesn't mean that you owe me, but since I didn't get what I wanted for helping you, I'll at least take that kiss."

Before I could react, Maxwell wrapped his arms around me and pulled me close, pressing his full lips against mine. I felt his tongue pushing against my lips, forcing my mouth to open. My body stiffened in surprise when he first reached for me, but I quickly relaxed and slid my arms around his waist, feeling his strong back against my hands. His lips and tongue were hot against mine, his high body temperature somehow making his kiss seem more intense.

I don't know how long we stood together like that, but finally he broke the kiss, though his arms were still wrapped around me. "Are you still mad?"

I shook my head numbly. "No."

"Good. Sweet dreams, Betty."

"Good night, Maxwell," I said, while he leaned in to kiss me again, softly this time. He released me then, and as soon as he walked over the threshold of my door, he seemed to disappear into the darkness beyond my doorway. Just a few seconds later I heard his car roar to life and I shut the door, leaning against it as a wave of ecstatic dizziness swept through me.

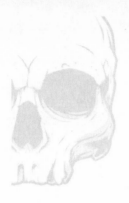

THIRTEEN

I felt like I was drifting through a fog the next day, the things going on around me somehow detached and shadowy. My boss noticed how distracted I was and suggested my brain had started the weekend early. I kept picturing Maxwell's blue eyes and remembering how warm and intense his kiss had been. I should have been focusing on the horrible vision of hell he'd shown me and the devastation I'd felt when Margaret turned her sad eyes on me. Those eyes were sad because of Maxwell, because he had destroyed Margaret, her husband and even her children. Yet every time I thought of the things that defined Maxwell as a demon, I pushed them out of my mind.

Was Maxwell somehow compelling me to fall for him? Could he force me to overlook his evil nature? Nope, I wasn't going to think about that right now, either.

I called Daisy on the way home to invite her and Shaun over for dinner. I figured we could eat at my place and then walk over to the Everett-Tattnall house together. She agreed, and I got home with enough time for a quick nap before I had to start dinner.

Shaun and Daisy showed up right at 6:30, and by then I was halfway through layering pasta, meat and sauce in a pan for lasagna. Daisy made a beeline for me and launched right into her questioning. "Okay, spill it, Betty! How was your date with Maxwell? What happened?"

I did my best to look casual. "Come on, Daze, it wasn't a date. Remember, this was just a celebration of our success at Sam MacIntosh's house."

"Celebration, date, whatever. Was it just the two of you?"

"Of course."

"See, if it had been a real celebration, he would have invited the entire team."

I laughed, picturing Maxwell hosting Carter and the rest of us at a party. "All right, I guess it does count as a date since I got a good-night kiss at the end of it."

"Ah-ha! I knew it!" Daisy punched her fist into the air. "I could hear you smiling when we talked on the phone earlier. So what new excuse has he found for taking you out again?"

"I don't know when I'm going to see him again. Things got a little weird at the end of the night." I told Daisy and Shaun about Maxwell running into Sam, and how disappointed he'd been that I hadn't revealed the true nature of the haunting to Sam.

"But he kissed you after all that?" Daisy asked.

"Yes."

She clapped her hands together. "Oh yes, you two will be going out again. I'm proud of you, Betty. When you promised to get a date within a month I had no idea you'd do it so quickly."

"We haven't actually met this guy," said Shaun. "For all we know, he's the spitting image of Mark the Mortician."

"Trust me, he's not," I said. "I'm never going to live that down, am I? A girl dates one weird guy and it haunts her forever." I heaved a dramatic sigh as I popped the lasagna into the oven.

"No, you're probably not going to," said Shaun. "Not as long as you're friends with us, anyway."

"Well, Maxwell sounds like a great guy for you. Successful businessman, good-looking, well-dressed, polite, romantic," Daisy counted off Maxwell's better attributes on her fingers.

"He just so happens to be a demon," I added.

"I thought that was just some joke of his?" Shaun asked.

"So did I, until last night." I gave them a brief account of the vision Maxwell had given me. I purposely left out some of the details, specifically that I'd felt a great deal of pain as the heat had pulsed through my arm and head. Even though I hadn't been injured, I knew Shaun and Daisy would be upset if they knew about that, and the last thing I wanted was for them to tell me I needed to stop seeing Maxwell.

Because, deep down, I knew they were right.

"Boo, if anyone else were telling me this, I wouldn't believe them," Daisy said slowly. "But it's not anyone else; it's you."

"Thanks, Daze. I know it's strange." Strange didn't begin to cover it. I was dating a demon who looked, acted and kissed like a man, and I wasn't nearly as concerned about it as I should be. "I'm still trying to sort it out, too."

Daisy put her arm around my shoulders, her tone light. "Okay, so he's a demon. Not all of us can be so lucky as to find a guy as perfect as my husband here."

Shaun flexed his biceps in mockery. "Oh, yes, I'm a perfect specimen. No man or demon alive can compare to my awesomeness."

My cell phone began to ring just then, and I rolled my eyes. "Oh, thank goodness, I'm saved from having to witness any more of your preening." My phone was on the coffee table, and I dashed over to pick it up.

"Hello?" I said.

"Hi, Betty. How was your day?" I immediately recognized Maxwell's smooth voice. Well, speak of the devil.

Completely boring until right now, I thought. "Pretty good, actually. We're getting all set to start our investigation at the Everett-Tattnall House tonight. How about you?"

"As a matter of fact, I thought about you all day. I'd like to take you out again tomorrow night." Wow, I thought, a real date. Finally, he's not offering to take me out using my work as an investigator for an excuse. No meeting, no celebration; just a date. This time, I hoped Maxwell wouldn't reveal any more of his deep, dark secrets to me. One was quite enough.

"That would be great." I turned and caught Daisy staring at me expectantly. I mouthed "Maxwell" to her and gave her a thumbs-up. She grinned and began blowing air kisses, so I had to try not to laugh into the phone.

"Okay, I'll be at your place at seven. Dress comfortably because we're going to be doing some walking. I'll see you tomorrow, Betty."

"Bye, Maxwell." I hung up and turned to Daisy and Shaun. I had no idea what Maxwell had in store for me, but I figured it would be something fun. "I have a real date tomorrow night!" I announced.

"That's three dates in the span of a week, Boo. I think this demon is falling for you," Shaun said.

"We'll see. Come on, I want to fill you guys in on the meeting Carter and I had with Alec Tuesday night." The three of us sat down, and I gave them all the details while we waited for the lasagna to finish cooking. I also told them about Carter's unexpected guest, and how I had to play nice for the media once again. Shaun found the entire scenario hilarious, but Daisy was indignant.

"I swear, Boo, I really am going to push him down a flight of stairs one of these days," she said.

Shaun patted Daisy's arm. "Such pent-up violence, honey. Maybe Betty's enjoying the limelight."

"Keep it up, Shaun, and I'm going to think that you're on Carter's side!" I said as I got up and went to check on dinner. The smell wafting from the oven made my stomach growl. "Food's ready, you two, come and get it."

We had to eat quickly since we wanted extra time for walking to the Everett-Tattnall House. I gathered up my paranormal pack and we left, stopping at Shaun's car to pick up his and Daisy's equipment.

When we arrived at the law firm, Alec was standing on the front porch of the old house, deep in conversation with Carter. "Hello again, Betty," Alec greeted me.

"Hello, gentlemen. Alec, this is Shaun and Daisy Tanner, two of The Seekers. Shaun, Daze, this is Alec Thornburn, one of the partners in the firm here."

After the introductions were finished, Carter gave me a disappointed look. "Alec says you've had no luck with the research."

"Not yet," I said. "None of Jasper's recent cases seemed of enough importance that a ghost would come back to try and get a message across about one of them. Alec's given me a box of the other things that Jasper's ghost has been moving around, and I hope to make some headway there."

"What do you make of the teddy bear?" asked Alec.

"I have no idea. Was it a gift from his wife, maybe?"

Alec shook his head. "I don't think so. As I remember, our other partner, Terrence, gave it to him as a joke one year. Something about them seeing each other more than they got to see their wives."

"Well, in the meantime, my team is already getting set up. Betty, your tech boy is here, too," said Carter.

"Cool, then let's go in and see what's happening. By the way, how is Kerri?"

Carter's tone was condescending. "More spooked than injured. Her arm is healing just fine, but she decided not to come out tonight."

"That's too bad. Tell her we hope she's doing better." Actually, I was kind of glad that Kerri wasn't joining us tonight. She was a little too haughty for my taste, so I wasn't going to miss her attitude.

We went into the house, where Lou was busy setting up a base of operations in the kitchen toward the back of the first floor. The house was designed like many of the early nineteenth-century houses in Savannah. The front door opened onto a long, wide hallway that ran the length of the building. Four rooms opened off of the hallway, one on each corner of the house. Now that the Everett-Tattnall house was a law firm, the room to the right of the front door was the receptionist's area, and the room to the left was a waiting area for clients. The two rooms at the back of the house were the kitchen, on the left, and Terrence Stiles's office on the right. The furnishings were mostly antiques, with plush leather chairs in the waiting area. Chandeliers hung from the high ceilings, and Persian rugs covered the hardwood floors. The law firm looked more like a house museum than an office.

A staircase in the hallway led up to the second floor, which had a similar four-room layout. Alec's and Jasper's offices took up the rooms at the front, with their floor-to-ceiling windows overlooking Chippewa Square. The rear rooms, once the master suite, were both used for storage. When I saw all of the filing cabinets crammed into the rooms, I believed Alec's claim that they kept every scrap of paperwork.

Lou, along with Jamie and Ron from Carter's team, was busy positioning the infrared video cameras. We didn't know where to expect Jasper's ghost to turn up, so we put a camera in each room and one on the landing halfway up the staircase, where Alec had seen Jasper's image in the mirror hanging there.

Alec already had a pretty good idea of what we were going to do, but we sat him down in the waiting room to explain the procedure to him anyway. "We'll be collecting video footage, taking pictures and using tape recorders to try and hear what Jasper might have to say to us," explained Carter. "If we're lucky, we'll also get some direct interaction with him, and maybe even see his apparition. I'll call you tomorrow to let you know how the night goes, but it may take a few days to go over all of the video and photos before we can tell you if we got any good evidence."

"If Jasper is half as eager to communicate with all of you as he has been with us, then I think you'll find plenty of evidence," said Alec. "You have my cell phone number, so if there's anything important that happens tonight, call me immediately no matter what the hour. I live about fifteen minutes away, and I can come over here if necessary."

"We should be just fine, but we'll keep it in mind," assured Carter. He checked his watch. "It's about 9:30. Shall we get started?"

"That's my cue to leave you professionals to your task," said Alec, standing. We saw him out the door, and he passed a key over to Carter. "Just arm the alarm before you leave tonight, like I showed you earlier. And please lock the front door once I leave, so no one can slip in while you're investigating."

"You got it," said Carter. As soon as Alec was gone, he locked the door and turned to all of us. "I think Betty and I should pair up tonight."

"Why, Carter, do you have a newspaper reporter

coming along on the investigation that you want me to entertain?" My sarcasm had the opposite effect on Carter than the one I intended.

"No, but that's a really good idea. The next time we come here we should do that. Brian from the Morning News would love to tag along, I'd bet."

"Yes, I'm sure he's a card-carrying member of your fan club. All right, I'll go with you. Daisy, Shaun, why don't you two work with Jamie to start?"

"And the two of us will be at our post in the kitchen," spoke up Lou, referring to himself and Ron. "I wonder what kind of coffee these fancy lawyer boys keep around here."

I followed the three of them to the kitchen, where I had stowed my gear. I popped a fresh set of batteries into my camera, put my little digital tape recorder in my pocket and returned to the front entrance, where Carter was waiting for me.

"The other three are going upstairs first," he told me. "I thought maybe you and I could start in the waiting room since a client saw Jasper's apparition there."

I agreed, and Carter and I settled into two of the leather chairs after he turned off the lights. The only window coverings were sheer white curtains, so there was still a lot of light filtering in from the streetlights outside and from the occasional sweep of a car's headlights as it drove around the square. An ornate mirror hung above the fireplace, directly across from the two windows facing the square, and I realized that the headlights reflecting off of the mirror created an odd effect. Someone could easily catch the quick right-to-left movement of the reflected light out of the corner of their eye and mistake it for something paranormal.

I said as much to Carter, but he answered with his usual air of authority. "Maybe, but clients are in here during the day, so they wouldn't be affected by headlights," he said.

"That's true," I said, feeling deflated. "But maybe the effect begins before it's completely dark, so clients in here late in the day might see something, especially in the winter when the sun sets so early."

"But this client saw the ghost recently, so it would have been in the middle of summer."

Carter one, Betty zero. I gave a quiet "Humph," then settled back in my chair. "Do you want to ask some questions first, or me?"

"I do. How can you have not found anything interesting in that huge stack of information Alec gave you?"

"What?"

"I thought you knew what you were doing when it came to research, so you should have found something. I think maybe you're not looking hard enough."

"Since you do everything so much better, I suggest you try going through all of those files."

Carter gave a sniff. "No, thanks, that's what I have people like you for."

"You are such a jerk, Carter!"

Before I could say more, our radios buzzed, and Daisy's voice spoke up. "Do we need to separate you two? We can hear you all the way up here." I could hear her barely-suppressed laughter.

I keyed my radio before Carter could pull his from his belt. "It's just a little spat. We'll try to argue quietly from now on."

Carter and I eyed each other in the dim room for a moment, but Daisy's amused voice had calmed me down. "What I meant originally was, did you want to ask questions of the ghost?"

"I'm not sure any ghosts would stick around after all the noise you just made, but I'll try." In the faint light I saw

Carter pick up his tape recorder, and the little red "record" light began to glow. "Is there anyone here with us tonight? My name is Carter, and this is Betty, and we're here to help you. We don't mean you any harm."

While Carter tried his best snake-oil salesman voice on Jasper or any other entity hanging around, I pulled out my camera and began snapping pictures.

I got all of three pictures taken before my low-battery light began to flash urgently, and within a minute my camera was dead. "Oh, you're kidding me!" I mumbled.

Carter, who had been wrapped up in his questioning, glanced over. "What's that?" he asked.

"My brand new camera batteries are drained already. There's something paranormal here, all right, and it's thirsty. I'll be right back. Radio me if anything happens." I got up and shuffled through the dark mansion, heading down the hallway toward the kitchen. The smell of fresh-brewed coffee greeted me as I got closer to the kitchen door, and when I went in I found Lou and Ron huddled in front of a bank of monitors, each with a steaming mug in their hands. "Don't you two look cozy," I said, pausing a moment to let my eyes adjust. There wasn't much light in the room, but after the dimness of the rest of the house, the kitchen seemed bright.

"It's gourmet," said Lou. "Want some?"

I gave him a wave as I went to my bag and began fishing for more batteries. "Nah, if I start drinking coffee then I'll wind up investigating in the ladies' room half the night. I just came to get some more batteries. My new set drained in about fifteen minutes."

"All right, it's going to be a fun night," said Ron.

I took the entire package of batteries with me, just in case. Lou called after me as I opened the kitchen door. "Don't be scared, Boo."

I turned and looked at him closely. "Why would I be scared?"

"Because you have to go back into that dark room all by yourself and face Carter." Lou laughed, but only after I noticed Ron snickering, too, did I feel comfortable joining in. I didn't want our two investigation teams to get caught up in some us-versus-them rivalry—well, any more than we already had—so it was nice to see that one of Carter's team members could enjoy the joke, too.

"My ego might get a little bruised, but otherwise I think I'll be okay." I gave Lou a wink and stepped out into the hallway, closing the door behind me. My eyes were no longer adjusted to the darkness, and the hallway seemed to disappear when the kitchen door clicked shut.

I stood still for a moment, letting my eyes adjust once again. Within a few seconds I could see a faint glow coming from the stained-glass windows flanking the front door, and as I waited, the railing of the staircase began to take shape, as well.

Then I realized that there was a shadow in front of me that didn't match any of the furniture I had seen earlier, before we turned the lights out. In fact, it was the right height and shape to be a man.

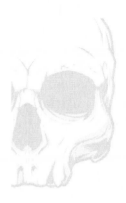

FOURTEEN

I still couldn't discern much in the darkness, but the shadowy form seemed to be about ten feet away, and only his right side was visible because it stood between my line of sight and the front windows. After several seconds, the form was still there, but it wasn't moving.

"Carter?" I called.

"Betty?" It was Carter's voice answering, but it seemed to be coming from more than ten feet away.

I groped for the radio on my hip and brought it to my lips, keeping my gaze on the mysterious shadow. "Carter, where are you?"

"Right where you left me," came his answer.

"I think there's an entity in the hallway between the kitchen and the front door. I'm going to try to talk to him." It was ironic that Lou had told me not to be scared, and now I was feeling a little nervous as I faced this shadowy figure all by myself. The distance from the waiting room to the kitchen was so short that I had never even considered bringing Carter with me. My paranormal experiences have run the gamut from eerie feelings to seeing apparitions that almost look corporeal, but I've always had at least one other person with me.

I considered opening the kitchen door to step back inside its light, but I was feeling more stubborn than scared. If the light from the kitchen poured into the hallway, it was likely that the shadow would disappear.

My hands were full, with my camera in one and my radio in the other, so I shoved my radio back onto my hip and dug my tape recorder out of my pocket without taking my eyes off the shadow, which still hadn't moved. I was beginning to wonder if I wasn't mistaking it for a coat tree or some other innocuous object, but I had the distinct feeling of another presence there in the hallway with me.

Once my finger found the button that turned on my tape recorder, I held it out. "What's your name?" I asked, fighting to make my voice sound stronger than I felt. "Are you Jasper Whitney? Why are you here? Is there something you would like to tell us?"

I knew I wouldn't hear an answer right then, but I paused between each question. If the ghost—if it really was one, and not just some ordinary shadow playing tricks on my mind—had anything to say, I would have to wait to hear it when I played back my tape recording. Still, I realized I was waiting anxiously, leaning forward onto the balls of my feet in anticipation. I held my breath, hoping for some kind of affirmation that I was getting somewhere, when I heard a loud thump behind me. Something pushed hard against my back and I went sprawling, landing on my hands and knees as my camera and tape recorder skittered away into the dark hall.

I shouted and craned my head around to see what had happened, and a dark mass loomed over me, the light from the kitchen creating a halo around it. I gasped, and then heard Lou's urgent voice. "Betty? I'm so sorry! Are you okay?"

My knees were beginning to sting, so I rolled over so that I was sitting on the floor, facing the kitchen. Lou was the dark shape in the doorway, and I looked over my shoulder to find the shadow figure I'd been talking to.

It was gone. I now had a clear view of the stained-glass windows.

I turned back to Lou. "What happened?" I asked, as I heard the same words shouted by Carter, who was running out of the waiting room behind me. Lou reached down to give me a hand up and began to explain. "We heard you tell Carter you thought there was a ghost in the hallway, but then our radio in here went dead. Right when that happened, the screen showing the video feed from the camera set up in the hallway got so much static that we couldn't see any kind of picture anymore. I guess I panicked a little and thought something might have happened to you. I didn't realize you were just outside the kitchen door."

"Something was in the hallway, standing perfectly still." I described the shadow to the others, then turned to get my camera and tape recorder. They hadn't gone far, and luckily both of them seemed none the worse for wear after my tumble.

Shaun, Daisy and Jamie came running down the stairs then, and Daisy's eyes were wide. "What happened? We heard a huge noise from down here."

Lou actually blushed a little as I repeated my story. He felt guilty, but when I told him that a couple of skinned knees weren't so bad, he looked even more embarrassed. "Actually, I feel more guilty about the fact that the entity you saw got scared off," he said, "but I am sorry I knocked you over."

Ron leaned in toward Lou and me and whispered, "I guess he warned you about the wrong guy, Betty. Here it was one of your own team members all along." Lou gave Ron a friendly nudge with his elbow as they both glanced surreptitiously at Carter.

"Betty, why don't you and I sit out here in the hallway

instead of the waiting room? Maybe your new buddy will come back," said Carter.

"You got it, but I'm not sitting anywhere near the kitchen door."

Shaun, Daisy and Jamie began to move toward the staircase when Carter stopped them. "Have you three had any luck upstairs?"

"Not yet," Jamie answered, "but then, we haven't been up there for long. We were just getting settled into those nice big chairs in Alec's office."

"If what I saw was Jasper, then he must be anxious to communicate. He materialized quickly," I said.

Carter gave a derisive snort. "If you saw anything at all."

I turned to him, momentarily forgetting all pretense of politeness. "What makes you think I made it up?"

"I didn't say you made it up. I just think that maybe you're trying too hard to see something. It is awfully early in the night for apparitions to be materializing in front of us. Maybe you're just being over-eager. Sometimes investigators want a paranormal experience so badly that they'll mistake ordinary shadows for ghosts."

I stared at Carter. I didn't know if he was jealous because I saw something first, or if his attitude toward me made him skeptical, but through my anger I felt something else: hurt. Carter had managed to hurt my feelings, and that made me even angrier. I'd never cared what he thought before, and I reminded myself that I still shouldn't care. I guess that our working together had led me to believe Carter had some fraction of respect for my work, even though I knew he would always see himself as the superior investigator.

Finally, I just nodded my head. "Fine, Carter. You believe what you want. I sincerely hope that Jasper's ghost shows up in front of you tonight, so that once you're done screaming about it I can say, 'I told you so.'" I turned my head and called down the hallway, feeling bold. "Hey, Jasper, are you hearing this? Carter thinks I made you up. I'd sure appreciate it if you could prove him wrong tonight."

I turned back to Carter. "Lights out, let's go." Without another word, I turned and sat on the hardwood floor of the hallway, facing the front door. This time, though, I put a few feet between my backside and the kitchen door.

Daisy caught my eye as she followed Shaun and Jamie upstairs, and her face looked as livid as I felt. I knew that once we finished tonight, she'd go on a tirade about Carter's attitude, and I couldn't wait to hear it. Once everyone was in their spots, Carter flicked off the hall light and settled in next to me on the floor.

"I'm sorry," he said stiffly, "but you have to stay objective, Betty."

"And you think I wasn't? I considered that the shadow could be a piece of furniture, or drapes or even my over-active imagination. None of those options made sense, Carter, and besides, I got the feeling that something was present in here with me."

"It's just that everything went from perfectly calm to total chaos in the span of two seconds."

"It's not my fault that Lou decided to come crashing through the kitchen door," I said, and then I sighed. "Carter, look, I understand your point and you're right, we have to be objective. I've seen other ghost hunters who think every speck of dust in a picture is an orb, and I don't want to be like that. Maybe you could have expressed yourself a little better, though. Accusing me of seeing things isn't going to do anything but make me mad."

"Yeah." Carter's voice still had a defiant edge, but he spoke so quietly I had to strain to hear. "I guess Lou wasn't the only one who over-reacted a little."

"Were you a little scared for me?" I joked.

Carter paused, and when he replied, his voice was even quieter. "Maybe a little."

Maybe Carter was beginning to come around. I still didn't like him, but in that moment I felt a little sorry for him. Carter was the type who always got what he wanted using his charm and his money, but I suspected that he didn't have a lot of genuine friends. I didn't get the idea that he spent a lot of time with the rest of his team outside of their investigations, but I really didn't know a lot about Carter's life outside of the paranormal. I made a mental note to ask him about it sometime. At the moment, though, I was thinking more about Jasper.

"I'm sorry I asked Jasper to come scare the hell out of you," I said. I'm just not good at staying mad at people.

Carter cheered a little. "Don't apologize. I want to see him. Of course, if we want that to happen, we ought to get started. You're asking the questions this time."

Since it was my turn, I turned on my tape recorder and held it out while Carter snapped pictures down the length of the hallway. "Jasper, are you still here with us?" I asked.

The hallway illuminated with a flash from Carter's camera, then he grabbed my arm and whispered loudly. "There's something down there! I saw it moving from the waiting room into the hallway."

"Jasper, would you like to come talk to us?" Carter and I waited silently, but I couldn't see any shadow against the windows like I had before. Carter took another picture, and when he looked at the digital image on the camera's view screen, he started to laugh self-consciously.

"I'm the one seeing things this time," he said, passing the camera to me. The picture showed an empty hallway, save for a little dog in the bottom of the frame. Just then, I felt something warm and wet against my arm. A little white Shih Tzu was nuzzling me.

"I forgot: Alec told me that one of the partners keeps his dog here. Something about his kid being allergic." If the lights had been on, I'm sure I would have seen Carter blushing over his gaffe.

"You know, Carter, it's important that we maintain our objectivity. It's the only way we'll ever become respected in our field," I said, keeping my voice deadpan.

Carter ignored me, instead reaching over to stroke the dog's ears. He apparently didn't like Carter any more than me, because he swiped at him with a paw. "Ow! He's sharp."

"He's smart. Dogs can sense things that people can't." Like who's a jerk and who's not, I added silently.

"Like right now?" Carter asked, still looking at the Shih Tzu.

"What?" I looked down. The dog's ears were pressed back against its head, and in the dark hallway I could see huge eyes staring toward the front door. Carter and I followed its gaze, and the shadow was back, perfectly framed by the stained-glass windows.

"It's Jasper," Carter whispered. "You weren't seeing things."

"I told you so," I whispered back.

I held out my tape recorder once again. "Jasper Whitney, is that you? Your partner Alec believes there is something you want to tell us. If you'll come and talk to us, we'll be able to hear your voice when we play back my tape recorder."

The shadow finally began to move, shuffling forward slowly.

"We don't want to hurt you; we just want to talk to you," said Carter, and I could hear the tension in his voice. He lowered his voice and whispered in my ear, "Think I should take a picture, or will it scare him off?"

"I don't know," I answered. "Let's wait a minute and

see what he does." I continued to ask the ghost questions, pausing between each to let him answer.

Carter shifted next to me, and I realized he was talking on his radio when he said, "There's an entity in the hallway. Maintain radio silence and stay upstairs."

The shadowy figure continued to approach, and I kept my arm extended in front of me, my tape recorder hopefully catching some EVPs. The apparition, whether it was Jasper or not, was now only a foot from the tips of my fingers.

"Please, tell us the message you want Alec to hear," I said. I leaned back instinctively; the close proximity of the ghost was making me feel uncomfortable. As I shrank backwards, Carter leaned toward me until his upper body was wedged in behind mine, keeping me between him and the ghost. We sat there together in total silence; not even our breathing could be heard. The air in the hallway turned ice cold, like we had been transported to a freezer, and I shivered. Carter mistook my shivering as a sign of fear, and he whispered, "It's okay," into my hair, though he sounded on edge himself. When he spoke, the ghost stopped short and stood there, within our reach. Even at such close proximity, I still couldn't see any details. It was like a shadow had detached itself from its human counterpart and was standing in front of us. It seemed solid because the hallway behind its human shape wasn't visible, but the blackness was featureless.

Carter reached out with one of his hands. "Can you touch me?" he asked. We both waited anxiously, but instead, a heavy knocking noise began to sound.

I jumped and felt Carter do the same, and the ghost in front of us disappeared again. "Damn it!" Carter shouted.

The knocking sound came again, and I realized that it was emanating from the other end of the hallway. "Is someone at the door? You've got to be kidding me!" I said, exasperated. Our interruptions were coming at the worst times tonight.

Carter got up and turned on the light, then stomped down the hall to open the door. "What do you want?" I heard him ask loudly, but his tone immediately changed.

Over Carter's shoulder I could see a policeman standing on the doorstep. "Do you have permission to be here?" the man asked.

"Yes, of course, sir," answered Carter. "We're here with the permission of Alec Thornburn, one of the partners in the firm that uses this house for their offices."

"Is Mr. Thornburn here with you?"

"No, sir, he's gone home for the evening."

The policeman caught sight of me, then, and smoothly sidestepped Carter so that he was standing inside the house. "How many of you are there?"

Carter paused. "There are seven of us."

"We're conducting a paranormal investigation here," I jumped in. "Mr. Thornburn and his staff believe this building is haunted, and he asked us to investigate this evening to help determine what might be responsible for the paranormal activity here."

The policeman looked at me skeptically at first, but then his eyes widened. "You're that group that was on the news," he said.

Carter's face lit up in triumph. "Yes, that's right. We had a press conference announcing that we'd be investigating here because it's a historic landmark."

"Yeah, I remember her from the story." The officer nodded at me. I was tempted to respond with a snarky comment about me being the cute sidekick, but I figured it wasn't the best time for joking around.

By this time everyone else had joined us, and we were crowded together in the hallway. "I'm really sorry, but I'm going to have to ask all of you to leave since you don't actually have someone here who's an owner of the business."

"Is that really necessary?" asked Carter, his tone turning persuasive.

"I'm afraid so." To the policeman's credit, he really did look apologetic. "We got an anonymous call from someone who thought this place had been broken into. I can see that's not really what's going on, but since you're not actually affiliated with the firm, I can't let you stay."

Carter looked like he wanted to argue, but he finally gave in. "All right. Next time we'll ask Mr. Thornburn to stick around for the night. We'll need a little time to gather our equipment."

"That's fine," said the officer. "I'll wait to make sure everyone gets out."

I turned and addressed the others. "All right, kids, the cops are breaking up the party. Let's get packed up." I was incredibly disappointed since we had been making such great progress, and I was anxious to hear what my tape recorder might have waiting on it. I consoled myself with the fact that if Jasper was willing to show up this soon in the investigation, then things could only get better when we returned.

We got packed up fairly quickly, and after all of our equipment was piled onto the front porch, Carter set the security alarm and locked up. The policeman apologized several times for kicking us out, but we knew he was just doing his job. Of course, Carter was convinced that his press conference was the only thing that had saved us from getting arrested for breaking and entering.

As we helped Lou load our video cameras and monitors into his car, I filled the group in on what Carter and I had witnessed. I wanted to go home and play my tape recorder back myself, but Lou insisted on taking it with him.

"I promise to call you the second I find anything," he promised. "My equipment is better than yours. I can isolate EVPs that you might not even hear with just your headphones."

"I know," I said. "You're right, but that's not going to stop me from pouting about it. That ghost manifested twice, and both times we got interrupted. It's not fair."

"We did have pretty bad timing tonight," Carter said. "Next time we'll get better results. Our luck has to change, right?"

I shrugged. "I hope so. Lou, at least you can get an early start on reviewing video." I glanced at my watch and realized it was only eleven. It was still early for the bar-hopping crowd. In fact, there was still a fair amount of traffic driving around the square and a few college kids wandering the sidewalks.

Daisy seemed to read my mind. "I bet we can get a back table at the Burglar Bar, so we can hide out and drown our sorrows," she said.

I agreed, and then Daisy did something that shocked me. "Carter, would you three like to join us?" she asked. My jaw dropped, and I caught Shaun's eye. He looked as surprised as me.

Ron declined because he wanted to start looking over his own video footage, and Jamie said he needed to get home to Kerri. Apparently the two of them were dating, which made me really glad I hadn't expressed my relief over her absence out loud.

That only left Carter. "Thanks, but no. Some friends of mine were heading to that tapas bar on Barnard tonight for martinis, so I'm going to catch up with them there."

I exhaled the breath that I didn't realize I'd been holding. A little bit of Carter went a long way, and I'd definitely had my fill.

With our video equipment loaded up, we all said good

night and I turned to walk to the bar with Daisy and Shaun. We were still toting our cameras, even though Lou had confiscated all of our memory cards so he could review each picture. As soon as we were out of earshot of the others, I turned to Daisy, but Shaun was faster than me.

"What's gotten into you?" he demanded.

Daisy smiled. "I knew he wouldn't say yes. Now we look like the good guys, though, asking him along even though he was a jerk to Betty. Did you see the way he squirmed when I asked him?"

"I missed that," I said. "I was too busy staring at you, and wondering how Shaun would cope once we threw you into an institution."

We teased Daisy all the way to the Burglar Bar, where we snagged the last outdoor table. It was a little chilly out, but the usual Friday night crowd was spilling over from inside.

A pitcher of beer was brought to our table in short order, but I barely touched the glass in front of me. I was too busy mulling over the night's events. I felt almost desperate to know if we had captured any EVPs, and I wondered why the ghost we saw had no discernable features, while Alec had reported actually seeing Jasper's image. Then again, with the low light and the glow of the windows behind him, the ghost could have looked like Daisy, and I still wouldn't have recognized it.

Two hours flew past while the three of us recounted the night's events, pondering the high level of paranormal activity (for me, at least), lamenting the interruptions that kept us from getting any further and wishing we could return the next night. Unfortunately, Carter was going to be out of town, and Daisy's parents were coming from Macon to visit for a few days. And I had a date with Maxwell.

Finally, I stood up and stretched. It was getting cooler as the night wore on, and I was feeling cold and stiff. "I think it's time for me to head for bed," I said. "Spending time one-on-one with Carter wears a girl out."

Shaun and Daisy echoed the sentiment, and we paid and left. After the short walk back to my apartment, I hugged both of them and said goodbye while they climbed into Shaun's car.

I turned and rounded the corner to my apartment, and when I opened my front door, I got a horrifying feeling of déjà vu. Someone had broken into my apartment again, only this time, they had been a lot less cautious.

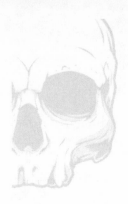

FIFTEEN

Every book I owned had been thrown off the bookshelf, small pieces of furniture, like the chairs in the dining room and the little table next to my couch, were all turned over. I glanced around quickly, and once again my valuables—my TV, my laptop—were untouched.

Then I saw that my little ceramic angel, a gift from my grandmother, had been pushed off my bookshelf and lay shattered among my discarded books. Tears instantly welled up in my eyes. I wondered what else might have been damaged and knew I had to go look in my bedroom, but when I tried to walk forward, my knees buckled and I sank to the floor.

I began to cry in earnest, and I gave in for a moment, sitting there on the floor with my face in my hands. Finally, I heaved several deep breaths and wiped at my eyes.

It wasn't until then that I noticed what was sitting right in front of me. A huge dead rat was sprawled on my floor, and a piece of paper was tied with string to its long, worm-like tail. I leaned forward, fighting the urge to gag, and read the words scrawled on the paper: "No police this time."

I stared, horrified, at the words as their meaning sank in. Whoever had broken in before was responsible for this latest invasion, and they somehow knew that I'd called the police that first time. Which meant they had been watching my apartment. And probably still were.

If I couldn't call the police, then I had to call someone. The idea of being left alone to deal with this made my heart pound.

Daisy. I had to call Daisy. She and Shaun wouldn't be far away yet, and they could come back and help me make sense of everything.

I fished my cell phone out of my pocket, feeling my way because I still couldn't tear my eyes away from the hideous dead rat and the awful words that it bore. I had called Daisy on my way home from work, so I knew that if I hit the "call" button twice on my phone, it would automatically dial the last number I'd been connected to. My thumb found the button, and I pressed it twice, even though it was hard to do because I was shaking. I brought the phone to my ear, and it seemed like an eternity before I heard the first ring.

Finally, I heard a voice, but it wasn't Daisy's.

"Maxwell," the voice said.

I'd forgotten about Maxwell's call earlier that evening, which came after my conversation with Daisy.

"Maxwell? Oh, shit," I said.

He became instantly alert. "Betty, what's wrong?"

"I – Nothing, I was trying to call Daisy. I'm sorry."

"Are you in danger? Are you hurt?"

How did he know? Did I sound that distraught? "No, no, I'm okay. They broke into my apartment again and it's awful. There's a dead rat and my little angel is broken and I can't call the police." I started crying again. Okay, so I did sound pretty upset.

Maxwell's voice was tense. "Are they still there?"

"No," I said, then dropped my voice as if I might be overheard, "but I think they're watching my apartment."

"Betty, I want you to stay exactly where you are. I'm on my way."

The phone went dead and I stared at it. I didn't know how far away Maxwell lived, but the idea of waiting here alone for longer than a few minutes was horrifying.

I was still on the floor, my legs curled up underneath me, sitting in front of the rat and staring at my phone when I heard a soft "pop." The sound came from behind me, and I realized with dismay that I had left the front door standing wide open.

Before I could turn my head, a pair of strong hands clamped down on my shoulders. I shrieked and jumped to my feet, whirling to meet my attacker. Instead, I found myself gazing into Maxwell's impossibly blue eyes.

"It's just me," he said. "It's all right."

"Maxwell," was all I could get out. I threw my arms around him and buried my face in his chest. His skin was hot against my cheek. Wait a minute, I thought, his skin?

I stood back and looked at him. "Maxwell! You're naked!" I shouted. I didn't know whether to be amused or horrified, but my sense of decency made me look up into his eyes so I wouldn't stare at the rest of him. I was sorely tempted.

"I was asleep when you called," Maxwell said casually. "I could tell something was wrong, and I didn't want to waste any time."

"But you're naked!" I could hear the hysterical edge in my voice. The absurdity of a naked man (demon, I reminded myself) standing in the middle of my living room was going to push me past my limit for how much I could handle in one night.

"Would you like me to leave?"

"No, don't go." I reached out and laid my hand on his arm, as if my touch could keep him there with me. A bare Maxwell was vastly better than being alone. I closed my eyes and tried to force the jumble of thoughts and emotions in my head into something coherent. "First of all, how did you get here so fast?"

Maxwell shrugged, and one corner of his mouth turned up. "One of the perks of being a demon. I can materialize anywhere I want."

I moved past Maxwell to shut and lock the front door. "But it's not safe for you to be here," I said. "They're watching, and if it's a demon hunter like you think it is, then you can't be here."

"With all of these things happening to you, you're concerned about my safety? You really are a good woman, Betty." Maxwell pulled me back into his embrace. "But unless anyone can actually see inside, then you're safe. It's not like I walked up and rang your doorbell."

"They may have seen you through the open door," I argued.

"Maybe. I'm willing to take that risk. Now tell me everything."

Maxwell sat me down on the couch, and I told him what I knew, which wasn't much. The story was pretty much told by my ransacked apartment and the dead rat.

When I finished and had calmed down considerably, Maxwell was quiet. He rubbed the fingers of his left hand together absent-mindedly, sparks flying from them. "I'm sorry if I brought this on you, Betty. If I was a nice guy I'd say we shouldn't see each other anymore because I might be putting you in danger."

I looked up at him, horrified. The last thing I wanted was to not see Maxwell again, but a small smile was on his lips. "I'm not a nice guy, though."

"You came over here to keep me from going insane," I said. "That counts as nice in my book."

"Yes, dating you is going to turn me into a good guy if I'm not careful." Maxwell said it so quietly that he was almost talking to himself, but when he spoke again his voice was firm. "Come on, I know it's late, but you'll feel better if we get some of this cleaned up tonight."

I shook my head. "Maxwell, you don't have to stay. You've already been wonderful."

When Maxwell insisted, I shook my head again, but this time I was smiling. "Fine, you can stay, but you have to put some clothes on."

Maxwell laughed. "If you insist. Give me three minutes." With that, he disappeared off the couch, and I heard the same quiet "pop" that I had earlier. He was back in only two minutes, dressed in a pair of jeans and a white tee-shirt. Even dressed casually, he still looked good.

Now that I could look at Maxwell without blushing, we got to work cleaning up. He took care of the dead rat for me while I arranged my books on the shelves where they belonged. It was sad to see the shards of my ceramic angel as I swept the pieces into a dustpan, but I did feel better as my apartment began to look normal again.

The intruder had come in through my window again, even though I remembered locking the window after the first break-in. Curious, Maxwell banged against the window and discovered that the lock was so loose that a few solid knocks made it slip out of position. I found a screwdriver, and Maxwell tightened the lock while I continued sweeping.

The cleanup really didn't take that long. The furniture that had been toppled was easily righted, all of the things scattered on the floor were put back where they belonged and, despite my worry, my bedroom had barely been touched.

I surveyed the apartment when we finished. "Thanks, Maxwell," I said.

"You're welcome." He gave me a long look, and finally said, "I think I should stay here tonight."

I dropped my gaze, wondering how to respond. Part of me wanted him to stay because he made me feel safe and calm. Plus, the thought of curling up in bed with him sounded blissful. But my independent side argued that I just wanted to be alone after such an exhausting night. "Maxwell, that's so nice of you," I finally said, "but I'm exhausted, and I think I'll sleep just fine by myself. I don't think they'll come back tonight."

"Maybe you would sleep fine, but I wouldn't. I'd be too worried about you," Maxwell said. As he spoke, he reached out and took my hand. "Let's go to bed."

I just couldn't argue with that suggestion. "Okay," I said, and as soon as I was resolved to go to bed, I realized how numb my body felt. It was three o'clock in the morning, and my night had involved two encounters with a ghost, a break-in, and a naked demon. And a dead rat, I reminded myself.

I went into the bathroom to get ready for bed, and when I came out Maxwell was already under the covers, sitting up with one hand stretched toward Mina. She was standing tentatively on the bed, leaning forward to sniff at Maxwell's hand. As I watched, she crept forward a couple steps and let Maxwell stroke her head. Maxwell was shirtless again, and I glanced at my dresser to see his jeans and tee folded up neatly on top of it. By that point, though, I was too tired to care what he was (or wasn't) wearing. I flicked off my bedroom light and crawled into bed next to Maxwell. We both rolled onto our sides so that we were facing each other. His eyes almost seemed to glow in the darkness of my room.

"Maxwell," I began. I wasn't sure how to say what I felt. We'd only met a week before, and yet he had come over instantly when I called, helped me clean up my wrecked apartment, and was now staying so I wouldn't have to be alone. Finally, I sighed. "Thank you."

Maxwell draped his arm over me and rubbed my back. "You're welcome." He leaned forward and kissed me softly, and I was reminded of his goodnight kiss on Thursday. With a jolt, I realized that our dinner on the beach had only been the night before, even though it seemed like weeks ago.

Our kiss deepened, and Maxwell's fingers curled under, his nails lightly grazing my back. Despite the warmth of my bed, I felt my skin break out in goose bumps. I snuggled closer to Maxwell: he was definitely naked. When he broke our kiss, I sighed.

My sigh turned into a yawn. I put a hand to my mouth to stifle it, but even Maxwell's charms couldn't hold back the exhaustion I felt. "Sorry," I mumbled.

Maxwell laughed and gave me another light kiss. "Sweet dreams, Betty," he said.

"Good night," I answered, and I was asleep almost before the words left my mouth, my exhausted body cradled in the demon's arms.

When I woke up Saturday morning, all I could think about was how sore my body felt. Whether it was from the general stress of the night, or from piling my books back onto their shelves, I ached from head to toe.

As I lay in bed, willing my body to feel better, I realized that I was really, really warm. I cracked one eye open and looked over to see Maxwell pressed up against my side, apparently still asleep. I don't know why, but the idea of a demon having to sleep struck me as funny. I glanced at the clock; it was only eight. My eyes shut again, and even though I couldn't fall asleep again, I enjoyed just laying there, feeling Maxwell's skin against mine and listening to his soft breathing. There was something almost vulnerable about him when he was asleep.

As if he knew I was thinking of him, Maxwell stirred and mumbled, "Morning."

"Hi," I said, "Coffee?"

"Yes, please."

I stretched and climbed out of bed, making my way to the kitchen for my morning ritual. The coffee was brewing when Maxwell joined me, already dressed. I pulled two mugs from the cabinet and filled them, handing one over to him. "Let's go sit outside," I suggested.

Maxwell nodded and we walked outside to sit at a little table in the courtyard. It was a nice day, and the sun was shining through the old magnolia tree planted there.

"Do you normally go out in your pajamas?" Maxwell asked, glancing at my pants and tank top set with their bright cherry print.

I shrugged. "It's Savannah. Once in a while I'll bring my coffee out here. It's not like I'm prancing out here in a negligee."

"Now that I would like to see," he said, taking a long sip of coffee. "So what's on your agenda today?"

"I'll probably head over to Lou's place," I said. "He's our tech guy, so he reviews all of the pictures, video and tape recordings from each investigation. We got done so early last night that I'll bet he's halfway through everything by now. I just hope that he finds some good evidence."

"Is that all you have planned?"

"Yeah."

Maxwell laughed. "Aren't you forgetting something?"

I frowned. "I don't think so. There aren't any other investigations going on right now and – oh. Oh, yeah. I'm supposed to go out with you tonight."

"You're still up for it, I hope."

"Of course," I said, nodding my head emphatically.

161

"Last night was just so crazy that I forgot we'd made plans."

"Good," Maxwell said, smiling. "Once we finish up here I'll head home. I think you're going to have a lot of fun tonight."

"I hope so. I could stand to have a little fun after my adventures of late. So can I get a hint about what we're doing tonight?"

Maxwell raised his eyebrows. "No. A little suspense never hurt."

We finished our coffee and went back inside, where Maxwell promised to pick me up at seven. He pulled me close, and he was still kissing me when he disappeared.

Since I hadn't heard anything from Lou yet, I decided to forego a shower in favor of a bath. I ran the water as hot as I could tolerate it and dumped in a few handfuls of Epsom salts, hoping it would help relax my sore body. I eased down into the water until even my shoulders were submerged and closed my eyes. When I opened them again, I realized I must have fallen asleep because the water was only lukewarm. I climbed out and put on a light blue tee-shirt and jeans.

My suspicions about falling asleep in the tub were confirmed when I realized I had a voicemail from Lou. I had never even heard the phone ring. He wanted all of us to come over at noon, and since it was fifteen minutes 'til, I finished getting ready and headed out. Like my last trip to Lou's, everyone else was waiting by the time I arrived.

"We didn't get much," he began, "but I think you'll be happy with what evidence I did find. The ghost—whether or not it's really Jasper—has a bad habit of disrupting the video cameras. Betty, what happened with the hallway camera when you first spied Jasper is the same thing that happened when you and Carter saw him again. If we could consider the static on the video screens as evidence, then we'd have a great case for a haunting. Since so many other factors could be to blame, though, we need something more definitive."

"And we're hoping you have that," said Shaun, clearly impatient for Lou to reveal what else he found.

"Ron went over Carter and Jamie's evidence, and he emailed me a picture Carter took in the hallway. Here." Lou handed us a printout of the picture, and the shadowy figure was clearly outlined in the glow from the front doors. We all agreed that it looked great, and Lou continued. "The EVPs are where we really got something telling. Listen to this clip from Betty's tape recorder and tell me what you think."

Lou turned to his computer and pulled up a digital track that he had isolated from the question and answer sessions I'd recorded. I could hear my own voice asking, "What's your name?" There was a response in another voice, one that was deeper but barely more than a whisper. "…asp…" the voice said, along with some softer muttering. Lou played the clip again, but the disembodied voice was so quiet that it was hard to make out anything but the "asp" sound.

"'Asp'…as in 'Jasper'?" I asked. "That's all I can make out."

Everyone agreed that it was the most likely explanation, but it didn't convince me entirely. The EVP was so short and could have been some other noise. Perhaps we were just imagining it was a voice trying to articulate "Jasper."

"Maybe you'll like this better," said Lou, pulling up another track on his computer screen. Carter's voice suddenly filled the room, beginning mid-sentence: "…to hurt you, we just want to talk to you." Then a voice, more distinct than the first EVP, answered, "Tell him… not…"

Shaun, Daisy and I all sat up straight, sucking in our

breath at the same moment. "Wow," said Daisy, "that was crystal clear." Shaun and I agreed. EVPs are often so muffled that we have to make a guess as to what the ghost is saying, but those three words were as audible as if Carter had spoken them.

"Tell him what, I wonder?" I assumed that the "him" was Alec.

"Whatever it is," broke in Lou, "I think we've confirmed Alec's suspicions that Jasper is trying to communicate something."

"Definitely. I'll call Alec and fill him in. Great work, Lou."

Instead of waiting until later, I decided to call Alec before I left so that I could play the EVPs for him. He was understandably impressed, and relieved to know that the ghost's persistence wasn't imaginary. Like us, though, he was anxious to know what Jasper was actually trying to communicate.

Alec asked us to return that night, and I filled him in on our visit from the police, adding that we would need him to be present at all future investigations. He seemed slightly annoyed at the news about the police officer paying us a visit. When he and the other partners spent so many late evenings in the office, he couldn't believe that someone would call and report us to the police. "They should have figured it was business as usual," he concluded. I reminded him that it was nice he had neighbors looking out for him, thinking to myself that it would have been nice if any of my neighbors had spotted the intruder at my apartment and called the police. The note on the rat had specified no police involvement, so I wondered what would have happened if someone other than me had called them. I finally decided that I didn't want to know.

I told Alec that a few of us might be able to rearrange our schedules to return to the Everett-Tattnall House that night, although I was definitely out (no way was I going to cancel my mystery date with Maxwell). He had plans with his family, though, so we agreed to try something next week. Friday, a whole week away, was the earliest we'd be able to all get together again.

Once I got off the phone, Daisy gave me a hard look. "Boo, you look awfully tired considering that we didn't have a very late night."

On the drive over, I had debated whether or not to tell the others about the latest drama at my apartment, and I had pretty much made up my mind not to mention it because I didn't want to make everyone worry. By the tone of Daisy's voice, though, I could tell that she sensed something was amiss. I told her the details of the previous night, leaving out only the method of Maxwell's arrival and departure since Lou, who was listening in along with Shaun, didn't know that my new romantic interest wasn't entirely human.

Everyone's reactions were what I expected, ranging from shock to horror to outrage on my behalf. Daisy suggested that I stay with her and Shaun for a few days, but I declined. "If I do that, then Maxwell won't get any more opportunities to play hero," I said, trying to lighten the mood. "Besides, you two are going to have a full house with your family coming to town. And Shaun, don't you dare breathe a word of this to your mother!"

Shaun had the courtesy to look remorseful, but his tone was mocking. "I can't help it if you're the biggest thing in Savannah," he said. "When you start doing press conferences and getting on TV, then your personal life becomes the talk of the town. It's the downside of stardom, Betty."

"And on that note, I'm going to go home and do some house cleaning before my big date tonight," I said.

I got all the way home, only to get a phone call from Lou, asking me to meet him at the historic cathedral on

Abercorn Street. He wouldn't explain why, other than to say that he wanted to speak with me. I found it odd, considering we had just seen each other at his apartment, but I agreed. Lou wasn't usually the type to open up, and all he would tell me on the phone was, "It's about you, and it's important."

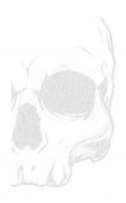

SIXTEEN

I walked to the Cathedral of St. John the Baptist, wondering the whole time why Lou had asked to meet me there. It seemed like a bizarre spot to talk with me. The cathedral is beautiful, though, and I love popping inside when I'm out on a hot day. It's always so cool and quiet inside, and the stained glass windows are just stunning. As I walked in to meet Lou, however, my mind was too occupied by his urgency to notice the beauty around me.

Lou was already there, seated in one of the back pews. His head was bent, and he rested his forehead on his hands, almost as though he were in prayer. The wood of the old pew creaked when I sat down, and he instantly sat up, his face concerned.

"What's wrong?" I asked in a hushed voice. There were a number of tourists walking through the cathedral, taking pictures and talking quietly, as well as a few parishioners sitting silently in reflection and prayer. I didn't want to disturb anyone, nor did I want people overhearing our conversation.

Lou hesitated, but after a moment he gripped the back of the pew ahead of us, almost as though he was bracing himself for an impact. "This guy you've been seeing, he's the one who exorcised the demon at Sam MacIntosh's house?"

"Well, banished the demon, yes."

"He's not a priest."

"Obviously." Where was Lou going with this line of conversation?

Lou sighed and gave me a sad look. "Betty, I'm concerned. What he did, well, sometimes it takes a demon to get rid of a demon."

I raised my eyebrows, waiting for Lou to continue. Apparently, I didn't react as he'd expected, because he sighed again. "I think your new guy might be in league with demons."

I actually laughed. I should have known that Lou would catch on to my secret. He was quiet, sure, but he was sharp, and he was well versed in both the paranormal and religion. Probably more so than any of us. I wasn't sure how Lou had made the demon connection, but I was impressed. No point in holding back now, I thought. "You're close. He is a demon."

Lou was quiet for a full half minute, staring at me in disbelief. Finally, he spoke, stuttering over his words in his surprise. "But, Betty, do you know what you're saying? How can you laugh at that?"

"Oh, I'm not laughing at what Maxwell is. I just laughed because you figured it out so quickly."

"He could hurt you. And I don't mean just physically. Your soul is in danger."

"But you can't deny he helped us with Sam." I glanced away, trying to think of what I could say that would alleviate Lou's concern, and my eyes fell on a gilt cross in a nearby alcove. "Is that why you wanted to meet me here?"

Lou followed my gaze. "There's a belief that anyone under the influence of a demon will be uneasy in a house of God. A demon himself can't even step foot on holy ground."

"Is that so? Luckily, I'm not uneasy. I love this cathedral. Where did you learn that?"

Lou shrugged. "I've been studying."

I could tell it was the only answer I was going to get. I put my hand over one of Lou's, which was still clutching the back of the pew. "I'm very aware of what Maxwell is capable of doing. And I promise you, I don't want to be influenced by his demonic tendencies any more than you. So far, Maxwell has treated me like a gentleman. So long as that continues, then maybe I can have an influence on him."

Lou nodded reluctantly. "I still don't like it."

"I know. I appreciate your concern for me. And you can meet me here whenever you wish, to make sure I'm still one of the good guys." I gave Lou's hand a squeeze and stood. "I'll see you later, okay?"

Lou nodded again, but looked reassured. I was thoughtful during the walk home, and reminded myself more than once that I ought to visit the cathedral regularly, just to make sure I didn't start feeling any ill effects from Maxwell's influence.

Maxwell knocked on my door at seven sharp, and I was ready to go in jeans and a short-sleeved black knit top. I slipped into a pair of cute black tennis shoes since I had to be prepared for whatever adventure Maxwell had in store for us.

Maxwell was dressed similarly in jeans and a rugby shirt with burgundy stripes. It was only the second time I'd seen him dressed so casually. He greeted me by wrapping his arms around me and pulling me close for a quick kiss.

"You decided to arrive in normal human fashion, I see," I said.

"I try to maintain an appearance of 'normalcy,'" he answered. "We don't want the neighbors to start talking."

I grabbed a light jacket because the temperature was supposed to dip down into the sixties tonight, and once we reached the sidewalk outside the carriage house I spotted Maxwell's car and began to head for it. Instead, he took me by the elbow and steered me in the opposite direction. "We're walking tonight," he reminded me.

"Are you ready to reveal your grand scheme yet?"

"Not yet. I will confess that I thought we'd grab dinner at the Sixpence over on Bull. Pub fare okay with you?"

"Shepherd's pie is always okay with me," I said. We took our time walking over to the Sixpence Pub, which was only one block south of the Everett-Tattnall House. While we walked, Maxwell asked me about the results of the investigation last night. He was intrigued with the ghost's odd message, too.

The Sixpence Pub was bustling when we got there, but through either sheer luck or some demon trick of Maxwell's, we got a table immediately. When I saw the way the hostess was looking at Maxwell, I realized that it may have been his charm and good looks that got us seated. We weaved through the crowd of people packed inside the narrow pub, sitting down at a table in the back.

We settled in and I gave the menu a precursory glance. Since I already knew what I wanted, I put it down and looked out over the crowd of people in the pub. A woman sitting a few tables away was staring at us, her eyes wide and her mouth slack. The man with her was so involved in eating his fish and chips that he took no notice. I looked down at myself, wondering why we had drawn the woman's attention, but when I turned to her again, I knew that Maxwell was the only person she saw. I bit my lip to keep from laughing. What was it about Maxwell that mesmerized women so much?

Women had reacted the same way the first night we went out.

Curious, I looked around the room and noticed two women at the bar, both swiveled around in their seats to stare at Maxwell. The women were about my age, and although one of them looked like she was in a mild state of shock, the other was clearly thinking about what she'd do if she had Maxwell to herself. The shocked girl continued to stare, but Little Miss Lustful's gaze shifted slightly, and she met my eyes with a look that clearly said, "You got him tonight, but he'd rather be with me."

"I don't think I'm getting any new fan club members tonight," I said, still looking back at the woman.

"Fan club?" Maxwell asked. Out of the corner of my eye, I saw him close his menu, apparently unaware of the attention he was garnering. He turned and followed my gaze. "Oh."

I blinked and turned my gaze back to him. "Half the women in here are staring at you, and thinking evil thoughts about me."

"Well, that's good," Maxwell said. "Lust and envy are two of the seven deadly sins. Sometimes my job is so easy." He gave me a wide smile.

"Whatever your job may be," I said, my tone cold, "we girls don't really like it when every other girl in the room wants to scratch our eyes out and take our date home for themselves."

Maxwell leaned forward and took my hand, his smile still in place. "No one is going to scratch your eyes out, and you're the only one allowed to take me home. You should be proud: every woman here wishes she were you." He brought my hand to his lips and kissed it, his eyes never leaving mine. I was enthralled, and my expression probably looked like the one Shocked Girl at the bar had—I had to remind myself to close my mouth.

"I can't really blame them for feeling that way," I conceded. "It's just a little unnerving to think that you could have your pick of any woman here."

"No, I couldn't. I've already chosen."

Our waitress had to pick that moment to come over, and I wondered if she was purposely interrupting our romantic moment. Oh, well, I thought, maybe I'll just have to get used to having the most desired man in town. Yes, I could definitely deal with that.

It was still hard for me to believe that Maxwell and I had only met just over a week before; we fell easily and comfortably into conversation with each other as we waited for our food. I kept prodding Maxwell to tell me what was in store, but he refused to give me any hints until we were finally finished eating.

Maxwell glanced at his watch. "It's almost time for the real fun to begin," he said.

"I'm having fun already, but if you're about to reveal your deep, dark secret, then I'm all ears."

"I was looking at the website for The Seekers," Maxwell began, giving me an impish smile, "and I noticed something interesting in your bio. It says that you, Betty Boo, Ghost Hunter, have never been on a ghost tour here in Savannah."

I laughed. "You're taking me on a ghost tour?"

"Yes. I thought it would be fun. And I'm sure you know all the stories our tour guide has, so once we've heard the tourist-friendly version, you can tell me the real ghost story."

"I've been on ghost tours in other cities, but you're right, I never bothered going on one here because I think I've heard every story there is to tell about Savannah. Finding out if our precious tourists are getting the correct story sounds like fun." At first, the idea of me going on a ghost tour seemed ridiculous, but with Maxwell's suggestion that the "tourist-friendly" stories might be different from my own experiences, I was intrigued. Ghost tours went past my old carriage house all the time, and it was fun to walk by the groups always roaming around the historic district. Some of the guides around here like to dress in period costumes, with the male guides typically in Civil War-style uniforms and the women often in Victorian dresses.

Maxwell had chosen the Sixpence because the tour we were taking met there in front of the pub. By the time we wrapped up and went outside, several people were already milling around a man wearing a gray wool coat and hat. "So, Betty," Maxwell said conspiratorially, "is that our tour guide or the ghost of a Confederate soldier?"

"Considering he's got a cell phone clipped to his pants, I'm guessing it's our tour guide," I said, smiling.

Maxwell paid the guide for our tickets, and we were given little stickers to put on our shirts identifying ourselves as tour members. Once we were ready to go, we stood to the side and watched as more people joined the group. An interesting mix of people began to assemble, including a few families, two other couples, and a group of Girl Scouts surrounding a tired-looking adult, who I assumed was their troop leader.

When it was finally time to start, the tour guide called everyone to attention. After introducing himself as William, he asked how many of us were local residents. Only Maxwell and I raised our hands, and William arched his eyebrows. "Hmmm, let's hope I don't stop in front of your house tonight to tell a tale!" The others in the tour chuckled, while Maxwell and I shared a knowing look. I know a lot of the paranormal investigators in Savannah, but few of the tour guides. Most of them just learn the ghost stories from a script compiled by the tour company owner, so William had no idea who I was. I decided it might be nice to experience the paranormal as a casual observer for a change.

William finished his introduction and began to walk, heading for our first haunted destination. Maxwell and I lingered near the back, and as we walked he reached over and took my hand. I squeezed his fingers and glanced up at him, thinking again that I could definitely get used to this.

Our walk took us straight through Chippewa Square, and William raised his voice so that we could all hear. "That house over to our right is the Everett-Tattnall House. It's a law firm now, and they've called in a team of ghost hunters to investigate there. We don't know what sort of ghostly activity is going on there yet, so you'll have to come back to Savannah on your next vacation so you can find out," he said.

At that, Maxwell and I both began to laugh. Even though he was at the front of our group, the guide heard our laughter and called back to us. "Our locals seem to find some humor in that."

"We saw the press conference on the news!" I answered him.

We turned right on McDonough Street and after a short two blocks we arrived at Colonial Park Cemetery. It's the oldest cemetery in Savannah, and it is smack in the middle of downtown. It's more of a public park now, and it's a popular spot for tourists and dog-walkers alike. William stopped at the locked entrance gate, turning around to motion all of us to draw closer together.

Maxwell and I crowded in along with everyone else, and William related stories about apparitions hiding in the shadows of the old oak trees along the back wall of the cemetery, even on the sunniest of days. It was nothing I hadn't heard before, but I enjoyed how he worked the history of the cemetery into his story. The next couple of stops along the tour were mostly the same—local lore combined with history—but I was still enjoying myself. Watching the others in our group was especially entertaining, since most of the men seemed to find the whole thing humorous, while several of the women definitely looked a little nervous. The Girl Scouts were obviously wrapped up in the stories, but the closer they huddled to each other, the more they giggled. Even their troop leader giggled along with them, when she wasn't staring at Maxwell. I've always been fascinated how non-threatening frights like ghost stories can actually be fun. Of course, I've been to plenty of haunted houses—the kind that people create for Halloween fund-raisers—where I spent half my time screaming and the other half laughing.

I didn't see any ghosts, but as we turned and walked past a row of dark townhouses—signs of renovation apparent everywhere—I glanced down a narrow gap between two of the houses and saw the shadowy figure of a man. Why would someone be lurking back there? I wondered. I tried to pass it off, telling myself that maybe it was just a homeless guy who had wandered back there. Still, after having seen the mysterious man watching the press conference, I got an odd tingle on the back of my neck at the sight.

Maxwell hadn't seen him, and I didn't mention it. We were at the back of the tour group, though, and when we crossed the street to head to the next block, a glance back showed the figure standing on the sidewalk, staring in our direction. He was still too shrouded in shadow for me to see any recognizable features.

I took a deep breath and shook my head to clear it. The man wasn't doing anything wrong, and he certainly wasn't threatening. I told myself I was being paranoid, but I snuggled a little closer to Maxwell after that.

Our fourth stop was the 17-Hundred-90 Inn, one of

Savannah's most famous haunted spots. The story there revolves around a girl named Anna, a maid at the inn back in the nineteenth century, when it was a boarding house. She committed suicide there after having her heart broken, but the details of her story had always been vague. William's story differed quite a bit from the one I'd always heard. In his version, Anna fell in love with one of the sailors who came into Savannah's busy port and took a room at the boarding house. They had an affair, but when she told him she was pregnant with his child, the sailor jumped on the next ship and left town. In her grief, Anna flung herself out of a window of the house and died. Her ghost lingered, though, and still harasses guests at the inn, especially those staying in room 204, which had belonged to her.

After he related the story, William ushered all of us inside the street-level restaurant and bar for a brief break, adding that the ghost of a former cook sometimes caused trouble there and that we should be wary.

I found an unoccupied couch right in front of one of the bar's fireplaces, and it was suitably cozy since there was almost no electric lighting on that side of the room. Maxwell joined me after he went to the bar for wine. "So, what do you think so far?" he asked.

"This is fun," I told him. "Most of the stories sound like the versions I've always heard, except for the one here. I always thought that the sailor loved Anna back, and he only left because the ship he was on was sailing, and he had no choice but to go. He promised to return, but after a couple of years she got tired of waiting and killed herself. She was never pregnant in that version of the story."

Maxwell took a sip of his wine and stared into the fire. "No, she wasn't pregnant. And the real story is quite different than what you and our guide have both heard."

I shifted on the couch so that I was facing Maxwell, my eyebrows raised.

"Anna had a crush on the man, but he wasn't a sailor and their relationship never went beyond saying hello to each other in the hallway," he explained. "She was a little unstable mentally, and she began to get obsessed with him. She started leaving love notes when she cleaned his room, and small possessions of his would often turn up missing. He assumed that Anna was taking them as keepsakes— handkerchiefs, cufflinks, that sort of thing. It was her obsession that finally drove him away, though his exit wasn't on a ship. He went north to Charleston for a while."

"Where did you hear that story?"

Maxwell looked at me seriously. "I've been in Savannah for a long time."

"I've never heard that version. Are you saying the story has just changed over the years?"

"I'm saying I know the truth because I was there."

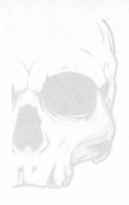

SEVENTEEN

I stared at Maxwell. "Define 'I was there,'" I said. My mouth went dry as I waited for his answer.

"You're smart, Betty. I think you understand."

I wasn't sure how to respond. The idea that Maxwell had played a role in one of Savannah's most famous ghost stories seemed absolutely ridiculous, but then so did the idea that he was a demon who could materialize out of thin air. I opened my mouth to speak several times, but nothing I tried to say seemed quite right. Finally I gave up and sat back, sipping my own wine and thinking over Maxwell's words.

When Maxwell realized that I wasn't going to say anything, he began speaking again. "I felt bad about her committing suicide, of course. Tonight's the first time I've stepped foot in this inn since I left it all those years ago."

"Does she know you're here?"

"Who, Anna?" Maxwell seemed surprised by my question. "I don't even know if the stories about her ghost are true. You'd know that better than me."

"Did you really feel bad that she killed herself? I'd think as a demon that it was part of your 'job,' like the lust and envy and chaos."

"Yes, I really did." Maxwell paused, as if he was trying to phrase his words carefully. "Preying on someone who's mentally unable to understand right from wrong is, believe it or not, unscrupulous even for a demon. Plus, it's just not something you can brag about. It's much more impressive to damn a woman like Margaret, whom you met Thursday night: an intelligent, stable, God-fearing soul."

"You knew we were coming here tonight, didn't you?" It wasn't really a question. "This is a little weird for me, you know. You're talking about a legend from a couple hundred years ago, and one that most of us think of as half-fictional, at that. And now you're telling me that you, the guy I'm out with tonight, were a part of it."

"You know what I am, Betty," Maxwell said. He leaned in close to me, speaking softly. "I can understand that it's going to take you a while to get used to the idea. I actually thought you'd enjoy knowing that I was a part of the ghost story. Just think: there are probably a dozen tour guides that lead people past here every day, and they all talk about me."

I still wasn't sure what to say. "You're right, it is going to take me a while," I said finally. In truth, I realized that it wasn't the idea of him being a part of the story that caught me off-guard. It was the idea of the maid being so desperately in love with him. Even though Maxwell said the feeling wasn't returned, I still felt an odd flare of jealousy at the thought, maybe because the popular stories about Anna included them being in love with each other, or at least having an affair. Besides, was Anna really mentally unstable, like Maxwell said, or did he have some weird sort of demonic thrall that made women fall for him? I'd certainly fallen for him in a heartbeat, though I wasn't stealing his cufflinks or sending him "I love you" text messages. I decided, for my own sanity, to stick to the idea of Anna having been a bit off her rocker.

Relationships can be so complicated, especially when you're dating a demon.

Maxwell put his glass on the coffee table in front of us so he could take my free hand in both of his. "I promise I'm not in any other popular ghost stories around here," he said.

I nodded and tried to smile for him. "Okay. I'm going to run to the restroom here before the tour starts up again. If Anna's ghost attacks me in a jealous rage, do you promise to come save me?"

"I promise."

Thankfully the only other creature I met in the bathroom was a very drunk woman, who was making so much noise tottering around in her black stilettos that I doubted any ghosts were within a mile of us.

The rest of the tour was fun, and I actually heard some details during two of the stories that I'd never heard before. I felt proud when William backed up one story by citing evidence by "some local ghost hunters," because I realized it was an investigation The Seekers had done. I told Maxwell that it was our EVPs and photos William mentioned, and he slid his arms around my waist. "You're a pretty cool date, you know. If all these ghost stories get me scared, can I stay with you tonight?"

"You're the one starring in the ghost stories," I reminded him, "so you're going to have to find a better excuse than that!"

"We only have one stop left on the tour, so I'd better think fast," Maxwell answered.

The tour wrapped up at The Marshall House, an ornate old hotel on Broughton Street. It was only one block back to my apartment, but Maxwell suggested we walk four blocks in the other direction first so we could wander along River Street. The bars, restaurants and gift shops lining River Street are usually packed with tourists on Saturday nights, so we skipped all of them and crossed to the other side of the street, which sits on the Savannah

River. The little bit of a chill in the air gave me the perfect excuse for snuggling up against Maxwell. We walked along the water's edge, stopping to watch a huge cargo ship glide past.

"What was it like in Savannah back then?" I asked.

"Hot and dirty."

I gave Maxwell a playful nudge. "Seriously."

"I am serious. Living in Georgia before the age of air conditioning wasn't pleasant. At least in hell I never had to deal with humidity. And it really was dirty. Most of the main roads in town were cobblestone, but smaller roads were still hard-packed clay. When it rained, they were muddy, and when we had a dry spell, they were dusty. All of the horses in the streets…I'm sure you can imagine. The winters weren't so bad because the smells were diminished."

"And here I think of those times as romantic."

"A lot of people do," Maxwell assured me. "History tends to forget the little details, like how rarely some people bathed, and how indoor plumbing as we know it didn't exist."

I wrinkled my nose. "Yuck. I get the picture. But did it really seem that bad at the time? It's not like you knew any other lifestyle."

"You're right, it was tolerable because I didn't know what I was missing out on." Maxwell stopped walking and sat on the low barrier separating us from the river. He pulled me down next to him and wrapped his arm around my waist, but his expression was distant, like he was seeing something else. "There were a lot of things I didn't like, but I took it in stride like everyone else. Today we put up with exhaust fumes from cars, but people in a couple hundred years might wonder how we ever dealt with it. Back then we put up with dirt, sweat and a lot of diseases."

Maxwell turned his head to gaze thoughtfully upriver

at the suspension bridge linking Savannah with the southern edge of South Carolina. Headlights from a steady stream of cars rushed over the river. "On the flip-side," he continued, "there were things we took for granted that I have a greater appreciation for now."

"Such as?" I asked.

"Gas lamps, tall ships sailing into the port of Savannah with their maze of masts, riding only a few miles out of town and feeling like you'd left the entire world behind."

I smiled. "I'd like to have seen you in a frock coat and top hat."

Maxwell smiled back. "And I'm sure you would have been lovely in a ruffled muslin dress over a hoop skirt." He ran his fingers lightly up my back, and I shivered. "But you would have hated getting laced into a corset every day."

"Yes, I much prefer being able to breathe. You're going to have to be content with me in jeans and a tee, I'm afraid."

"I'm more than content with that. Besides, if this were really 150 years ago, we'd have a chaperone with us. That wouldn't be any fun."

"Sure it would. It would be like a game, trying to push the limits of what we could get away with."

"The temptation of the forbidden," Maxwell agreed, eyeing me appreciatively. "You have a little bit of wickedness hidden underneath that sweet exterior."

"I just know that being denied something makes you desire it that much more."

"And what do you desire, Betty?" Maxwell's voice dropped to a low murmur.

I felt my cheeks flush under Maxwell's gaze. I was definitely having wicked thoughts now, but I wasn't sure I could say them out loud. I opened my mouth to say something—anything to fill the silence—but no words came out.

Maxwell seemed to sense my embarrassment, obviously

taking great delight in it. He drew me closer to him so his lips were only inches from mine, and his eyes were all I could see. The rest of the world disappeared, the noise of the river and passersby extinguished.

"Do you desire me?"

I nodded slowly, like someone in a trance.

Maxwell moved even closer, his lips brushing against my cheek as he spoke. "Right here, right now?"

I put one hand up to Maxwell's cheek; to draw him to me or to push him back I didn't know. Part of me—most of me—wanted to answer "Yes, here, right now, never mind all these people walking past." But one question kept forming in my mind: Was it a desire like this that had driven Anna to suicide?

Maxwell had said he never intended to ruin Anna's life. She was just an innocent bystander, a girl without enough intellect to make her worthy of Maxwell's attention.

On the other hand, I was very much the center of Maxwell's attention. A half century from now, would tour guides be telling the story of the ghost hunter turned ghost, a woman who killed herself after a handsome, mysterious man broke her heart? "Betty's ghost can still be spotted sitting by the river, waiting for him to fulfill her desires," they'd say, gesturing dramatically.

I laughed before I could stop myself. Maxwell pulled back and looked at me quizzically. "Is there something funny?"

I shook my head. "I was just wondering what kind of story tour guides would tell if I were a ghost."

"I'm trying to seduce you, and you're making up ghost stories?"

"Well, Margaret and Anna both ended up as ghosts. There's a precedent." I regretted saying it as soon as the words came out of my mouth. Sometimes I talk before I think, and this was one of those times. Things had been progressing so nicely until I had to ruin it.

Maxwell looked at me thoughtfully. "I didn't go out with either woman. Their loss was of no consequence to me. Losing you, however, would be quite painful. Trust me, I don't want you becoming a ghost anytime soon."

"Thanks." I wanted to add, "You can continue with the seduction," but by then I'd broken the spell, and the revelry around us was suddenly blaringly loud.

Maxwell offered me his hand to help me up, and he kept his fingers entwined with mine as we turned to head back to my apartment. I think we were both reluctant to see our date nearing its end, but short of wandering around town all night, we didn't really have a choice.

We walked hand-in-hand, making up our own ghost stories about some of the buildings that we passed on our route down Abercorn Street. We were making up ridiculous details about the ghost of an opera singer at the ornate Lucas Theatre when movement in an alleyway to our right caught our eyes.

Maxwell and I both stopped as a man stepped out of the shadows with a gun in his hand. He wore a black leather jacket and pants, and his hulking frame towered above both of us. He motioned us into the alley with his free hand.

"I suggest you both step off the sidewalk."

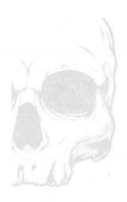

EIGHTEEN

My feet were frozen in place, and Maxwell squeezed my hand reassuringly. "It's okay, Betty, come on," he said, though his voice had a twinge of worry. My first thought was that we were being mugged, but I always thought those guys just grabbed your valuables and ran. Instead, we were being led somewhere. My heart caught in my throat when I realized that this man must be a demon hunter, maybe even the same one who had broken into my apartment twice and called to warn me about Maxwell. I hadn't listened to him, and now I was going to face the same fate that was in store for Maxwell.

I stepped into the alley with him, and it felt like a curtain had been lowered behind us as we sank into the darkness of the narrow space. The man continued to motion us forward, walking backwards so he could keep his gun trained on us. Finally, when we were hidden from the street by several dumpsters and a delivery truck that took up nearly the entire width of the alley, the man stopped.

"I didn't expect to have to deal with two of you," the man said, running his free hand through the greasy blonde hair that tumbled over his eyes, "but that's just more fun for me, right?"

"I'm the one you're concerned with," Maxwell said.

"You're not going to harm her unless you've forgotten who you work for."

"You know who I work for?"

"I know all of you claim to be doing God's work, though I'll argue that some of you are as evil as the bounty you track down. If your work is truly divine, you won't hurt an innocent mortal like her."

The man narrowed his eyes at Maxwell. "What the hell are you talking about? She's the one I want. You're just a little something extra for me to shoot."

Maxwell and I glanced at each other, and I could clearly see the surprise on his face. "Aren't you a –," he began to ask, but he seemed to think better of it. "Why are you interested in her?" he asked instead.

"Because she was too dumb to listen to me," the man answered.

"You're the one who called my house," I said.

"That's right. But you didn't listen to me, did you?"

I gave Maxwell another sidelong glance. "I didn't really understand what you were trying to tell me. It seemed like a warning, but I didn't know what you were talking about."

The man gave an exaggerated sigh. "Do I have to spell it out for you? You've been looking into things that you shouldn't, and somebody isn't happy about it. I took back some of the things you weren't supposed to see, and I tried to warn you away, but it hasn't stopped you. I'm being paid to make sure you stop, and apparently shooting you is the only option."

I was beginning to feel frustrated, even through my fear. "But I don't understand! Stop what?"

"Stop messing around with your little ghost hunt at the law firm." As he spoke, the man took several steps toward me, his gun clearly pointing at me and not Maxwell.

Definitely not the answer I'd been expecting. "This is about the Everett-Tattnall House? You broke into my apartment because of a ghost we're looking for at the law firm? No one else doing the investigation has been getting threats." Why me? I wanted to shout.

"That's because the rest of them are just running around looking for a ghostie. You're the one looking through all those records."

"Oh," was all I managed to say. I had no idea what was in the files Alec had given me, but it was obvious there was something incriminating in them that I had failed to notice. But who had something to hide, something so bad that they would rather have me killed than own up to the truth?

The man smiled grimly at me. "So you see, that's why I have to shoot you. It's nothing personal." I saw his finger press against the trigger, but everything after that was a blur. I felt something crash into my side at the same time I heard the gun fire. Instead of the bullet I expected to feel ripping through me, I felt a blinding pain in the back of my head as my body sailed backward into the brick wall lining the alley. I heard a yell, and then everything went dark.

I don't know how long I was unconscious, but the pain in my head was still sharp when I finally opened my eyes again. It took me a moment to remember where I was and what had happened. I wondered why my bedroom wall had been replaced with a grimy dumpster and a dirt-blackened brick wall.

Oh, yeah, I thought, I was about to get shot. I'm not in bed; I'm in an alley.

I was still slumped against the wall where I'd collapsed, and I cautiously wiggled my toes and fingers. All of my parts still moved and the rest of my body felt okay, so my head was the only real injury. And I hadn't been shot, which was definitely a bonus.

Then what had happened? One moment I had

expected to feel a bullet tearing into my chest, and the next I was on the ground. Something had hit me hard enough to push me out of harm's way. Not something, I realized, someone. Maxwell.

Which meant that Maxwell got shot instead of me. I sat straight up with that realization, gasping as the pain in the back of my head flared and my vision blurred. I blinked several times, and as my eyes came back into focus, I looked down the dark alley for any sign of Maxwell.

I saw him a short distance away, crouched on the ground. It was hard to see him as he huddled there in the shadows, nearly obscured by another dumpster, but I could tell he had his back to me.

Moving slowly, I got my feet under me and stood up, leaning against the wall in case my head protested again. I took several tentative steps toward Maxwell, anxious to know if he was okay, when I realized that he wasn't alone.

The man who had tried to shoot me was sprawled on the ground in front of Maxwell. I couldn't tell if he was alive or not, but he was perfectly still. As I watched, Maxwell leaned over and put his hands palms-down against the man's chest. A soft glow began to emanate from Maxwell's hands, and I was reminded of his demonstration the week before, when he'd proven to me that he was a demon.

The glow began to grow brighter, and the scene became clear. Our prone attacker was at least unconscious, and by the angle of his neck, I suspected he was dead. I wondered if Maxwell had killed him with his bare hands, then decided I didn't want the mental image that conjured.

The light from Maxwell's hands radiated over the man's body, beginning at his chest where Maxwell was touching him and spreading down through his legs and up through his shoulders. Soon his entire body was glowing in an eerie orange light. The light brightened so much that I had to shade my eyes, and as it began to turn red, the body started to collapse into itself. The skin darkened and turned black, seeming to shrink as I watched. Finally the glow began to fade, and in the diminishing light I could see that the man had been reduced to a charred skeleton. Maxwell pulled his hands away, and as he did so a breeze swept past me down the alley, and the body broke into millions of tiny pieces of ash, which blew away into the darkness.

I was worried about Maxwell's safety, and I wanted to make sure he was okay, but I couldn't make myself move. Seeing what he was really capable of doing also had me worried in a completely different way. As much as I was concerned for Maxwell, I was, at that moment, absolutely terrified of him. Seeing him produce fire and summon ghosts on command was one thing; watching him incinerate a body was another.

As I debated internally about what to do, Maxwell began to stand. He got about halfway up when he lurched forward and sank to his knees. Any fear I had for myself was eclipsed by the wave of pity I felt for Maxwell in that moment, and I made myself move. I walked forward, every step echoing in my throbbing head.

When I reached Maxwell, I sank down and put a hand against his back. I tried to speak, but between my shock and pain, words just wouldn't form. He looked up at me with a pained expression, and it was frightening to see Maxwell, who was always so strong and confident, looking so vulnerable.

My breath caught in my throat, and I put my arms around him, not knowing what else to do. Maxwell collapsed into me, and I could feel his heart pounding against my own chest. "I'm so sorry," I finally whispered.

This is all my fault, was all I could think. I didn't know what I'd stumbled into with the investigation at the

Everett-Tattnall House, but it was because of my work there that someone had been sent to shoot me. I pulled back from Maxwell a few inches and glanced down at his body. Blood soaked his shirt, running down from a hole in the material on the right side of his chest.

"Oh, no, Maxwell," I said, feeling panic begin to take hold. "We have to get you to a hospital."

Maxwell gave me a weak smile. "No, I'll heal. Demon, remember?"

"But you're hurt!"

"It takes a lot of energy to heal from a gunshot like this." Maxwell paused and coughed, then shut his eyes in pain. "It also takes a lot of energy to take care of guys like that."

I glanced over at the scorched asphalt where the greasy-haired man had recently lain. Yes, I was sure it took a lot of energy to kill a man and then incinerate all traces of him.

Maxwell seemed to know what I was thinking, and his weak voice broke into my memory. "I'm sorry you had to see that."

The fear I'd felt toward him earlier disappeared as something like pride flooded through me. "You saved my life," I said. "You did what you had to do to save me, and now you're hurt. This is all my fault." My voice broke on the last word, and I bit my lip, willing myself not to cry. That was the last thing I needed to do.

"I just need rest," Maxwell reassured me. "Think you can go get my car and come back to pick me up?"

I nodded, and Maxwell passed me his keys. "Hurry," he said, with a faint smile.

Maxwell eased into a more comfortable sitting position, and I set off to retrieve his car from the street outside my apartment. It felt odd walking out of the blackness of the alley onto the brightly-lit sidewalk along Abercorn Street.

Cars passed by, and several people walked along the other side of the street, oblivious to the horrific things that had happened only feet away.

I ran my hand through my hair to smooth it down, and was happy to realize that despite the pain, at least my head wasn't bleeding. When I brushed my hands down the front of my jacket, though, my left hand came away wet. I glanced down, surprised to see blood on my hand. I realized that it must be Maxwell's, and I was glad that my jacket was black, so it kept the blood from being obvious to anyone I might pass. I wiped my hand against my right sleeve, vowing to burn the jacket in my fireplace as soon as I could.

When I reached Maxwell's car, it took me a minute to figure out how to unlock it. By the time I slid into the sleek sports car and got the engine running, the shock that had kept me calm up until then was wearing off, and I was beginning to shake as the night's events continued to flash through my head. I took a deep breath and pushed it out in a rush of air, willing myself not to think of anything but maneuvering the car. I silently thanked my dad for teaching me to drive in his old Thunderbird with a manual transmission. Otherwise, I would have never gotten Maxwell's Audi out of its parking space.

The short drive down Abercorn seemed to last an eternity, but finally I pulled up in front of the alley. With a quick glance to make sure there was no traffic, I threw the car into reverse and eased into the alley. The front of the car blocked the sidewalk since the parked delivery truck barred my way into the alley, so I turned on the hazard lights.

By the time I sprang out of the car, Maxwell had already gotten up and eased himself a few steps toward me. I slid my arm around his waist and helped him gingerly into the passenger side of the car. As I shut the door, I heard a woman's brisk voice behind me.

"You're blocking the sidewalk."

I turned and saw a well-dressed couple behind me. "Sorry," I mumbled. I made a beeline for the driver's side door, wanting nothing more than to get away as quickly as I could, when the man spoke up.

"Is he okay?"

He had seen Maxwell, and I could only hope that he hadn't realized Maxwell was covered in blood. I turned to the man, making up a lie as fast as I could. "Uh, he had a few too many drinks tonight. He had to duck into the alley so he wouldn't get sick in the car."

The concern on the man's face turned to disgust, and his date uttered a disdainful, "Oh!" They quickly skirted the car and continued on their way. I was in the car a few seconds later, ready to flee before anyone else could ask questions.

"Go right," Maxwell instructed. I pulled out and glanced over at him. His skin had a sickly grayness to it, and even his eyes seemed to have dimmed, but he reached over and gave my leg a weak squeeze. "I'll be fine. I'm more worried about you."

I shrugged. "I just hit my head. That's better than being shot any day."

"You might have a concussion."

"I think all I need is a couple of Excedrin and a hot cup of tea."

Maxwell nodded, but remained silent. He continued to direct me, and eventually we pulled into a narrow street behind a row of townhouses in Savannah's Victorian neighborhood, not far from Lou's apartment. Maxwell reached up to press a button that opened his garage door. Everyone along the street had detached garages, most of them converted from the original carriage houses.

Once we were inside and the garage door was safely shut against anyone who might see us, I came around to Maxwell's side to help him out. "Why didn't you just materialize yourself back home?" I asked.

"Couldn't," he answered through gritted teeth. "I'm too weak right now."

We walked slowly through an immaculate garden that separated the garage from the back of the house, and Maxwell showed me which key on his key ring opened the back door. When we stepped inside, he leaned over and punched in the code to turn off the security alarm, then flipped a light switch.

We were standing in a kitchen with beautiful hardwood cabinets and granite countertops. Everything was in perfect order, and the décor looked like it had been professionally done. "Wow," I said.

Maxwell grimaced. "This isn't exactly how I wanted to bring you home with me."

I looked over at him. "What do you need to do?"

"I just need to go to bed and sleep for a very long time, but I'm taking a shower first."

I nodded, and we started walking down the hallway that led to the staircase at the front of the house. We only got a few feet when Maxwell stopped and looked at me with a pleading look that was heartbreaking. "You'll stay with me, won't you?"

"Of course," I answered. I hadn't even considered leaving him in his weakened state, and I was surprised that he felt the need to ask. I wondered if he was concerned that his…evidence disposal (I didn't know how else to think of it) had made me think twice about dating a demon.

Maybe it had, but how could I abandon him when he was in this state because of me? Maxwell had taken a bullet for me tonight. Plus, there was something strangely attractive about me finally getting to help Maxwell, instead of the other way around.

We made our way slowly up the stairs, and more than once I had to grip the railing as my eyes unfocused again. A feeling of dizziness began to grow as we ascended, and the further we got, the more I prayed that I wouldn't pass out and send us both tumbling down.

"You're hurt worse than you let on," Maxwell said between shallow breaths.

I grit my teeth, using all my concentration to stay upright. "I'm fine." I glanced up at him, and suddenly a giggle escaped my lips. It must have stemmed from the shock of the night's events, but part of my mirth was because we really did make a pitiful pair. Sometimes, all you can do is laugh.

Finally, we reached the top of the stairs, and we shuffled our way into an expansive bedroom at the front of the house. The hardwood floor was covered with an ornate rug, and the high bed looked like it had been carved from oak. A chair and table in one corner and a wide dresser all looked as antique as the bed, but signs of Maxwell's modern lifestyle were everywhere: a laptop sat with the lid closed on the table, a flatscreen TV was mounted on the wall above the dresser, and there were chargers laid out for his cell phone and whatever other gadgets a businessman like him had to tote around.

"Tell me what I can do to help," I said.

Maxwell released his grip on me and lurched toward the open door of the master bathroom. He gestured vaguely toward the dresser. "Tee-shirts in the second drawer, pajama pants in the fourth. Grab some for you, too."

"Do you have a first-aid kit somewhere? We need to wrap up your chest."

"I have one, but there's nothing in it that's going to take

care of a wound like this. There are some old towels in the hall closet that might be better."

Maxwell moved into the bathroom, but he left the door open, and I heard the sound of the shower as I pulled two shirts and two pair of pajama pants out of his dresser. All of his clothes were neatly folded, but after seeing the rest of his house, that didn't surprise me. I had to handle the clothes carefully since my left hand was still stained with Maxwell's blood.

Since the bathroom door was wide open, I figured Maxwell wouldn't mind if I wandered in. After all, it wasn't like I hadn't seen him naked already. Even amid my pain and shock, I still wondered idly if I'd ever get to see him naked on an occasion that didn't involve criminal activity.

Maxwell was already in the shower, and his bloody clothes were piled in a heap on the tile floor. He must like his showers as hot as hell, I thought, because the shower's glass walls were already fogged over. I set our clean clothes down on the counter, then shrugged out of my bloodied jacket, carefully turning the arms inside-out as I did. I folded it and laid it on top of Maxwell's clothes, then took a look at the rest of me. There were a few drops of blood on my jeans, and I was sure my backside was filthy from laying in the alley. My shirt, at least, had survived unscathed.

I pushed my sleeves up and washed my hands in the sink, running the water as hot as I could tolerate while I tried to scrub the blood off my hands. I got most of it—a few dried bits clung stubbornly to the undersides of my fingernails—then splashed the water over my face. When I was done, my reflection in the mirror was at least clean, but I looked tired and haggard. I guess I needed a good night's sleep almost as much as Maxwell.

I carried my pajamas back into the bedroom and

changed into them before I went down the hall in search of the old towels Maxwell had mentioned. The hall closet was easy to find, and I found a threadbare gray towel near the back that would make a good bandage for Maxwell's gunshot wound.

Maxwell was still in the shower when I returned, and I popped my head into the bathroom. "You okay?" I asked.

"Yes, but I think I might need to stay in here a week to get all the blood off."

"I think permanent marker might be easier to get out. Where do you have scissors?"

"Downstairs, in the kitchen drawer by the fridge. Are you okay to get them?"

"Sure." I couldn't hide the sarcasm in my voice. I would either be okay, or I'd faint halfway down the stairs.

Fortunately, I didn't faint on the stairs, and I found the scissors easily. I also got two glasses out of a cabinet and filled them with water, so I had to do a balancing act going back up since I didn't trust myself to walk without keeping a hand on the railing.

Maxwell was out of the shower but still shirtless when I returned, and fresh blood was trickling out of the wound on his chest. I noticed that the towel he'd used to dry off was covered in dark splotches. I set the glasses down and began cutting up the old towel, clipping off two wide strips. The first I folded into a thick square to put over Maxwell's chest.

"Are you sure this will be enough?" I asked.

"As long as you get enough pressure on it, this will be fine." Maxwell was still dragging, but his voice sounded stronger.

Maxwell held the folded towel against his chest while I looped the other strip around his torso and tied it in a tight knot. I was afraid I would suffocate him, but Maxwell assured me that it had to be tight to get the bleeding under control.

I eased Maxwell's shirt over his head and helped him lay down in the bed. He winced as he tried to settle in on his back. It was a little disconcerting to see Maxwell so weak. If someone attacked us when he was in a state like this, neither one of us would stand a chance.

I climbed into the other side of the bed after I fished a couple of Excedrin out of my purse. Maxwell sipped at his glass of water gingerly, his head raised forward off his pillow, then he set it down and turned his face to me.

"Thanks," was all he said, but I could hear the sincerity in that single word.

I turned on my side so we were face-to-face and kissed him gently. "I'm just sorry I put you in this situation," I said.

Maxwell gave me a small smile and turned his body toward me. "It's okay. Now I get to look like a hero. I feel bad about your head; I should have been more careful."

"It's not like you had time to figure out where I was going to land. I'm still alive because of you."

"I told you I didn't want you becoming a ghost anytime soon. Keeping you alive is much better." Maxwell ran his fingers gently down my arm. "I can touch your skin…feel you shiver when I do this." As he spoke, his fingers slid down to my waist, then my hip. Maxwell deftly slipped his hand under the waistband of my (well, his) pants, and he continued tracing the contours of my body. I gasped as his hand traveled further down, until he found the spot he was looking for. His warm fingers worked slowly, softly, building up a tension inside me that felt nearly unbearable. I was on the verge of protesting when he covered my mouth with his. I think I forgot to breathe while Maxwell's fingers brought me to my climax, and I broke our kiss with a moan.

We were both quiet for a few moments, our faces still close together. It was Maxwell who finally broke the silence. "I'd been hoping to give you a lot more than that tonight. Maybe next time I won't get shot."

"You're not going to hear any complaints from me." Complaints? Maxwell had just been shot, yet he was making the effort to gratify my needs. And with a great deal of success, no less.

"Good, I think I'm too tired for complaints." Maxwell smiled, but I could see the weariness on his face as he rolled onto his back. His eyes closed and he took several breaths before he opened his eyes again. "Sweet dreams, Betty."

"Good night, Maxwell." I turned off the light and curled up on my side, facing Maxwell. He fell asleep within a few seconds; I could hear his breathing slow down and become deeper. He moaned softly once in a while, and I lay awake for at least an hour while I watched him in the soft glow from the streetlights outside. I was exhausted, but I was too worried about Maxwell to relax until I felt assured that he wasn't getting any worse.

When I awoke the next morning, Maxwell looked like he hadn't moved all night. He was still asleep on his back, and his chest still rose and fell with his soft, deep breaths. His color already looked better, and although his shirt had a dark red stain where the blood had soaked through his makeshift bandage, it wasn't an excessive amount. The bleeding had obviously stopped at some point, but I didn't know what Maxwell was going to do about the bullet now trapped inside his body.

My head felt better, and since the clock on the night-stand read eleven o'clock, I slid out of bed. We hadn't stayed out late last night, so I figured we must have slept close to twelve hours. I shut the bedroom door softly behind me and walked downstairs, the wooden floorboards cool beneath my bare feet.

Maxwell's coffee maker was one of the high-end models that makes one cup at a time, but it was easy to figure out, and I had hot coffee in my hands in just a few minutes. I gave myself a tour of the downstairs and ended up in the living room at the front of the house. A bay window looked out onto the narrow street outside, and I settled onto the couch sitting in front of it. The sunshine steaming through the floor-to-ceiling panes felt glorious against my face, and I enjoyed just watching the few cars and pedestrians who went past.

I checked on Maxwell at noon, but he was still fast asleep, so I went back downstairs. I was anxious to get home, and I knew Mina would be aware of my long absence, but I didn't want Maxwell to wake up alone. I found a tattered copy of Frankenstein on a bookshelf in the living room, so I pulled it out to read while I waited for him to wake up. The book was dated 1892, and I wondered if it had been new when Maxwell bought it.

Two hours later, Maxwell's soft footsteps on the stairs brought me out of the story with a start. I turned around and saw a nearly-recovered Maxwell. He was smiling, and he moved much easier.

"Hey, sleepyhead," I said.

Maxwell came over and sat down next to me. "Hi."

"You look so much better."

"The rest was exactly what I needed. Thanks for taking such good care of me last night. Let's see what the results are, shall we?" Without another word, Maxwell stripped off his shirt and untied the length of towel around his chest. He removed the material carefully, and where the gaping bullet-wound had been I saw nothing but a tiny scab.

"No way!" I said. I reached out a tentative hand and

199

touched the spot, almost as if what I was seeing was an illusion and I needed to prove to myself it was real. "Being a demon really does have some cool perks."

Maxwell laughed. "Well, this demon needs some coffee and breakfast." He got up and led the way into the kitchen, stuffing his stained shirt into a trash can before opening the fridge to pull out eggs, cheese and sausage. "Omelets okay?"

"Sure. Living dangerously really works up a girl's appetite." I sat down at a small table in one corner of the sizable kitchen. I had spotted a formal dining room off the downstairs hallway, but it looked like the kind of setting that was only used for really nice occasions. The long table I had glimpsed was covered in a delicate lace tablecloth, and a crystal chandelier stood sentinel above. The antique gilt chairs with red upholstery were probably used to cushioning women swathed in brocade dresses, not cotton pajamas on loan from a demon.

I yawned widely, and Maxwell turned away from the stovetop as I put a hand up to cover my mouth. "You're still tired. When did you get up?"

"A few hours ago," I answered. "Once I woke up my brain got too busy for me to fall back asleep."

"Wondering what prompted that visit from our alleyway friend last night?"

"Yes." I hesitated. There was something else I had begun to wonder about, and I wasn't sure I should bring it up with Maxwell. I watched him for a moment as he slid the first omelet out of the pan and onto a plate with an easy movement. I guess he's had a few years to practice making breakfast for women who sleep over, I thought suddenly. A stab of jealousy went through me as I considered how many centuries Maxwell had been around, and how many relationships that might equal. The thought spurred me to tell him the theory that had been forming in my head. "There's something else I'm trying to figure out, too."

"What is it?" Maxwell encouraged me casually.

I stared into my empty coffee mug, looking for the right words. "Well, I've been thinking about how you're a demon," I began.

Maxwell nodded knowingly as he slid the second omelet onto another plate. "So we've come to that question. The answer is yes, I can."

I felt my eyebrows come together as I frowned. "It wasn't a 'yes, I can' or 'no, I can't' question."

Maxwell seemed surprised as he carried the plates over to the table and sat down across from me. "Oh."

"What did you think I was asking?"

There was a pause, and I suddenly noticed that Maxwell looked a little sheepish, almost embarrassed. "Nothing. I've obviously proven that mind reading is not on the list of demon skills. Now, what's your question?"

I looked up at him, steeling myself. "When I met you, I was just starting on the investigation at Sam MacIntosh's house. Since then, a demon has set my hair on fire, my apartment has been broken into twice and someone tried to shoot me last night. Since you, as a demon, love chaos and disruption, I have to wonder if there's a link."

Maxwell put his fork down and gave me a long look. I couldn't interpret his expression, and I didn't know whether he was going to agree, be offended or even laugh at me for my accusation. "You think I'm coordinating all these events to purposely cause you harm?"

"I'm just saying that I've considered it as a possible explanation."

"If you've considered it, then why are you still here with me?"

I shrugged. How could I explain that I'd probably do anything for Maxwell, no matter what he was or what he might be doing to me? I was falling in love with him; I'd known that as soon as he'd collapsed in the alley last night. The way my heart jumped when I realized he was hurt, how comforted I felt hearing his reassurance and feeling him warm in my arms, how fiercely proud I was of being the one to help him. But I couldn't say all of that, not yet. Instead, I said, "Because I'd like to think it's the least-likely option."

"Betty, I'm impressed that you've made a correlation between what I do and what's been going on in your life. You're a smart woman, so I can't say I'm surprised that you would think of that. However, I can assure you that I'd never contrive something that gets me shot. I might be immortal, but I'm still in a human body, and that means I feel the same pain as anyone else."

"You're saying it's all just a coincidence."

"If I said I was behind it all, would you stop seeing me?"

I considered Maxwell's question. If he was orchestrating the insane turn my life had taken recently, then the smartest thing I could do would be to run as far away from him as possible. Of course, if he was going to create chaos everywhere I turned, then at least I got some reprieve by dating him—not that I was going to admit that to Maxwell. "I can dodge questions, too," I finally said.

Maxwell chuckled, but his expression was grave. "No, I didn't have anything to do with what happened last night or with the break-ins. I don't know what's going on with the Everett-Tattnall House, and if I did, I'd do whatever it took to make it stop. I don't like knowing you're in danger."

I nodded, satisfied that Maxwell was telling the truth. I was beginning to think that he might have had something to do with the demon at Sam's house, though. Maxwell had pointedly not answered whether he'd been involved in that, but since Sam's demon hadn't been the one pointing a gun at me, I decided to let it go. "Thanks," I said quietly.

We ate in silence for a few minutes, until Maxwell spoke up again. "I enjoy my work here on Earth, but ultimately I'm a selfish creature. I wouldn't bring trouble to someone I care about. You're more safe from me than anyone."

"I hope I didn't offend you," I said.

"No, not at all. I just want you to understand that I care about you, Betty. I want to see you happy and safe." Maxwell looked up at me, his eyes bright. "The question I thought you were going to ask before was whether or not a demon can fall in love."

I felt my cheeks grow warm, remembering his answer to the assumed question. I wasn't sure how to respond, but Maxwell's admission made me lose my nerve and change the subject. "Maybe all these events and you coming into my life are more than a coincidence, but in a different way. It was you who gave me a way to banish that demon, you who came over the second time my apartment was broken into and you who saved my life last night."

A corner of Maxwell's mouth turned up as he answered me with a wry tone. "Are you saying we're together through some kind of divine intervention?"

I raised my eyebrows and gave Maxwell a smile in return. "You know what they say: God moves in mysterious ways. Maybe you're my guardian demon, or something."

I was relieved to hear Maxwell laugh and glad he hadn't taken offense to my suggestion. I was even more relieved to know that my brush with death wasn't due to any fault of his. Maxwell made it sound like I was under his protection, in a way, and I decided that I liked that idea a lot. I finished up my omelet with renewed zest and stood up to take our empty plates and mugs over to the sink.

"I really ought to get home," I said with reluctance.

Part of me didn't want to be more than ten feet from Maxwell, especially since he was the one keeping me safe, but I knew Mina would be waiting, and I was anxious to make sure my apartment was still in one piece. After the break-ins, I was getting a little paranoid.

"I'll drive you. Why don't you just wear that home? I'll get your outfit from last night cleaned."

I screwed up my face in disgust. "You can burn my jacket. It's covered in blood. My jeans are in pretty sad shape, too. In fact, I think my shirt is the only survivor. I'll take it home with me, but thanks for the offer."

I followed Maxwell back upstairs and pulled on my socks and shoes. My outfit wasn't exactly made for going outdoors, but the walk from the street to my front door was short enough that I doubted anyone would notice. Maxwell seemed to be thinking along the same lines, because we were heading out the back door when he said, "This is the second time you've been outside in your pajamas with me."

"We'd better watch out, or people are going to talk."

When we arrived at my apartment, I was surprised when Maxwell pulled into a parking spot instead of dropping me off at the curb. He insisted on coming inside with me to make sure everything was okay.

Much to my relief, it was. Mina walked up to me, purring loudly when I picked her up, and even though I could tell everything was in order, we still made a tour of the apartment. Maxwell checked every window lock before he was satisfied that everything was as it should be.

Finally, he turned to me with reluctance. "I hate leaving you alone," he said.

"I'll be fine," I said, though internally I was screaming please, stay with me!

Maxwell reached behind him and pulled a small handgun out of the waist of his jeans. "This is for you. The safety is here, on the trigger. Pull the trigger halfway to disengage it, then keep pulling to fire. Do you know how to use a gun?"

"Most of us Southern girls know how to fire a gun, but I'm not sure I want one in my home."

Maxwell held the gun out to me. "Please. We already know that whoever is after you isn't afraid to shoot, so you can't be, either. You need to be prepared."

The gun felt heavy in my hand as I took it, but it was also reassuring. "Thanks." I put the gun down on my coffee table, hoping I'd never have to use it.

"Would it be too forward of me to invite myself over tonight? I'm mostly thinking of your safety."

Mostly? That had potential. "Actually, I think I'll sleep a lot better with my guardian demon here. If you want to come over around seven, I'll even cook dinner for you."

"Perfect. I'll see you soon, then. In the meantime, try not to have your life threatened." Maxwell leaned in and kissed me, and after he broke the kiss, I pulled him closer to me in a tight hug.

"You really did save my life last night," I said. "Thank you so much."

"You're welcome. I just hope it's something I never have to do again."

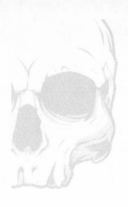

NINETEEN

Taking a shower was my utmost priority. Only after I was clean—the traces of dried blood finally scrubbed away thanks to a loofah and a lot of elbow grease—could I even think about what to do next. Maxwell wasn't going to be able to spend every night with me to keep me safe, nor did I really want him to. As much as I liked him, I wasn't ready for that kind of togetherness.

I considered giving Alec all of Jasper's files back and politely telling him that it was beyond my skills to find any connection. We could close the investigation and just walk away from the whole thing. Convincing Carter to go along with that plan would be nearly impossible, but it might be better to put up with his protesting than to continue investigating under the watch of whoever had it out for me.

At this point, though, I didn't even know if giving up on the investigation at the Everett-Tattnall House would remove me from danger. I assumed that my opportunity to just walk away had been when my attacker called to warn me from investigating further. He should have been more explicit; I hadn't even suspected that the call had anything to do with the investigation at the law firm until I was staring at a gun. Or, I reasoned, maybe he'd been vague on purpose so I wouldn't catch on and he'd get to kill me. He had looked like the kind of guy who might enjoy killing someone just because he could.

If Maxwell's life had been threatened because someone was after me, then there was also the potential for Daisy, Shaun and Lou to become entangled in the mess. Carter and his team were in danger, too. It was only coincidence that I'd been out with Maxwell when I was attacked, instead of one of them. In fact, since they were investigating at the law firm, too, there was an even better chance that they would get into trouble. I realized that any decision I made had to involve them.

I called Daisy, but her voicemail picked up, and I remembered that her parents were in town. They were probably out at Tybee, and I doubted that Daisy would carry her phone onto the beach with her. I left a voicemail, trying to sound as casual as possible. Shaun's cell phone went to voicemail, too, and when I heard his recorded voice I had a fleeting worry that maybe whoever ordered the attack on me had gone after the two of them, as well.

Lou was at home, at least, and even though there was no point in me speaking to him without Shaun and Daisy present, it still felt good to hear Lou's calm voice. Things might have become a little tense between Lou and I, but he was still my friend, and I still trusted him. If only he knew, I thought. Of course, there was no way I wanted him to know what Maxwell had done to our attacker. Whether he had saved my life or not, a demon killing a man would definitely not go over well with Lou. No, he was too on edge about my relationship with Maxwell as it was.

I was sitting outside, lost in a book, when Daisy returned my call and reality came crashing back. Her parents were staying through Monday night, so we agreed to meet on Tuesday. I only told her that we had some important things to discuss regarding Jasper's ghost, leaving out the really significant details, like Maxwell taking a bullet that had been intended for me.

As the afternoon wore on, a breeze picked up, sending tendrils of Spanish moss floating down from the tree branches overhead. Clouds were rolling in from the east, and I took that as my cue to move inside. I felt like I was in some weird state of limbo between waiting for Maxwell to arrive and waiting to know what the rest of The Seekers would have to say when we met Tuesday.

When Maxwell finally rang my doorbell, I was sitting on the couch with my legs curled up under me, and on my TV Julie Andrews was expounding on the virtues of a spoonful of sugar.

I stopped the DVD and answered the door, but Maxwell hadn't come five steps inside before he noticed the DVD case on my coffee table. "*Mary Poppins?*" he asked.

I shrugged. "A childhood favorite. It's like comfort food in visual form."

"That's right, and when you were five years old, your mother dressed you as Mary Poppins for Halloween."

"Wow, good memory."

Maxwell gave me a nonchalant shrug, as if he remembered tidbits from people's life stories all the time. I was impressed that he'd not only listened to me ramble on about Halloweens past in an earlier conversation, but that he'd even remembered some of what I said.

"You getting hungry?" I asked him.

"Actually, there's something I'd like to do before we eat dinner," he answered. In one graceful movement, Maxwell stepped toward me and pulled me against his body so tightly that my feet nearly came off the ground. He kissed me deeply, and I was reminded of the restrained passion between the two of us the first night he'd kissed me. This time, though, I could tell he wasn't holding back.

I wrapped my arms around Maxwell's shoulders, letting my fingers entwine themselves in his dark hair. His lips pulled away from mine, and he bent his head to my neck, where he began to kiss and nip at the sensitive skin there. I giggled when his lips brushed my skin so softly that it tickled, but my giggle soon turned into a gasp.

"Maxwell," I breathed against his ear, and I felt him tremble as he let out a low moan. His fingers began to tug at the bottom of my shirt, and we parted just long enough for him to pull my shirt up over my head. He continued to undress me while he steered me in the direction of my bedroom.

Maxwell quickly pulled his own clothes off, somehow accomplishing the task without ever letting his lips part with my skin. He pushed me onto the bed, following me down in a graceful crash as his blue eyes met mine. I felt my breath catch when his gaze made my entire body freeze, as if I could prolong the moment by holding perfectly still.

"Betty," Maxwell whispered raggedly, "I need you."

Maxwell's lips moved lower, his teeth grazing across my breasts slowly, teasingly. One of his hands slid around my waist, and when he tightened his grip, a red haze tinged my vision. The heat from his body seemed to flow into mine, but instead of pain I felt only the desire to lose myself in that warmth.

Maxwell's hardness pressed against my thigh, and I tentatively slid one hand down to stroke him. I felt so self-conscious; Maxwell was obviously very skilled, and I was so inexperienced compared to him. When he gasped and moaned again, though, I felt a renewed confidence. I continued my motions while Maxwell slowly kissed his way up my neck, and he put his lips to my ear. "Now," he whispered.

I guided him forward with my hand, and when

Maxwell finally entered me, it felt like a flame was racing up my spine.

I started to cry out, but my voice caught in my throat. The heat continued to surge through my body, pulsing with Maxwell's rhythmic movements. This time, I wasn't worried about getting burned. Instead, I felt enveloped and protected, as if nothing else existed but the two of us.

My body began to tremble as I neared my climax, and Maxwell sent me over the edge, thrusting deep inside me with a burst of heat. I clung to him, my nails digging into his back, and as I cried out I felt Maxwell's own release.

As I lay there, struggling to catch my breath, the fire I'd felt began to subside, but I still felt warm and protected. When our bodies finally parted, it seemed like my exhausted body could barely contain the tingling satisfaction that I felt. Maxwell rolled onto his back and pulled my head down onto his chest. Neither one of us spoke for a few minutes, and I could feel the sharp rise and fall of Maxwell's breathing.

One of Maxwell's hands idly played with my hair, and finally he said, "I hope that was worth delaying dinner for."

I smiled against his warm chest. "Just forgive me if I can't speak coherently for the rest of the night." We lay quietly together for so long that I nearly dozed off. Finally, I rolled away from Maxwell and stretched languidly. "So, now are you getting hungry?"

"Yes."

"Good, because I'm starving." I stood up and looked around the room. My clothes were in a trail leading from the living room to the bed, but since we weren't going out I stepped over them and selected a set of red pajamas from my dresser. I pulled them on and faced Maxwell, spreading my hands. "Not very sexy, I know, but it's dangerous to cook dinner in an itty-bitty nightie."

"I think you look gorgeous just like that," he answered. Of course, I'm sure he knew that any other answer might have gotten him into trouble.

Maxwell stood up and started dressing as I made my way to the kitchen to start making dinner. I was feeling so good that someone could have broken into my apartment right then and I probably would have pulled out an extra plate for them.

Before long we had sesame chicken with broccoli and rice in front of us, and after we ate we made the short trip to the couch, too tired and full to want to do much of anything. Maxwell, with good humor, talked me into putting on an old romance film.

"Okay, but if you hate it, it's your own fault," I told him, popping a copy of It Happened One Night into the DVD player.

"I vaguely remember seeing this when it first came out and liking it then."

I picked up the remote and collapsed onto the couch next to Maxwell as I heaved a dramatic sigh. "It was made in the thirties! It's tough dating an immortal demon."

Maxwell put his arm around my shoulders and pulled me toward him. "Is it really that bad?" he asked.

I gave him a long look. "No, it's actually pretty great."

The rest of the night was quiet, and we finally went to bed around eleven. No one broke in while we slept, and when I got up in the morning, there were no dead animals in my living room. Maxwell was up by the time I was ready for work, and before he left he asked if I wanted him to come over again.

Part of me wanted that very much, but I couldn't be a coward forever. "I appreciate it, Maxwell, but I think it will be good for me to face my fears and stay here alone. I've got the gun you gave me, and if something happens, you can be here in an instant."

"All right. If you change your mind, let me know. I'll call you later." He gave me a kiss and left, and I followed him out the door just a few minutes later.

My whole day was fairly agreeable. Until I got home, at least. As the sun sank behind the old buildings of Savannah and the shadows crept out of the corners to fill up the streets, I started to feel nervous. It was my first night alone since I'd found the dead rat, and I was worried that there would be a return visit by whomever had put it there. This time, though, I was sure they'd come not for the files from the law office, but for me. Maxwell called early in the evening, and he offered to come over again, but I heard myself turn him down even while my brain was begging him to come over without losing a moment.

I woke up numerous times during the night, sometimes going so far as to crawl out of bed and make a tour of the apartment, checking every single window like Maxwell had done on each of his visits. I would clutch the little gun he'd loaned me each time, as if I might come face-to-face with someone on the other side of a window. I was careful to keep my finger off the trigger: I didn't want to make a mistake and accidentally shoot a hole through my living room wall.

By the time I got to the office Tuesday morning, I was already three cups of coffee in and needing more. The day dragged along, and the only thing that really kept my mind engaged was knowing that my meeting with the other Seekers was that night. I kept going over the things I wanted to discuss with them, trying to find a way to impart the danger we were all in without telling them the full details of the attack Saturday night. I wasn't ready for Lou to know that Maxwell was a demon, and I certainly couldn't tell anyone that I'd seen him kill and then dispose of a body.

I got a strange feeling every time I thought of

Maxwell crouched over that body, but it wasn't guilt. In fact, the odd feeling was because I didn't feel guilty. I should have. Whatever that man's intentions had been, and regardless of how much evil he'd done in his lifetime, it wasn't up to us whether he lived or died. We should have called the police and let them put him in jail.

Of course, calling the police was just what I wasn't allowed to do.

The more I thought about it, the more I realized that someone would have died Saturday night, and thanks to Maxwell's status as an immortal creature, that left just me or old greasy-hair. Better him than me, I supposed. I even tried to feel guilty, playing the scene over and over again in my head and trying to envision the dead man leaving behind a wife and children, or maybe a sick relative for whom he'd had to care, but nothing worked. All I felt was relief.

We were all going to meet at my apartment at seven, and by the time I got home from work, I already had a script in my head for what I wanted to say. We usually met somewhere like the Burglar Bar, but tonight I didn't want to go anywhere public, where I might be overheard. I still suspected that I was being watched, and I didn't want to give anyone a chance to overhear my plans.

Daisy and Shaun arrived first, and as soon as I opened my front door for them, Daisy pulled me into a hug, then stepped back and gave me a hard look. "Tell us what's going on," she said, her tone sounding both worried and chastising, like I was an errant child who'd been getting into trouble behind her back.

"I'm going to," I answered, "but I'm going to tell you right now that what you'll hear tonight is an abridged version. Lou knows that Maxwell is a demon, but I don't care to remind him of that fact."

Daisy narrowed her eyes. "What kind of demon things has Maxwell been doing that you can't talk about?"

"Well, the kind I can't talk about." I knew it wasn't the answer Daisy wanted, but she would have to let it suffice. "But everything he's done has been to keep me safe," I added.

Daisy was still peering at me suspiciously.

"Like how he materialized here when I called him about my apartment being broken into. Little things like that." If Daisy kept staring me down, I'd eventually give up all of my secrets to her.

I laughed suddenly. "You know, you're going to make a great mom someday. You've got the 'you're lying to me' face mastered."

I could tell that Daisy was trying to maintain her serious face, but the corners of her mouth twitched, and she smiled back. "I just worry about you, Boo. I'd feel better if we at least met Maxwell."

"You will," I assured her. Lou knocked on my door then, so we dropped the subject of Maxwell. I pulled two dining room chairs into the living room, sitting on one while Lou took the other. Shaun and Daisy settled onto the couch.

I let out a breath, giving myself time to gather my thoughts. "Thanks for coming tonight, guys. I don't want to worry any of you, but we have a big decision to make about our involvement in the Everett-Tattnall House," I began.

"Is this about Carter?" Lou asked.

"Despite my feelings about him, he's actually blameless in this case. No, unfortunately, we're dealing with someone who's dangerous, not just annoying." I briefly related how my break-ins were related to the law firm and told them about the phone call I'd received telling me to back off from investigating further. I left out the attack in the alley

Saturday night, hoping everyone would assume I learned about the link between the break-ins and the Everett-Tattnall House from the mysterious phone call.

I held my breath when I finished my monologue, afraid that one of my three friends would find some hole in my story or question some of the details that related to Maxwell. I'd had to tell them how he came over to help me when I accidentally dialed him instead of Daisy on Friday, but talking about Saturday night was out of the question. Luckily, my story was coherent enough that even Daisy seemed satisfied.

Lou was shaking his head. "You have to give up the investigation, Boo."

"I at least need to appear that I've given it up," I conceded. "Obviously I have to worry about my own safety, but if there's someone dangerous keeping an eye on things, then I have to worry about all of you and Alec, too. Are we obligated to help him at risk to ourselves? Or, if we back away from this, will any danger he might have been in be removed?" Maybe Alec really would be safer if we told him he'd just have to put up with his former law partner popping up all the time. There were just so many "ifs" and "maybes."

"You said that the caller didn't care about us trying to make contact with Jasper's ghost," began Shaun.

"That's right."

"Then I think the rest of us should continue to investigate. If we can help Alec in any way possible, then we need to."

The others all nodded in agreement, and finally Lou spoke up. "Betty, you should give back all of the files and things Alec loaned you, and I think you should do it in the most blatant way possible so anyone who might be keeping tabs on you can't miss it."

"I agree," I said. "But Alec needs to know what's going

on. Once he has the files in his possession again, maybe he can go through them and see what's missing. If he can pinpoint a certain case or list of notes that have disappeared, it might help."

"But if he does so, it's at his own risk." Shaun was frowning. "He needs to understand that, and if he still wants to go through the files, then it needs to be done as quietly as possible."

Lou and I nodded in tandem.

Daisy smiled around at everyone. "That was easy. I guess it wasn't such a big decision, after all."

"I just want all of you to be certain this is what you want. Please don't discount the danger you might be putting yourselves in," I said. I was proud of them for wanting to continue the investigation, but at the same time I had almost hoped they would be so horrified that they would insist on calling Alec tonight to decline the chance to investigate further. "Carter and his team need to be filled in, too. I'll call and discuss it with him."

I wasn't sure that Carter would be as determined as my team. He was definitely a big fan of self-preservation, and he wouldn't like this news one bit. Then again, it might make good fodder for a press conference someday, especially if Carter could spin himself as the hero.

With our meeting wrapped up so early and a plan in place for me to return everything to Alec, I offered to make dinner for everyone rather than going out. Having so many people over always makes my little apartment seem a little crowded, but for once I reveled in the feeling. It was impossible not to feel perfectly safe with my closest friends around me, and we all lingered over our food, momentarily forgetting any lurking evil.

When everyone finally left, I made the round of the apartment windows, which was quickly becoming an obsessive habit. On this night, though, I fell asleep thinking warmly of my friends, and instead of lying awake in worry, I rested dreamlessly.

I couldn't wait to call Carter on Wednesday, and I planned to contact him as soon as my lunch break began. It turned out that Carter couldn't wait to talk to me, either, and I was still walking to my car when my cell phone rang. He was calling to let me know that he'd scheduled our second investigation at the Everett-Tatnall House for that Friday, and that Alec had already agreed to stay with us just in case the police decided to drop by again. "I just assumed you wouldn't be busy on Friday," he told me, "because you don't seem to have a normal social life outside of ghost hunting."

Only Carter could infuriate me just thirty seconds into a conversation. I informed him that I had a great social life, thank you very much, and was dating a nice business-man. I wondered if Maxwell would assent to putting his demon powers to work against Carter. Then I wondered if dating Maxwell was going to turn me into a bad person. No, I decided, I only got fired up like that about Carter. He was the bad influence, not Maxwell.

I promised to pass along the plan for Friday night but told Carter I wouldn't actually be there. He was beyond surprised—stunned, really—and I gave him an overview of my life lately.

"You definitely do not have a normal social life," he concluded. Despite my effort to impart the danger of his situation, Carter refused to back down. I was almost proud of him for not wimping out, but he confirmed my theory that he'd gladly risk taking a bullet if there was potential for good PR: Carter went so far as to suggest that this case might be a good focal point for his next book.

I couldn't even go to the police, and Carter was already mentally signing autographs on the title page of his next paranormal tell-all.

Once I wrapped up with Carter, Alec was next on my list. I wanted to talk with him in person, so all I said was that I needed to return the files and belongings I'd gone through. To my dismay, he said he was actually in Macon all week and wouldn't be back until Friday. I reluctantly agreed to meet him after I got off work at the end of the week, just a few hours before the others would begin their investigation.

Just two more days until I would be finished with the investigation, or at least I'd appear to be, and the threat of danger would pass. Hopefully. Maxwell also called me during my lunch break, offering to take a turn cooking dinner. I instantly agreed, glad to have a reprieve from thinking about the Everett-Tattnall House.

That was the only good thing that happened the rest of the day. About an hour after lunch, my office phone rang. When I picked it up, Jeanie's voice was both excited and curious. "Betty, it's a man for you, says his name is Sam MacIntosh, and he says that he's calling about a personal matter."

Why was Sam calling me? "Okay, Jeanie, thanks." While Jeanie connected the call, I worried that Sam's demon had somehow come back. "Sam?" I asked hesitantly.

"You didn't tell me that it was a demon." Sam sounded affronted, almost accusatory.

Wow, at least he wasn't beating around the bush. I knew I would have to choose my words carefully. "I didn't know it was a demon until I was given the solution which finally banished it. You were so frightened already that I didn't want to worry you any more."

"But it was a demon! That's a lot more serious than a ghost."

"Has it come back?"

"No."

"Then it's as harmless as a ghost now. I'm sorry if you're upset that I didn't tell you. I was just trying to protect you."

Sam exhaled so loudly that I could hear it over the phone. "I know. I'm sorry. It's just that I got blindsided with the information."

"Who told you?"

"A guy I've done business with once or twice. An acquaintance named Maxwell. He said he knows you and that you'd told him it was a demon."

Uh-oh. So much for me being able to protect Sam from Maxwell's scheming. "That's not exactly how it happened," I said. "Again, Sam, I am so sorry. Really, you have nothing to be worried about now. Everything is fine."

"For now. How do I know it won't come back? Why did a demon want to hurt me in the first place?"

That was a very good question, one that I'd wondered about before. "I don't know. No one knows the answers to those things. Sam, please, you know that if anything else should happen, we'll come help you."

"I know. All right. Sorry, Betty, it just really shocked me. Next time, just be honest about what's inside my house."

"Of course. Goodbye, Sam." I hung up the phone, feeling like someone had kicked me in the stomach. I'd tried so hard to protect Sam, and now he was accusing me of not being honest. To make it even worse, it was all Maxwell's doing.

I was staring at my computer screen, not even seeing the words written there, when my boss walked in. "Betty, I'm a little concerned," he began.

Great, my afternoon was about to get worse.

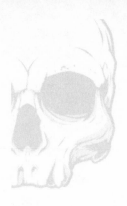

TWENTY

"I overheard part of your phone call. I'm worried that your ghost hunting might impede your work. It's bad enough that you're probably up at all hours of the night so you're not as fresh as you should be when you come here, but I'm willing to overlook that because you do good work. However, bringing drama from your ghost hunting into the office isn't acceptable."

"It wasn't about ghost hunting, exactly," I started to explain. "It was..." What? About Maxwell? I shook my head and started over. "I'm sorry. It won't happen again."

"I know." With a curt nod, he walked away, leaving me feeling even worse.

Somehow I slogged through the rest of the day, my brain never really on my work. When five o'clock came, I rushed out to my car, anxious to get home. Instead, as soon as the door was shut, I started to cry. I leaned my head against the steering wheel as the tears rolled down my cheeks, hoping none of my co-workers would notice me. A client of The Seekers had called my integrity into question today, my boss had lectured me about letting ghost hunting interfere with my job and Maxwell had flat-out lied to Sam about me. I didn't know which of those things was worse, but one thing stood out in my mind: Maxwell was behind all of those things. If he hadn't talked to Sam, then Sam wouldn't have gotten upset and called me, and paranormal drama would have never been an issue at work.

Maxwell kept claiming that he wanted me to be safe and happy. And yet, the chaos and fear that he loved so much had affected me in three different ways today. If Sam hadn't mentioned Maxwell's name, I knew that I'd be turning to the demon for comfort. Maybe he was doing it on purpose: creating one disaster after another in my life, then silently laughing as I ran to him for help. Maxwell had said he had nothing to do with the shooter in the alley, but my suspicions about his involvement with the demon at Sam's house were growing.

By the time I got home, I had enough time to change clothes and feed Mina before heading to Maxwell's house. I had considered calling to cancel our dinner plans, but I knew what I had to do needed to be done in person.

I parked on the street in front of Maxwell's Victorian townhouse, and he answered the door so quickly that he had either heard me walking up the steps, or he'd materialized to the front door. I followed him into the kitchen, the smell of dough growing stronger the further I walked into the house.

"Hope homemade pizza is all right. So, how did it go with everyone last night?"

"You dive right in, don't you? It actually went well, even better than I'd expected." I told him briefly about the resolve (or was it stubbornness?) of the other Seekers, and outlined the plan for me to return everything to Alec in broad daylight, where hopefully the right eyes would notice.

"But there's something else I need to talk to you about," I added. As I said the words, I felt sick to my stomach.

"Uh-oh. What have I done?" Maxwell was laughing as he slid the pizza in the oven.

"I'm serious."

Maxwell turned to me, his face instantly alert. He motioned to the kitchen table. "Sit. Tell me what's on your mind."

"Sam called me today."

"Come on, Betty, are you really surprised that I told him the truth? You know I wanted him to understand what was happening from the start."

"What you told him wasn't exactly the truth, and it made me look bad. He accused me of being dishonest. He was so mad that I'd held something back from him."

Maxwell sat back in his chair. "Ah, I hadn't thought about him getting upset with you. I'm sure you smoothed things over with him."

"That's not the point! He accused me of being dishonest," I repeated. Even if Maxwell was a demon, surely he could understand how much it hurt to be falsely accused. "My boss overheard the conversation, so he came in and gave me a lecture about my ghost hunting interfering with work, so now I'm on thin ice with him. Someone is questioning my investigations, things are going wrong with my job and I can't even sleep at night without worrying that someone is going to break in and shoot me. You couldn't have done a more thorough job of messing up everything I have, Maxwell, so congratulations."

Despite my agitation, Maxwell remained calm. "Are you pinning all of those things on me?"

"If you hadn't told Sam, he wouldn't have doubted me. He also wouldn't have called me, and I wouldn't be in trouble at work."

"I guess you do have a point there, though I certainly hadn't expected those repercussions when I spoke to Sam. I should remind you, though, that I'm the one trying to keep anyone from shooting you."

I waved my hand. "Yeah, I know you claim you had

nothing to do with that. There's something else, though. Tell me how that demon wound up at Sam's house in the first place."

"I thought you didn't like hearing about my 'job.'"

"I also don't like being manipulated."

Maxwell shook his head. "Betty, how many times do I have to tell you that I don't want to bring harm to you? I care about you; I want you to be happy. I all but told you I was falling in love with you the morning after I got shot, and yet you still think I'm doing things to hurt you."

I bit my lip. The sexiest, smartest man I'd ever met was falling in love with me, and here I was destroying the budding relationship we'd built over the past couple of weeks. Whatever Maxwell might feel for me, though, I knew I couldn't stop. "You can't deny that your comment to Sam has hurt me," I said.

"You're right." Maxwell was looking right into my eyes. "I'm sorry."

"I don't think 'sorry' is going to be good enough. If this is what dating you is going to be like, then it's not what I want."

Maxwell couldn't hide his surprise, and he was silent for a moment. When he finally spoke, his voice was tinged with disappointment. "Everything else has been what you wanted. I make one comment to someone and I'm condemned for it?"

"I just worry that you're trying to cause chaos in my life," I explained. "Instead of running away from you like I should, I keep running to you for help. I can't do that; I can't take the risk. You're the one always reminding me that you're a demon. Maybe it's time I listened."

"Betty, please don't do this."

I felt the first tear slide down my cheek. Great, I was going to cry again. How much could a girl cry in one day? I stood up. "I'm sorry, Maxwell. I have to go. Goodbye." I turned and walked down the hallway, but Maxwell followed. I was just reaching for the front door when he caught my arm. He spun me around, and before I could react, his arms were around me, my own pinned to my sides.

"Do you have any idea how much it takes for a demon to fall in love?" he asked. "Especially with a woman like you who, instead of embracing evil, is so full of happiness and goodness. You purposely kept the truth from Sam, and instead of being mad I just admired you that much more for doing what you thought was right. Everything you are goes against so much of what I am, and yet I can't help falling for you." Maxwell pulled me closer, our lips so close that they were nearly touching. "What you and I have is extraordinary," he whispered. "Please don't walk away from it."

I shut my eyes, knowing that I would give in if I had to keep seeing the sorrow on Maxwell's face. I was crying openly now, and I gently pushed his arms away from me. "I'm sorry," I said again. "I'm so sorry, Maxwell."

Before he could stop me, I opened the door and left.

I don't remember driving home. I was crying so hard that I'm not even sure how I could see the street ahead of me. When I got back inside my apartment, I lay down on my bed and sobbed until my whole body ached. I tried to remind myself that it was better this way and that being involved with a demon—no matter how wonderful he was—would only get me into trouble. As long as Maxwell didn't decide to get revenge on me, my life would be better. Well, back to normal, anyway.

Finally, I fell asleep, still fully clothed. As my mind drifted into a slumber full of nightmares, I had only one thought.

I could have had Maxwell's love, and I walked away from it.

Thursday felt like the calm before the storm. I didn't want to feel miserable for myself, and I was tired of crying, so I just tried to go about having a normal life, at least for one day.

I was beginning to forget what normal felt like. Ever since I'd stepped foot in Sam MacIntosh's house, I'd been having anything but normal days. I went to the grocery store and purposely spent more money than usual, stocking up on large quantities of cookie dough ice cream and candy: food for the brokenhearted. I had to remind myself that I was brokenhearted by choice, and that I should just move on. There were other guys out there, and there was an endless supply of cookie dough ice cream to get me through it.

After eating dinner, it still wasn't late. Wow, I wondered, how did I keep myself from a constant state of boredom before Maxwell and a crazed would-be killer came into my life? I watched TV, I called my mom and I checked my e-mail. In all, I did a lot of normal stuff, and even though it wasn't an interesting evening, it was nice to feel relaxed.

Friday morning, I packed all of the things I was returning to Alec into the trunk of my car so I could head straight to the Everett-Tattnall House after work. The day trudged along, but I felt like I was dashing out to the parking lot every ten minutes to check that everything was still in my car, like someone might come and snatch it out of there. Jeanie commented on my trips through the reception area, ticking off on her fingers how many times I had rushed out of the building, only to saunter back in with a relieved expression. According to her math, I was visiting the parking lot every hour. By my calculations, it just meant I was quite possibly losing my mind in my anxiety to be rid of everything tying me to the investigation.

When my day was finally over, I practically ran out the door of the office building in my rush to return Jasper Whitney's belongings. Parking downtown was pretty scarce, and the closest parking space I could find was one street behind the Everett-Tattnall House. I lugged one big box of things out of my trunk and tottered my way to the law firm. At least I'm tough to miss in case anyone is watching, I thought.

I stood on the front stoop of the old house, trying to figure out how to knock on the door or grasp the doorknob without putting the box down, when the receptionist—Annabelle, I remembered—came and opened it for me.

"You looked like you could use a hand," she said, smiling politely.

"Yes, thank you," I told her. "I have another stack of files in my car, so if you want to show me where to put this box, I'll go grab the rest."

Annabelle complied by just taking the box out of my hands. As I returned to my car for the second load, I felt my heart—and my mind—getting lighter. Look at me, I thought, I'm taking everything back to the law firm. I hope you're noticing.

As it turned out, someone was noticing.

He was standing in the square, on the opposite side from the Everett-Tatnall House. I could make out dark clothes, a cap pulled down low and wide sunglasses, but he was too distant and too shaded for me to see more. Despite the sunglasses, I knew he was looking right at me; it was as if I could feel his eyes boring into both my face and the stack of files in my hands.

My confident pace faltered, and my chest suddenly felt tight. I realized I was staring back at the stranger, and I quickly averted my eyes. I concentrated on making it up each step into the house, looking at the front door as if it were some sort of safe haven.

When I made it inside, Alec was already waiting for me in the front hall.

"It's good to see you, as always, Betty." Alec always seemed to be so pleasant and pulled together. I wondered if anything ever ruffled his feathers.

"And you, too, Alec. If you have some time, I'd like to sit down and speak with you about the investigation."

Alec gestured toward the staircase. "Certainly. Come on up."

Alec's spacious office was a lot more warm and inviting in the daytime, without a ghost hunt underway. He settled into a wide burgundy leather chair that creaked appropriately for a haunted house, and I sat on the other side of the giant slab of mahogany that he considered a desk. I instantly started to fidget in my chair, and Alec took notice of it almost before I did.

"Is everything okay?" he asked gently.

"No, it isn't." I folded my hands in my lap, willing them to stop their fussy movements. "Alec, I'm not sure where to start with this, so I'll dive right in. Whatever Jasper's reason is for haunting this place, it's dangerous."

Alec's face registered a look of surprise, and he sat up straight. "Would you care to explain what that means?"

I told him about my apartment, about my phone call, and I explained that "certain documents" had been removed from the stacks he'd given me. "I don't know what was taken, and I don't know why," I concluded. "Nothing you gave me seemed noteworthy, but then I didn't understand a lot of it. You might remember the files well enough that you'll recognize what's missing, but if you're going to look through them, please don't let anyone know about it. If it was dangerous for me to do so, then I'm guessing it would be even more dangerous for you."

The whole time I'd been talking, Alec's eyes had grown larger, until I thought they might be in danger of popping out of his head. He kept leaning further forward, too, until he finally had to put both hands on the desk to keep himself from toppling over. Now I had the answer to my question about whether or not Alec ever looked anything but collected and congenial.

Alec was silent for some moments after I finished, but eventually he let out a long breath and settled back into his chair. "I'll start going through the things tonight. I can go over them while Carter and the rest of you do your investigation."

I nodded. "Okay. And, just so you're aware, I won't be at the investigations anymore. I want to, but since I'm the one who's been targeted, I feel it's necessary to separate myself from this as much as possible."

"I'm sad to hear it, but of course I understand," he agreed. "I'm sorry if this investigation has turned into something dangerous for you. I really think we should call the police, even though you were threatened not to. They can protect you."

"I'm just not ready to do that yet, Alec. Let's see what the team finds tonight, and then I'll reconsider my options." The police probably could protect me: I'd be pretty hard to kill if I was locked up in a jail cell for just standing by while Maxwell murdered someone.

Alec and I spoke for a few more minutes, and then I stood up to leave. He walked me all the way to the front door of the mansion, where he turned and gave me a warm handshake. "Again, I'm sorry you won't be working on this anymore," he said, "but please keep in touch. I'd like to know your opinion on what Carter finds."

"Feel free to call me anytime," I said, feeling an unexpected wave of friendliness toward the lawyer. "And please, be careful."

As soon as I walked outside and Alec shut the door behind me, I scanned the square for my mystery man. He wasn't under any of the oak trees. I sighed and tried to reassure myself. I had washed my hands of the investigation, and had been, hopefully, obvious enough about it that everyone—whoever had ordered the attack on me, at least —would know.

I made the short drive home and walked in my front door. "I'm home," I called, though I'm not sure I was talking to myself or the cat, "and we're going to have a nice, normal night."

My phone rang just as I finished my pronouncement. I glanced at the caller ID and saw Maxwell's name. I laced my fingers together to keep myself from answering, and shortly after the ringing stopped, I got a new voicemail notification. I snatched the phone up to check Maxwell's message. "Betty, I'd really like to talk to you. I thought maybe I could come over to your place tonight. I can be there around nine, so just call and let me know."

"Nope, you can't come over," I said out loud.

I kept repeating that, like some sort of mantra, while I changed into a pair of jeans and a roomy sweatshirt. I was soon sprawled on the couch with a bowl of ice cream in my hand, Mina by my side and a movie playing on my TV.

My bowl had long been empty when there was a knock at my door. I bolted upright, startled at the sudden interruption. Had Maxwell come over even though I had ignored his request? I glanced at the clock, though, and it only read eight. Maxwell had suggested arriving at nine, and showing up early didn't seem like Maxwell's style, so I was immediately wary. People don't just randomly show up at my front door.

"Who is it?" I called, rising from the couch.

"John from across the street," responded a male voice.

"I'm getting signatures for a petition to save a historic building."

"Just a minute." I frowned and bit my lip, mentally checking off the names of my neighbors. I couldn't remember having met anyone named John, but I definitely didn't know everyone. Instead of answering the door right away, I went into my bedroom and grabbed the gun off my nightstand. Call me paranoid, but I wasn't going to take any chances. Halfway to the door I realized that it wouldn't seem very neighborly to open up with a gun clutched in my hand, so I shoved it into the deep pocket on the front of my sweatshirt. I didn't look like I had a gun, but I felt better knowing it was there.

When I opened the door, there were actually two men standing there, and they were nearly as tall and massively built as the guy from the alley. I didn't see any kind of clipboard in "John's" hands, but I wasn't yet willing to believe that they weren't just innocent neighbors circulating a petition.

"Can I help you?" I squeaked.

The one closest to me smiled broadly, showing off several chipped teeth. He had a wide scar on his forehead, which his shaggy dark hair nearly hid. "Yes, you can," he answered, and I knew right then that I was in trouble.

Before I could even get my hand to my pocket for Maxwell's gun, the man's right arm came up, and his fist hit my jaw so hard that I stumbled backward and fell. I tried to sit up, my mind screaming at me that I had to get up and run, but I barely got my hands underneath me before both men shoved their way through the door, towering over me.

The second man—Not-John—grabbed the lamp off the end table by my couch, yanking the cord out of the socket effortlessly. He brought it down toward my face, and I turned away just in time that the metal base of the lamp slammed into the side of my skull instead. I had a split-second of absolute clarity as I slumped down onto the floor: I could see Mina scoot underneath my bed with lightning speed, and just before I lost consciousness, I thought, "So much for normal."

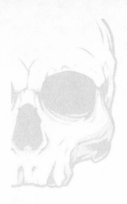

TWENTY-ONE

When I woke up, everything was still dark, only now I couldn't move, either. My arms were pinned behind the chair I was seated in, my wrists tied with rope or something like it. My stiff shoulder muscles burned. I didn't know how long I'd been unconscious, but I had been slumped forward in the chair, the weight of my upper body pulling against my arms.

After a few seconds, I realized I was in a small room, probably a basement. There were two small horizontal windows along the top of one wall, and the dim light filtering in through their brown, grimy panes was the only illumination in the room. The shapes that loomed over me were probably just your run of the mill junk—the type of stuff people stash in basements to die a slow, rusty death.

Maybe I was about to die a slow death.

My heart pounded in response to that thought, and I started to gasp for breath as my brain rose to a level of panic I'd never experienced before. I felt suffocated, and I realized slowly that it might have something to do with the rag tied tightly around my head as a gag. It smelled faintly of motor oil and tasted even worse. My dry lips felt like they were going to crack.

All of the dark shadows around me seemed to loom closer, like monsters closing in from the black corners of the room. I shut my eyes, trying to keep the feelings of panic and claustrophobia from consuming me, but I could feel tears sliding down my face. I gave in then, sobbing so hard that my body convulsed, pulling against my arms and the ropes holding my wrists captive. I knew the sounds of my desperate crying were muffled by the gag, but in my head the noise seemed deafening, too large for this bleak little room.

Was this Maxwell's doing? I thought of Margaret's ghost, trapped in that tiny room on Tybee Island after Maxwell had set her up to arrive moments too late to say goodbye to her dying husband. Maybe this was another elaborate setup of Maxwell's; now that I'd ended our relationship, there was nothing to stop him from ruining my life, too.

No, that didn't feel right. I believed that Maxwell really had been saddened by our breakup. Besides, if he wanted to ruin my life, he'd probably do it slowly and agonizingly, until suicide looked like the only viable option. Instead, I'd been kidnapped by a couple of thugs. This was about the Everett-Tattnall House. They hadn't killed me the first time, but now they would.

And now, I didn't have Maxwell to save me.

My hysterics eventually dulled into a sort of resigned apathy. The only question I had was why I wasn't already dead. If they just wanted to get rid of me, then John and Not-John could have killed me right there at my apartment. If only I'd had my gun in my hand when I opened the door, maybe I could have shot them before they knocked me out.

The gun: had they found it? My sweatshirt was too bulky for me to see the lines of the gun inside the pocket, if indeed it was still there. I leaned forward as far as my contorted position would allow, then drew my knees toward my chest. With my sweatshirt pressed between my stomach and my thighs, I could barely feel that the front pocket was empty. The hope I had felt so briefly faded. My cell phone, I could tell, had been taken from my jeans pocket, or it had fallen out somewhere between my apartment and wherever I was now.

I sat there, alone in that dark little room, for what seemed an interminable length of time. Strange thoughts floated through my head, like how dirty my socks were going to be from the basement floor since I had no shoes on. Mostly, though, I thought of Maxwell. Through all of this, he had been the one person—well, demon—to defend me, watch over me and keep me from feeling lost and alone. His evil nature, which had seemed like such an insurmountable barrier before, paled in comparison to the sacrifices he'd made for me. Sure, he'd gone to Sam MacIntosh with information I hadn't wanted Sam to know, but the resulting fallout wasn't what Maxwell had intended. It suddenly seemed like a petty reason to break things off with someone who had, in every other instance, taken such good care of me. I guess being tied up in a basement can really put things in perspective. I'd ended things with the one man who could help me now; the one man who had proven that he would take a bullet for me, if that's what it came to. I shut my eyes. Please, God, I prayed over and over again, let my demon come rescue me.

So when I heard footsteps somewhere nearby, my first thought was that Maxwell had found me, that somehow he knew I was in trouble. A door in the wall opposite the windows opened, and a shadow filled up the doorway, a shadow much larger than Maxwell's. An overhead light turned on with a click, and I had to squeeze my eyes shut against the sudden glare. When I cracked one eye open, I saw a burly man with a crew cut standing there. Not-John.

"How ya feelin', honey?" he asked with a mocking

234

smile. I glared back, trying my best to look daunting despite being gagged and tied up.

"Too bad we can't kill you ourselves," he continued, walking over to me and putting a dirty hand under my chin. The smell of rank sweat and stale alcohol made me wrinkle my nose in disgust. I swallowed back the urge to gag. "Boss says he wants to do it himself, make sure it gets done right this time. He also wants to know what you did to Pope, since you're still here and he's not."

Pope? I guess Not-John could see the confusion on my face, because he added, "Pope, big guy, long hair? You two were supposed to have a date last Saturday, but he's gone missing." What kind of a name was Pope?

"He's been shot so many times that he's full of holes, so he's 'holey' like the Pope." Not-John's head flew back as he laughed, obviously entertained by his own joke. At least he'd answered my unarticulated question.

Not-John went from mirth back to menacing in an instant, his laughter stopping abruptly. "So we just wait here for a while, until the boss arrives. He would have come earlier, but he waited to make sure all your little friends were safely inside that old building first." The way he said "safely" gave me chills. Was something going to happen to the others, as well? The thought made me even more afraid than I'd been for my own safety.

I was surprised when he reached forward and untied the gag, letting it fall into my lap. He hovered over me, his dirty face outlined by the overhead light. "You scream, and I knock you out again, got it?"

"Yes," I rasped. I swallowed hard a few times, trying to wet my parched mouth. "What's your name?"

"Shouldn't you be asking something more important, like, 'Am I gonna die?'"

I shrugged as best I could, trying to stay calm. "You've already made it obvious that the answer to that is yes."

"Then you ought to be begging me to let you go."

"You don't seem like the type to listen to begging."

He regarded me for a moment, then finally gave a barely perceptible nod. "Stake."

That was even worse than Pope. "How did you get that name?" I asked.

"Kid I used to know kept telling everyone he was a vampire, so I staked him to see if it was true. He lived, so I knew he'd been faking. Of course, he wound up in the hospital for a while." Stake smiled at the memory, and it was obvious that he took a lot of pride in the story.

I decided a change of subject was in order, before Stake could get any ideas. "Who is your boss, anyway? I can't imagine who might have something so big to hide."

"I'm not supposed to tell you that." Stake leaned in, until his face was only inches from mine. The heat of his putrid breath against my face made me pull back instinctively, and his brown eyes bored into my green ones with an odd look that hovered somewhere between murderous and lustful. Then he winked and gave me another creepy smile. "I'll make a deal with you. I'll untie you, and if you can get past me, and all the way up the stairs before I catch you, then I'll tell you who the boss is…right after I've tied you up again."

"Something tells me I won't be able to get past you," I said.

"Probably not, but it will be fun to try." Stake moved behind me, pulling out a knife. I shut my eyes and held my breath, afraid that his knife would slip and slice open one of my wrists. When my hands fell free instead, I let out my breath and wondered why I was even going to try to escape my captor. He was bigger, stronger and, I suspected, a whole lot crazier than me.

I slowly stood up, keeping an eye on Stake the whole time. He moved away, positioning himself in front of the door with his arms crossed. My legs didn't respond well, and I stumbled forward, catching myself on a pile of boxes with my hands. My wrists, I saw, were raw and red from the rope.

Then I saw what was lying on the topmost box: the gun Maxwell had given me.

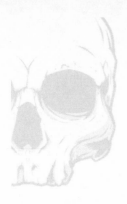

TWENTY-TWO

Stake and his cohort must have found my gun when they tied me up, and either they forgot about it, or they didn't bother to remove it from the room since I wouldn't be able to get it, anyway.

I could get it now. I glanced up at Stake, but he was watching me so closely that I knew he'd interfere before I ever managed to fire.

I straightened up and walked backward toward the corner opposite Stake. When I reached it, I leaned back against an old desk and crossed my ankles, casually sliding my hands inside my sweatshirt pocket as I did so.

"You're not trying very hard," he remarked, still motionless in the doorway.

"I'm strategizing," I told him. "I figure I'll only have one shot at making it past you, so I need to make sure I give myself the best chance possible." When I told Stake I was only going to have one shot, I'd meant it literally. I only had a slim chance as it was, but if I missed, I doubted there would be any second chance.

The seconds stretched as I waited, looking around the room and pretending to plan my escape route. That panicked feeling was returning, but when I finally pushed off the desk and began to walk straight forward toward my captor, my heart and my breath seemed to slow, and I felt calm again. It was now or never.

I passed the pile of boxes so closely that my sweatshirt rubbed against them. I kept my eyes straight ahead while my hand reached for the spot where I'd seen the gun. My fingers found it and wrapped tightly around the butt. The safety, I remembered, was built into the trigger: squeeze once to disengage the safety, squeeze again to fire.

I heard a shout as I raised the gun. The shout, though, didn't come from Stake. It was from someone upstairs, and even as I put pressure against the trigger, I heard heavy footsteps on the stairs.

Stake was so distracted by the noise behind him that it took him a moment to realize what I was doing, and it might have been that extra half-second that kept him from leaping on me before I could fire. I pulled the trigger all the way back, the gunshot echoing in the confined basement. Stake staggered backwards as a dark hole appeared right in the middle of his grimy shirt, and I fired again. His eyes widened in shock, and he swore loudly as he fell backwards. I kept moving forward, jumping over his body and through the stairwell door, and I came face to face with John, who was already drawing his own gun from his waistband.

Before I could react, the gun loomed in my vision, the barrel swinging toward me at the end of John's outstretched arm. I ducked as I heard the deafening shot just inches from me, and I found myself sprawled on the floor for the second time that night. John had fallen on top of me, his arms and legs flailing as he tried to get up. His skin began to grow hot against mine, and I scrambled away, stumbling back into the basement. John's body twisted around, and he looked up the stairs behind him. I followed his horrified eyes and saw Maxwell, his face contorted in fury and his hands clamped down on John's shoulders. Smoke began to rise in tendrils from John's chest, and he screamed until, in a strange act of murderous mercy, Maxwell slammed John's head into the brick wall of the stairwell, knocking him unconscious.

I knew what was going to come next, and I watched with little sympathy as John's body was reduced to a pile of ashes. When it was over, Maxwell finally looked up at me. His intense expression quickly softened into one of relief and concern, and he stepped neatly over my captors and reached out for me.

I stood and threw my arms around Maxwell's neck, holding onto him tightly, as if he might try to materialize away from there at any moment. His warm hands against my back felt so reassuring and safe, and he whispered my name over and over, his voice trembling.

"I knew you'd find me," I said, my voice cracking.

Maxwell pulled back and looked me over. "Are you okay?"

I nodded. My body, I knew, was sore and bruised, but at the moment I felt perfect.

"It wasn't just me who found you," Maxwell continued. He stepped to the side and looked back up at the stairs, and I saw an awed-looking Shaun and Carter standing there.

My panic rose up again in an instant. "Where's everybody else? You guys are in danger, the boss is planning something, everyone was supposed to be together!" I was so worked up that I wasn't even making sense.

"The boss?" Carter asked coolly. "If by boss you mean Terrence Stiles, then you don't have to worry about him."

"Terrence Stiles? The third partner in the firm?" Great, now I was panicked and confused.

Shaun smiled grimly. "Come on, Betty, let's get you somewhere that looks a little less like a horror movie.

Everyone else is at Maxwell's, so we'll explain everything there."

Maxwell gave me an encouraging nudge forward, simultaneously prying the gun out of my hand with gentle fingers. "Go on up with them, Betty. I'll take care of this guy, though it looks like you did most of the work for me."

"Is he dead?" I asked, the reality of what I'd done suddenly sinking in.

"He's not going to get up and come after you, at any rate. Now go; it's okay."

I trudged up the stairs, and Shaun took my arm to help me up the last few. Now that I was calming down, the adrenaline that had been keeping me going was disappearing fast, and I felt exhausted.

Upstairs, I found myself in a dingy house that looked barely lived in. The sparse furniture was old and sagging, nothing hung on the walls except torn and water-stained striped wallpaper, and the smell of decay was everywhere. "What is this place?" I asked.

"An old abandoned townhouse a couple blocks from the Everett-Tattnall House," Carter supplied. "Apparently these guys use the place from time to time. Well, used to use it. I guess they won't anymore."

"And everyone else is okay?" I asked, needing to hear the answer again.

"Everyone's fine, Boo," said Shaun. "Your new boyfriend made sure of that."

"About that, Betty," Carter jumped in. "You told me you were dating a businessman, and that you had a nice, normal social life."

"Maxwell is a businessman," I countered.

"Yeah, one who can cremate people with his bare hands." Carter sounded as impressed as he did shocked.

I shrugged. "Good thing I don't have to get approval from you on the guys I date, then."

"I can't say I disapprove. He did save your life tonight, and probably ours, too."

"He did," I agreed, then I sighed. "He's not my boyfriend, anyway. We broke up."

Shaun raised his eyebrows. "Considering what he did tonight, I'd say you two are officially back together."

I stared at Shaun. "Come on, you guys have to tell me what's going on!"

"We will, in a minute," Maxwell said. He had come up the stairs without making a sound, apparently finished with his clean-up job. He leaned against the wall, and his face looked drawn. "Shaun, Carter, you two leave first, and Betty and I will follow. If four of us troop out of an abandoned house, it's going to look suspicious. We'll meet you at the corner of Bull and Liberty."

Shaun and Carter looked out a front window until they saw that no one was nearby, then they dashed out. Maxwell stayed where he was, but he extended his hand to me. When I put my hand in his, he gently pulled me forward. "Shaun doesn't have to be wrong."

"What do you mean?"

"About us being officially back together. How did you know I was going to come for you?"

I shook my head. "I don't know. You were the only one I could think of when I was tied up in that room down there. How you'd already saved my life once, and how you kept coming to protect me when I was in trouble. It just," I shrugged, searching for the right words, "felt right that you should rescue me again."

Maxwell shifted, and I realized that instead of being held by him, he was actually leaning against me. Of course, I realized, disposing of two bodies like that must have exhausted him. Maxwell put his fingers under my chin and tilted my head up so that he could look in my eyes. "Why were you thinking of me?"

242

I felt my cheeks flush and tried to look away, but Maxwell's fingers held firm. "Because I'm falling in love with you," I whispered.

"And why do you think I came to rescue you?"

"Because…" I began, but my voice faltered. I knew what I wanted the answer to be, but what if I was wrong?

Maxwell nodded. "Maybe this time you'll actually believe me. Betty, I really don't try to make life hard for you. What happened with Sam…" Maxwell's voice trailed off, and finally he shook his head. "I came here to save you, because I want to be with you. It's as simple as that."

"It's not that simple, though. You're a demon; people have died because of you."

"I've saved your life twice now. Maybe I'm starting to make up for my past sins."

I thought about countering that a demon once is a demon forever. How many times would Maxwell have to save my life to make up for his future transgressions, too? He was right, though. I'd thought about him in that basement because I was falling for him—despite my best efforts to deny it—and because I'd been able to count on him in the past. If I had a dream man, Maxwell was it: charming, handsome, intelligent, caring, and reliable. Great in bed, too, which had to make up for some of his demonic nature. Someday, I knew, I would have to reconcile with the fact that Maxwell was a demon, but I hoped that day was far in the future.

Maxwell really was falling in love with me, and I wasn't going to walk away from that a second time.

My happiness at that thought must have been apparent in my expression, because Maxwell broke into a wide grin. "Officially back together, then?" he asked.

I smiled in return. "Officially." Maxwell leaned in and gave me a long kiss. When he pulled back, I made a face.

"I'm probably not really kissable right now. I need Chapstick and a gallon of water first," I said.

"I'll take care of you when we get to my house. Everyone is anxious to know you're safe," he responded, smoothing my hair back as he spoke.

"I shot a man."

"I know. You did what you had to do to take care of yourself, and I'm proud of you."

"And I'm in my socks."

Maxwell looked at me with a mixture of amusement and pity. "I don't think anyone is going to notice. Come on, let's get out of here."

TWENTY-THREE

We left the house, Maxwell walking slowly and leaning heavily on my shoulder. It didn't take long to meet up with Carter and Shaun, who had already called Daisy to let her and the others know that I was safe.

Carter and Shaun left, heading for Carter's car, and they promised to come directly to Maxwell's house. Maxwell was parked a few blocks away, closer to the Everett-Tattnall House, and I tried unsuccessfully to get Maxwell to fill me in during the slow walk there.

The drive over to the Victorian district was short, and I stayed silent the whole time. I was desperate to know what was going on, but I knew Maxwell wasn't going to say a word until we were with everyone else. I was safe, and that was all that really mattered at the moment. Maxwell watched me almost as much as he watched the road in front of him, reaching over to put his hand over mine whenever he wasn't shifting gears, almost like he couldn't believe I was really there.

We parked in the garage, and after I climbed out of the car, I reached down and stripped off my grungy socks, dropping them into a trash can near the garage door. I'd have to be barefoot for the rest of the night, but at least my feet were clean. I didn't want to track all that basement dirt and grime (not to mention blood) into Maxwell's pristine house.

I opened the back door and helped Maxwell into the kitchen. I wasn't even entirely inside the house before Daisy caught me in a crushing hug. "I'm so glad you're here!" she said, and I realized she was crying. I gave her a squeeze, and when she let go she grasped my arm firmly and pulled me into the kitchen. Everyone except Carter and Shaun was there; even Jamie, the tech guy from Carter's team, was looking at me anxiously.

"I am so glad to see all of you," I said, and I felt my entire body slump in relief. I hadn't realized how tense I was. "I'm going to go attempt to make myself look human, and then I want to hear everything!"

I went down the hall to the little downstairs bathroom. My reflection was pretty horrid: my face was dirty and scratched, and my hair stood out in a hundred different directions, except for one stiff tangle that was caked in blood. When Not-John (Stake just wasn't working for me as a name) had smashed the lamp into my head, he'd apparently drawn blood. My head had really been taking a beating lately.

I had to satisfy myself with washing my hands and face, and trying to rinse the blood out of my hair. When I was finished, I at least had a clean face, but my hair was still wild, and my clothes were going to join my socks before long. Attacks and kidnapping were really taking their toll on my wardrobe.

Back in the kitchen, I sank down into a chair at the table, and Shaun set a glass of water down in front of me. I took gulp after gulp, looking back at all the people staring at me. Shaun and Carter must have arrived while I'd been in the bathroom. Maxwell, though still weary-looking, was comfortably settled next to me, and Daisy was busy fussing over him. He kept waving his hand, as if he were halfheartedly swatting at a fly. "Really, I'm fine," he kept saying. "I just need rest." Finally I set my glass down and raised my eyebrows. It was time for some answers.

"You first," Carter said.

I rolled my eyes, but obliged, telling them about John and Not-John's arrival at my apartment, and my short-lived escape attempt that turned into a rescue. "That's it," I concluded. "Not-John kept referring to 'the boss,' and I'm dying to know what Terrence Stiles has to do with all this."

Shaun was the first to speak up. "We started the investi-gation around nine, and really early on we saw Jasper's ghost. I think having Alec with us is what made the ghost materialize so quickly. Carter had his tape recorder on, and we asked Jasper some questions. It lasted maybe a minute, and then he disappeared."

"I played back the tape recorder, because none of us wanted to wait to find out if we'd captured an EVP," broke in Carter. "What we got was clear as day. Here, have a listen." Carter pulled his tape recorder from his pocket, fast-forwarded through part of the recording and handed it to me.

I held the tape recorder up to my ear and heard Carter asking Jasper's ghost if he was trying to tell us something. A quiet but distinct voice answered, "I'm dead... Terrence's fault." Then there was a pause, before the disembodied voice said one more thing: "Betty."

I was surprised to hear my own name, and I looked up at the others in confusion. "How did the ghost know I was in trouble?" I asked.

"We think Jasper must have overheard Terrence plan-ning to have you killed," said Daisy. "If Terrence was calling people from the law firm, then it would have been easy for the ghost to eavesdrop."

"What did you do once you heard the EVP?" I was

eager to find out how they had found me and how Maxwell had gotten caught up in the search.

"At that point we didn't know Terrence was involved, but we knew Jasper must have been warning us," continued Daisy. "We tried to call you, but Maxwell answered your phone."

I glanced at Maxwell with a confused expression. "I came over hoping we could talk," he explained. "Your front door was closed, but unlocked, and your phone was in the middle of your living room floor, right next to a streak of blood. I had just arrived when Daisy called, so I answered."

"We told Maxwell what was going on and what the EVP said. He told us he'd come over to the Everett-Tattnall House right away," said Carter. "Fifteen minutes later, there's Maxwell on the doorstep with Terrence Stiles in his grip like the guy was a criminal. Maxwell brought him in and told us to start one of our video cameras because Terrence had something to say. He spilled his guts, telling us how he'd killed Jasper, who'd found out Terrence was embezzling money from the firm. Everyone thought it had been just a heart attack, so he thought he was in the clear, but then we started investigating. Terrence was nervous about it, but not really convinced that a ghost would be able to point the finger at him. All those files and notes of Jasper's that Alec gave you, on the other hand, had more potential for exposing him. Terrance hired some lowlifes to threaten you, but when that didn't work, he told them to get rid of you."

I was stunned. "How did you get a confession?" I asked.

Carter gave a short laugh. "Your boyfriend did that. I don't know what he did, but it worked. Terrence was almost hysterical, and every time Maxwell moved, he'd flinch back like he might get burned."

I looked at Maxwell, my eyebrows raised. Maxwell grinned at me and held up his hand, smoothly rubbing his thumb and forefinger together. "Guess I've got the magic touch," he said. "When I got to the house, I found Terrence just outside. He was on the phone with someone—probably one of your kidnappers—and I heard him mention you, Betty. I caught him and threatened him just enough to make him admit what he'd done."

Carter continued, saying, "Once we had his confession on video, we called the police. Maxwell told Terrence none of us would even mention he'd been trying to kill you if he would tell us where you were. He gave up the address pretty easily. Maxwell told Carter and me to head over there, and then he just disappeared." Carter gave Maxwell a frank stare. "What are you?"

Maxwell shrugged. "I think you already know."

"Anyway," Shaun said, picking up the story, "by the time Carter and I arrived, Maxwell was already there. You know the rest."

"What happened with Terrence?" I asked.

"The police took him away," Daisy spoke up. "He was still terrified, especially after Maxwell disappeared right in front of him, and he just kept babbling, telling them over and over that he'd killed Jasper. Alec gave the police a stack of financial records, similar to the info he'd given you to look through. To you, that stuff seemed unimportant, but apparently it was evidence Jasper was collecting against Terrence before he was killed. I don't think convicting him is going to be a problem."

"We all get to give statements to the police, too," Carter said, looking even more pleased with himself than usual.

"Wait, I don't understand one thing," I said, putting up my hands as if to ward off the overabundance of information. "Alec said Jasper died of a heart attack. How was that a murder?"

"It appeared to have been a heart attack, so no one questioned it," Shaun said. "I guess there are ways to kill someone that makes it look like a natural death." Shaun looked at Maxwell, the unspoken question clear on his face.

Maxwell made a dismissive gesture with his hand. "Sure. In this case, it was probably some kind of poison; brucine, strychnine, something like that. I'm sure they'll exhume Jasper's body and do a thorough autopsy."

I sat back in my chair, trying to absorb all the information. "Wow," I finally said. It felt inadequate, but words couldn't describe my amazement or my intense relief.

Maxwell cleared his throat. "I don't think I have to say this, but we're not going to mention Betty's kidnapping and rescue to the police. If anyone asks, she was at home tonight, with me." Maxwell looked around the room, and his usually bright blue eyes held something almost sinister. I could feel everyone else quail under his stare, and they all quickly agreed on the fake cover story. After all, how could I confess to shooting a guy, but not be able to produce a body as evidence? Plus, I knew that even though the others weren't entirely sure how Maxwell had coerced the confession from Terrence, they did know that Maxwell was capable of acts they couldn't imagine. The implication of Maxwell's request was clear: if anyone told a different story, he'd be happy to do to them the same thing he'd done to Terrence, or even to my kidnappers.

Once we were all agreed, I felt the need to lessen the tension in the room that Maxwell had produced with his unspoken threat. "Carter, you were limping at that abandoned house. What happened to you?"

Carter stiffened and looked at Daisy. "I was walking down the stairs at the law office. Daisy was behind me."

Daisy's eyes widened. "I don't know why you're mad, Carter. I missed a step and bumped into you. At least you only fell down the last few stairs and not the whole flight."

I put a hand to my mouth to muffle my snicker. As soon as Carter's gaze turned away from Daisy, she gave me a grin and a wink.

"I'm starving," I announced, changing the subject so I wouldn't laugh.

Shaun grinned at me. "You're not dressed to go out to dinner," he reminded me.

"Why don't we just order pizzas? You're all welcome to stay," Maxwell said. Everyone agreed, and he put in a call to have pizzas delivered.

Lou had been silent since I walked in the door, and I could tell by the look on his face that he wasn't comfortable being in Maxwell's home. While we waited on the pizza to arrive, he pulled me into the front room.

"I'm so glad you're safe," he began.

"Me, too."

"I had thought for sure that returning all of the files to the law firm would stop the threats to you. You were as blatant about it as you possibly could have been."

I was about to agree, but stopped myself. "How do you know that?"

Lou looked down at the floor sheepishly. "I've been, um, keeping an eye on you."

"That was you in the square."

"Yes. And I think you saw me the night you went on the ghost tour. I went home after that because I didn't want you to notice me again."

I let out a short laugh. "You should have stuck around. It got really interesting after the tour. You were following me in case I got more threats?"

"No. I was keeping watch to make sure that demon wasn't doing harm to you."

I just didn't know what to say to that. When the silence began to stretch, Lou spoke again. "I know he saved your life tonight. Just be careful, Betty. He's still a demon."

I nodded, and my voice was quiet when I finally spoke. Lou was right: I would have to watch out for myself. "I promise."

Lou gave me an awkward hug before we returned to the kitchen, where he quietly announced that he wanted to get home to start reviewing other recordings and video footage from the evening. I was the only one who knew why he was really leaving.

The rest of the night was relaxed, and as tired as both my body and mind felt, it was wonderful to be there, surrounded by my friends and my boyfriend (or whatever Maxwell qualified as; I still wasn't sure). I even enjoyed Carter's company, which was a first, but I was so happy just to be alive that everyone seemed agreeable to me.

Until he announced we'd be holding a press conference the next day.

"Carter, you have to be kidding me," I said, talking around the giant bite of pepperoni pizza I'd just taken.

"Alec has to issue a statement to the media about Terrence's arrest, since of the three partners, he's the only one left," Carter explained. "He wants us up there with him to explain how Jasper's ghost helped solve the case."

"Was that really his idea, or yours?"

At least Carter had the decency to look a little ashamed. "It was sort of both of our ideas."

"Fine," I conceded. "This is the last press conference I do for you, ever. What time does it start?"

"Two o'clock, so be there a little early so I can brief you on how it will proceed. We'll be on the front steps of the Everett-Tattnall House again." Carter's voice was triumphant.

It was well past midnight already, and since we now

had a press conference to attend on our Saturday afternoon, the party broke up soon after. Maxwell drove me
home and insisted on staying with me. I was grateful for his
company, and when I walked in the front door, I happily
saw that the only damage done was some blood on my
hardwood floor and a broken light bulb from the lamp
Not-John had used on my head. Both were cleaned up
quickly, and I jumped in the shower to get myself cleaned
up, too. My clock read three a.m. when I curled up in bed
with Maxwell's arms around me, and I knew I was really
and truly safe.

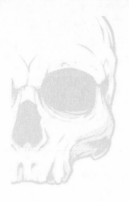

TWENTY-FOUR

The press conference turned out to be more tolerable than I'd anticipated, though there was one instance near the end that almost made me laugh out loud.

Carter and Alec handled the talking, like before, and I got to stand by and watch without anyone directing questions at me. We had an impressive turnout of media since Terrence's arrest was big news. He had been a lawyer in Savannah for years, and his family had lived in the area for generations. The arrest would, I knew, be front-page news on Sunday. There were a lot of other people in the audience, too, curious locals and tourists alike.

I held my composure until a local newspaper reporter called out the last question of the day, which he directed at Carter. "Was this the scariest thing that's happened to you as a ghost hunter?" he asked.

Carter, decked out in a navy-blue suit and looking as well-manicured as ever, kept an entirely straight face as he answered, "No. The zombies we had to take care of in Mexico were much more frightening than this."

Zombies? It was everything I could do to keep a straight face, but I looked down and saw Maxwell, Daisy and Shaun standing in a line, and they were doing all the laughing for me. Maxwell caught my eye and winked.

Once the press conference broke up, I shook Alec's

hand and told him to let me know if he had any more trouble with ghosts at the law firm.

"I think we've seen the last of Jasper, but who knows?" he said. "Jasper might stick around to keep an eye on the firm, and that's fine by me. Thanks for all of your help, Betty. I'm glad it all turned out okay."

"Me, too. Take care, Alec." I said a quick goodbye to Carter and headed down the steps to meet up with the others.

"We're talking about dinner tonight, at the Pink House. Just the four of us," said Shaun in greeting.

I looked at Maxwell. Now that Daisy had finally met him, she seemed to be approving. "Works for me," I agreed. Maxwell took my hand, and after Daisy and Shaun left to go home, we walked to his car and drove back to my apartment.

Maxwell fished a little box out of his car, which he carried tucked up under his arm as we walked to my front door. Once we were inside, he handed it to me. It was made of metal, probably iron, and it was blackened and rusty from time. "What's this?" I asked.

"That's just a box," Maxwell said, smiling mysteriously.

"What's in the box?"

"Lieutenant Ambrose Griffin."

I stared at Maxwell. "I think you might need to explain this one to me."

"Lieutenant Griffin was a Confederate soldier stationed out at Fort Pulaski. He was killed there when the Union Army attacked, and his ghost has been at the fort ever since, still keeping guard like he did when he was living. Of course, guarding the fort from tourists isn't a very exciting job for a soldier. I offered Lieutenant Griffin the chance to come here, to guard your home instead."

"You're telling me there's a ghost inside this box, and I can let him out so he'll keep watch for me."

"Yes. Think of him as your own personal sentry. A Spirit Sentry."

I nodded. "Thanks. It's definitely the most unusual gift I've ever gotten."

Maxwell smiled. "You're welcome. And don't worry, you'll get used to him." Maxwell reached down to pat Mina on the head. "You'll get used to him, too, little one."

Maxwell straightened up and continued, as if giving me a ghost wasn't out of the ordinary at all. "Hopefully the Lieutenant won't be busy here, but considering the way life has been for you these past few weeks, I thought it was a good idea to get you some sort of security around here."

"As long as he promises not to watch me when I'm showering," I joked.

Maxwell sighed and gave me a long look with his brilliant blue eyes. "If I was a good demon, I'd get more people to break in here to make you paranoid. Instead, I'm helping you."

"You also saved my life last night," I added. "I'm sorry I doubted you before. I can't tell you how happy I am to have you on my side. Who knows, maybe I'm a good influence on you."

"Or a bad influence, depending on the perspective."

"I shot a man, and I'm not even sure I feel bad about it, so maybe neither one of us is exactly what we seem to be."

Maxwell grinned at me suddenly. "I know exactly what you are: a woman who needs a double scoop of ice cream from Leopold's." He held out his hand and I took it, feeling the demon's warm fingers close over mine as we stepped out into the Savannah sunshine together.

Everything was back to normal.

A NOTE FROM THE AUTHOR

Thank you for reading *Ghost of a Threat*! I hope you're enjoying being a part of Betty's world.

Will you please leave a review for this book? Reviews mean everything to indie authors like me, and they help other readers connect with authors they might enjoy.

Thank you so much for your support!

Beth

ACKNOWLEDGMENTS

As always, I offer heartfelt thanks to my husband Ed, whose support has been invaluable. I'm indebted to my mom Ann for her amazing editing skills. Thanks to Dad, Karen and all of my test readers who offered such valuable feedback: Tim B., Jenny, Evelyne, Sean, Jess, Tim G. and Nancy. Finally, thanks to Denise Dumars, whose guidance made this a better story.

NEXT IN THE SERIES

GHOST OF A WHISPER

BETTY BOO, GHOST HUNTER BOOK TWO

THINGS GO TO HELL IN SAVANNAH.

Life is good for Betty "Boo" Boorman. Things are going great with her demon boyfriend Maxwell, and her paranormal investigation team is busier than ever as Halloween approaches.

But things go to hell—literally—when Maxwell is banished by a demon hunter. As Betty tries to cope with her grief, another demon enters her life, and he offers her a deal: Betty's soul for Maxwell's rescue.

Time is running out for Betty to make a decision, and the ghosts of Savannah, Georgia, aren't making the task any easier. Cryptic messages from the ghost of a little girl seem to be directed at Betty, but are they a warning or a plea for help?

BOOKS BY BETH DOLGNER

The Betty Boo, Ghost Hunter Series
Romantic Urban Fantasy
Ghost of a Threat
Ghost of a Whisper
Ghost of a Memory
Ghost of a Hope

The Nightmare, Arizona Series
Paranormal Cozy Mystery
Homicide at the Haunted House
Drowning at the Diner
Slaying at the Saloon

The Eternal Rest Bed and Breakfast Series
Paranormal Cozy Mystery
Sweet Dreams
Late Checkout
Picture Perfect
Scenic Views
Breakfast Included
Groups Welcome
Quiet Nights

Manifest
Young Adult Steampunk

A Talent for Death
Young Adult Urban Fantasy

Nonfiction
Georgia Spirits and Specters
Everyday Voodoo

ABOUT THE AUTHOR

Beth Dolgner writes paranormal fiction and nonfiction. Her interest in things that go bump in the night really took off on a trip to Savannah, Georgia, so it's fitting that the Betty Boo, Ghost Hunter paranormal romance series takes place in that spooky city. Beth's first book was the nonfiction *Georgia Spirits and Specters*, which is a collection of Georgia ghost stories.

Since Georgia is obviously on her mind, you might think Beth lives there. Well, she did, but these days she and her husband, Ed, live in Tucson, Arizona, with their three cats. Their Victorian bungalow is a lot smaller than Eternal Rest Bed and Breakfast, but Beth likes to think it's haunted, even though Ed swears it's just drafts.

Beth also enjoys giving presentations on Victorian death and mourning traditions as well as Victorian Spiritualism. She has been a volunteer at an historic cemetery, a ghost tour guide and a paranormal investigator.

Keep up with Beth and sign up for her newsletter at BethDolgner.com.

Made in United States
North Haven, CT
16 October 2023

42812550R00162